Noelle Holten is an av[...] [...]crimebookjunkie.co.uk. She [...] for Bookouture, a leading [...] worked as a Senior Probation Officer [...] covering a variety of risk cases as well as working in a multi-agency setting. She has three Hons BA's – Philosophy, Sociology (Crime & Deviance) and Community Justice – and a Master's in Criminology. Noelle's hobbies include reading, attending as many book festivals as she can afford and sharing the book love via her blog.

Dead Inside – her debut novel with One More Chapter / HarperCollins UK is an international Kindle bestseller and the start of a series featuring DC Maggie Jamieson. All books in the series can be found on her Amazon author page.

www.crimebookjunkie.co.uk

𝕏 x.com/nholten40
f facebook.com/noelleholtenauthor
⊙ instagram.com/author_noelleholten
BB bookbub.com/authors/noelle-holten

Also by Noelle Holten

HIS TRUTH HER TRUTH

NOELLE HOLTEN

One More Chapter
a division of HarperCollins*Publishers* Ltd
1 London Bridge Street
London SE1 9GF
www.harpercollins.co.uk
HarperCollins*Publishers*
Macken House, 39/40 Mayor Street Upper,
Dublin 1, D01 C9W8, Ireland

This paperback edition 2025
1
First published in Great Britain in ebook format
by HarperCollins*Publishers* 2025
Copyright © Noelle Holten 2025
Noelle Holten asserts the moral right to be identified
as the author of this work

A catalogue record of this book is available from the British Library

ISBN: 978-0-00-869403-6

Printed and bound in the UK using 100% Renewable Electricity
by CPI Group (UK) Ltd

This one is for you, Graham. I finally found my true partner-in-crime and am more than happy to serve a life sentence with you.

Prologue

The couple lay sprawled out on their kitchen floor. Beth Stanford's vibrant locks of dark brown hair matted with blood, making it impossible to distinguish where Joe Tasker's bearded bruised face ended and her own began.

The moonlight cast long, grotesque shadows on the worn-out floor tiles of what was once a picturesque semi-detached home in Gladstone Village. Gladstone is nestled in the lush countryside of North Warwickshire and exudes the charm of a quintessential rural village. At its heart lies a corner shop, a quaint establishment that has stood the test of time, offering everything from fresh produce to local gossip. Nearby, the village park invites both young and old for leisurely strolls and picnics under the canopy of ancient oaks and is the perfect cut-through to the local pub. The pub is the hub of community life, where laughter and stories echo against the backdrop of crackling firewood. All of Gladstone exudes the spirit of community and time-honoured traditions.

Except this night was different.

'You'd think they were just asleep.' PC Bradshaw kept his voice low as he spoke to his colleague, the irony of the peaceful scene, brutally interrupted by the splattered crimson that painted the walls and cabinets.

'They sure picked a hell of a way to nap.' PC Mitchell swallowed hard, his gaze fixed on the knives the pair held.

One in his hand.

One in hers.

Glinting, almost winking under the room's dim light and covered in blood.

The rustic charm of the house was marred by the chaos – the smell of a burnt meal, broken glasses, scattered utensils, and torn bits of paper that danced across the floor. A final, desperate struggle took place here.

'The call. Anonymous, was it?' PC Mitchell mumbled, wiping sweat from his brow with a gloved hand as he looked through post on the counter. 'Joe Tasker and Beth Stanford.' He held up a letter.

'Yeah, the caller said they heard screams or shouting of some sort. Guess they didn't want to be involved.' PC Bradshaw's eyes scanned the room, trying to piece together the violence.

As the two officers leaned closer to inspect the wounds, Mitchell's seasoned eyes caught a slight twitch in Joe's fingers, a movement so subtle it could easily be mistaken for a trick of the moonlight.

'Dammit, Bradshaw, he's alive.' Mitchell's voice was layered with its familiar rasp. 'Quick, check her pulse!'

Bradshaw, eyes wide with surprise, pressed two fingers to Beth's wrist. 'Alive. Just ... faint.'

Mitchell scrambled to his radio, his voice urgent. 'Where the hell's that ambulance?'

The hushed stillness of the night was broken by the distant wail of sirens. There was only one question on the officer's minds: What had happened in the once peaceful streets of Gladstone Village?

Part I

Chapter One

JOE

Joe and Beth drove to the train station in silence. She was angry with him, and as much as he understood, he'd explained he needed some time to sort things at work before he could head to Leek and be with her and her father.

'What if he dies, Joe? What will I do?'

Guilt punched him in the gut. 'Hey.' He reached across and took her hand, giving it a squeeze. 'He took a turn for the worse, but you know what your dad's like. He'll be all right.' He glanced over but she was staring out the window. He knew his words sounded insincere.

'Nearly there.' He turned left towards the front of the station. Pulling into a parking spot he got out and headed to the boot of the car, pulling out her case and placing it beside her. She was in her own world. 'Are you sure you're going to be all right? We could always ask if Kay can come and collect you.'

Beth and her Aunt Kay had one of those up and down

kinds of relationship. Although Kay had stepped in as a mother figure when Beth's own mother had abandoned her, Joe knew how Beth still held grudges.

She pulled the handle of her case up sharply. 'No, thanks. I'll be fine. It's only an hour and a half or so by train.'

Joe pulled her close. 'Call me as soon as you arrive, and make sure you eat something.' Beth had a bad habit of not eating when stressed, and worse, she drank to cope with the stress; a toxic mix. Fortunately, Joe only saw glimpses of this on a few occasions when they first started dating. With her anxiety and low tolerance for medication, anything that upset the balance caused mood swings and erratic behaviour.

'I will. Right.' She took a deep breath. 'My train will be here shortly. I'll go grab a coffee and snack for the journey.'

Joe kissed her on her forehead and watched as she walked away.

He got back into the car and drove into Langley town centre, parking his car in the lot behind the office building. Langley – conveniently located about a forty-minute drive from the village of Gladstone, though public transport extended the journey to around an hour – blends a bustling town centre with a strong community focus. The town centre itself is a hive of activity, boasting an array of businesses, with several pubs, cafés and a shopping mall.

A prominent feature of Langley is its park, a large, green oasis that serves as the town's lung and gathering place. The park includes well-maintained walking paths, open grassy areas for picnics and sports, and a children's play area. Community events, like local markets or outdoor concerts, are held here, fostering a sense of togetherness.

Central to Langley's community spirit is Tasker House, a local charity led by Joe. When Joe's grandfather died, he left a significant inheritance, which Joe used to start Tasker House. The organisation plays a crucial role in supporting vulnerable individuals in the area and works in collaboration with various agencies – health services, the police, and the council – to provide comprehensive support and advocacy. Their presence in the town centre underscores Langley's commitment to inclusivity and social welfare.

Joe was struggling with work commitments and illness was not something he coped with well. He always managed to say the wrong thing, which was probably why Beth was reluctant to share too much with him.

She was so close to her father, and if the worst happened ... well, he didn't want to think about that right now.

Joe walked into Tasker House and headed straight to his office, for once unable to make eye contact and smile for his team. He had always made it clear to his staff that work and home life should be separated, so much so that he didn't allow any personal items or photos in the office. This was partly due to the clients; some had criminal convictions and could use this to their own benefit. It was safer for his staff if the individuals they met with knew as little about their lives as possible. Joe also believed that it helped his team focus on why they were there ... to help others. He had enough on his plate dealing with the community. Beth had once commented on how impersonal it sounded. Yet to Joe, he was thinking about his team as well as the individuals seeking their services. Private should stay private.

Within minutes, AJ – a part-time counsellor on his team – was at his door. 'Everything okay? You don't seem your usual self.'

'My fiancée's father is in the hospital ... and it's not looking good.'

'Oh, shit. Sorry to hear that. What are you doing here, then? We'll manage...'

Joe appreciated the offer but there were a few big meetings for funding planned in the next few days. He didn't trust anyone else to deliver and ensure that the charity got what was needed. 'I'm sure you would, thanks, but I'm meeting with the council and I'm still working on the forms and my presentation. You know how important this is to me ... to all of us, really. If we don't get this funding, who knows what the next six months will look like. Or what will happen after that.'

'Well, the offer's there ... between us all, I'm sure we could figure things out.' The dig from AJ wasn't missed by Joe.

'If there's nothing else? Only I really need to get on with this...' Joe pointed at the application forms open on his desktop screen, his voice tight, a forced politeness that barely masked his impatience. Frankly, he could do without any interference from his team, it was bad enough having Beth mad at him. Joe swallowed hard, his hand hovering over the mouse. He needed space, time – just enough to keep the questions at bay and the records looking clean. Just enough to keep everything from unravelling.

Over the next few hours, he'd reviewed the financials, dropping figures into the presentation that he hoped would impress his audience next week. Charities were ridiculously underfunded and his was no exception. If the money didn't come through, he'd need to consider lay-offs, and this would have a ripple effect on the community they served. He'd screwed up and put his charity in jeopardy ... he didn't want to think about that now.

When his mobile rang, he nearly jumped out of his chair. 'Hey, love. You've arrived, then?' He glanced up at the computer screen to see the time.

'Not yet. Bloody train delays, and Kay says Pops is in a bad way. I knew I should've travelled last night...'

Joe could hear the blame in her voice. It was he who'd convinced her to go this morning after her aunt had rung yesterday. In either case, they wouldn't have made it in time for the last train and Joe had had a drink so couldn't drive her. He'd have loaned her his car, but he'd needed it to get to work and she had told him that long drives triggered her anxiety. As urgent as Beth's situation was, she wasn't the only person who relied on him. 'I'm sorry. Hopefully you'll be there soon.'

'Yeah ... look, I've got to go. Just didn't want you to worry.'

Guilt, again. His thoughts drifted to Beth's father, Kevin, and their first meeting only a couple of months ago.

Her father hadn't looked ill at the time. The cancer had spread quickly and now he was in hospital. If he died, Joe doubted if Beth would want to walk down the aisle without her beloved Pops by her side. Joe paused for a moment, feeling the weight of it all pressing in on him. Their wedding was set for May next year, and he hoped – truly hoped – that Kevin Stanford would pull through. And not just for Beth's sake. It wasn't that Joe didn't care for Beth; he did, in his way. But sometimes, love was more complicated than feelings. It was timing, circumstance, survival. And right now, the last thing he needed was any more complications – especially not from the woman he was supposed to build a future with. He didn't think he could handle navigating her grief, not with everything else teetering so close to the edge.

Chapter Two

BETH

'I still remember, Pops.' She smiled, holding his hand tight. 'Matilda – the ghost. You said she was a mistreated young stable hand and died giving birth to the child of the master of the house...' Beth wiped her father's forehead with a cool towel. 'But before she died, she cursed both the Craven family that owned the house and any future child that they had. Legend has it that not only were the Craven family afflicted with several children dying, but sightings from guests attribute self-slamming doors and footsteps to her.'

Every time her father had taken her to Coombe Abbey as a child, he would tell her Matilda's story and then sneak off to stomp on the floors or slam a door. She spent the next hour confessing her failings as a daughter, saying she was sorry. She had put him through the wringer in her younger years – anger and feeling abandoned by her mother led her down some dark trails. She knew he loved her, she knew he was proud of her despite everything ... but she just wasn't prepared or ready to say goodbye. He was.

Beth clutched her father's hand, listening to his final breaths. The death rattle they called it. His jaw hung open and Beth lodged the towel she had been holding under his chin to close it. She stared at his face as it changed before her. Kevin Stanford had been a burly man – his hair, grey with matching beard, was always well groomed, but now he was a shadow of his former self.

In less than a week after diagnosis he was on palliative care and within two days of that, here he was, dead, before her. She'd just made it in time to say her goodbyes, no thanks to her fiancé, Joe. She shook her head. It wasn't Joe's fault the trains were delayed. He couldn't know her father would take a turn when he'd had that drink.

She was projecting again. Beth twirled the ring on her finger. Joe was a good man ... she wasn't totally alone.

A nurse walked into the room and gently touched her shoulder.

'Do I have to go now?' Beth wasn't sure she was ready just yet.

'Not at all, love. Take whatever time you need.' The nurse was kind. Beth wondered how she coped with death and pain on a daily basis. She stood back and waited as the nurse lowered the bed, laying her father flat and placing an additional pillow behind his head.

And just like that, he was gone. She couldn't accept it. He'd put up with Beth while she was growing up – rebellion, drugs, alcohol, depressive episodes, crippling anxiety – and despite it all, he'd never kicked her out. Instead, he pushed the GPs to get her into programmes and therapy, and when she'd screwed it up, he was there to do it all again. The therapy had made her realise that her issues were about her mother.

She still had crippling anxiety, but the medication helped. And now wasn't the time or place to dwell on her past, or that woman.

It was only last month she'd visited Leek, where her father had lived all his life. Even though the outside of the house had changed over the years, the inside remained much the same. She had happy memories there. Her father always made her feel that no matter where she was in her life he always had a place for her.

She'd put off telling her father about her engagement initially. It was a big moment for Beth, one she thought would never happen. When she'd turned thirty, her father had joked that he wanted grandchildren and if she didn't get a move on, at her age, it would only get more difficult. Now thirty-four, she wished she had made more of an effort to see him and not taken those moments for granted.

When she'd finally felt ready to share the news at her last visit, it had been one of the few times she'd seen her father show emotion. He was happy his little girl had finally found someone to share her life with. After a bit of banter and teasing, Joe was welcomed into their small family with a hug and a handshake that turned her father's knuckles white.

———————

'You're a good man, Joe ... but know this'—her father had leaned in close to his ear—'if you hurt her in any way, you'd better disappear because you won't want to be around to find out what I'll do...'

Sitting next to him, Beth remembers her reaction as if it was yesterday. Her eyes widening. 'Dad!' She tapped his arm. 'Would you stop now. I'll never get married if you scare them all away!' She laughed. Joe laughed. Her dad glanced her way, dropped Joe's hand and stepped back. Beth saw the lines by his eyes seconds before he burst out in the biggest belly laugh, bringing tears to all their eyes.

'Your faces!' Her father had pointed at Joe. 'I couldn't resist!'

Beth rubbed her father's lifeless hand. 'How did we get here, Pops? You were supposed to walk me down the aisle, be the best granddad to my kids...' Her chest constricted. It felt as if someone had her heart in their hands and was squeezing with all their might. She took a few deep breaths, but the pain didn't go away.

'C'mon love, let's get you home for a cuppa.'

Beth turned when she heard her Aunt Kay's voice. Kay was like a mother to Beth, not that she knew what that meant. Their relationship was fraught, especially as Kay insisted on calling Beth by her birth name, Lisbeth, which she only used in a professional capacity. But Beth knew Kay always meant well, and on this occasion, her aunt was right.

Beth struggled to let go of her father's hand. Letting go would mean an ending; he was never coming back. Logically, she knew this, but her heart was telling her to keep hold as long as she could. As her dad's older sister, Kay had her own grief to deal with, but she'd hidden it to give Beth the comfort she needed.

Beth felt like she was having an out-of-body experience – she watched as Aunt Kay came up to her and removed her fingers one by one from her father's hand, until all Beth could feel was a draught on her palm.

She let Kay lead her into the corridor and a wave of sadness gripped her. Every part of her ached. Beth's knees buckled and Kay couldn't keep hold as she slid into a heap on the cold floor and cried with abandon.

Chapter Three

JOE

Joe's mind wandered to when he'd first met Beth. His job often took him out of town and to the surrounding areas. After a meeting in Stafford, some colleagues had suggested going out for a few drinks to the pub. It was there he saw Beth singing by herself, as if no one was watching. There was something about the way she carried herself – confident, but not arrogant; vulnerable, but with a quiet determination. He knew, in that moment, he was going to marry her.

He often wondered what she'd seen in him that night. Maybe it was his confidence, his ambition, the way he could make things happen. Beth had always appreciated someone who could match her drive, someone with a clear sense of where they were going. She liked that about him, how he seemed to have it all figured out. And for a while, Joe had believed that about himself, too.

As they'd talked that evening, Beth shared stories about her troubles in the past, her plans for the future, her hopes for a family. There was a strength in her that intrigued Joe. She was

resilient, and that made him believe they co
ups and downs of life, despite their differences.
saw the possibility of stability, a secure future. It w.
he'd always imagined – if only he could keep everythin
from falling apart long enough to make it real.

They had a whirlwind romance. Within a year he'd popped
the question, and despite his friends telling him to tread
carefully, he went for it. Although he and Beth were complete
opposites, they shared important interests: their love of the
outdoors, their interest in books and their passion to succeed in
life. He was impressed when he found out that Beth worked as
a paralegal and had hopes that one day, she would go on to get
her law degree and practise as a lawyer.

Beth was relieved to learn that neither of them had to
worry about money. She'd told Joe that she'd had issues in the
past but had worked hard to get herself out of debt. Joe's
parents were wealthy, and his grandfather had left him a
substantial inheritance, which he'd used to start the charity,
but after a few bad investments this was dwindling fast. A
further lump sum had been set up in a trust by his grandfather
and could be accessed once he was married. He needed the
wedding to go as planned or he'd lose everything.

He shook the thought out of his head. He didn't want to
think about that now.

Back then, when he'd seen Beth singing karaoke at the pub,
he'd taken a shot of whisky for courage and walked straight
up to her. 'Your voice isn't bad...'

'It isn't that great either,' she'd said, and there'd been a split
second before they both burst out laughing. They'd spent
every moment they could together since that encounter, and
after a hike around Bluebell Forest in Hartshill Hayes Country

'ark, Joe had set out a romantic picnic and found the courage to pop the question.

Beth had squealed and jumped around, shouting 'Yes! Yes! Yes!' before throwing her arms around his neck and kissing him. 'We're going to have such a good life, Joe Tasker'.

———————

Joe picked up his phone and listened to Beth's message again.

'He's gone, Joe. He's really gone. What am I going to do without him?'

A part of him was furious that he hadn't made the time to be with her when she needed him – but she understood, didn't she?

He called her back.

'Hey...' Her voice was a whisper.

'I'm so sorry. I wish I was there with you but ... well ... you know. I'll be up by the end of the week. Do you need anything from here?' His words sounded hollow. He never knew what to say when there was bad news, so he tried to keep the conversation practical. He was a logical thinker and left the feelings to those better suited.

'I need my father, Joe. That's what I need. How can you be so blasé about Pops – didn't you hear what I said?' Her voice became louder. 'It would have been nice to have my fiancé by my side as I said goodbye to him, but of course, your job is more important than me.'

'Hey, you know that's not true. Let me see what—'

'I know.' Her voice cracked. 'I'm sorry. Aunt Kay is here. She's driving me nuts but she's here.'

Joe couldn't tell if she was being sarcastic or understanding.

He had responsibilities to a lot of other people besides her, but her father had just died, and he didn't want to push her. If he did, who knows what she'd do.

'I'm going to go now. It's just been a bad day. The worst day of my life, in fact.'

'I love you. I'll be there as soon as I can. When's the funeral?'

She hung up.

Chapter Four

JOE

Joe had been staring at his computer screen since the call with Beth, trying to figure out what he could do to make it up to her.

When they'd got serious about each other, she'd told him about her anxiety, but it had been a conversation she'd started while sweat was still cooling on their skin, and he hadn't really been listening. At the time, he'd brushed it off as a fleeting admission, something they'd circle back to later. Now, as she told him today had been the most difficult day of her life, the weight of that earlier conversation hit him with a force he hadn't expected. He realised, belatedly, that he'd never truly understood the depth of her struggles. He'd only ever seen glimpses – moments when she'd retreat into herself or snap at him unexpectedly – but he'd assumed it wasn't about him, not really.

But today... her anger *was* directed at him. He could hear it in her voice, in the way she spoke to him as if she were holding back something much larger. He felt a knot forming in his chest, an uncomfortable mix of guilt and frustration. Joe sent her numerous texts in the hours following the call, trying to smooth things over, but her replies were cold – one-word responses, if she replied at all.

Did she even want him there? Was he wasting his time organising cover? What if she shut him out when he got there? Should he wait for her to reach out to him or should he take the initiative and go to her? All his questions led him nowhere.

What was he even thinking? Of course he needed to be with her.

He tried calling her one more time via the landline and was surprised when she picked up, but her voice was distant and cold.

'I was worried after we last spoke. How are you holding up?' Joe tried to sound as supportive as he could.

'I'm fine. Kay's still here. I don't really have the time or energy to talk right now.' Her voice was little more than a whisper.

Joe felt a lump form in his throat. 'Beth, please. I want to be there for you. Can we talk about what's going on? I feel like you're shutting me out.'

The line went quiet, and Joe feared Beth had hung up again, but then he heard her sigh.

'What do you expect me to say? I'm overwhelmed right now. I need some time to process things without everyone asking me how I am every five minutes or giving me the side eye because I feel like having a drink to forget everything for the briefest of fucking moments.'

It wasn't the answer he'd expected, but at least she was still talking to him. The fact that she had mentioned having a drink hung heavy on his mind. He'd need to speak to her about that another time. With her medication and her history, alcohol was the last thing she needed. Why hadn't Kay done anything to stop her?

'I get it. I'm sorry for pushing and I'll give you whatever space you need. I hate to see you this way.' He reassured her.

'Mmm…' Beth mumbled.

'Is Kay nearby? I'd like to say hello...'

Beth didn't respond but the next voice he heard was her aunt's.

'Hello? Give me a minute while I just go and grab my cuppa from the kitchen.'

Joe scanned his emails as he waited.

––––––––––

'I don't know what to do.' Kay's voice was hushed. 'Beth's a mess, and she needs you. Are you coming up soon? The funeral is not far off and if she isn't coping well, I can't imagine what she'll be like then. I've invited some of Kevin's friends around, many who can't attend the cremation, and she'll make a show of herself at this rate. Her behaviour is worrying, and her drinking... Well, you know about her mother ... it's a slippery slope and she's standing right at the top of it. When can you come up?'

Joe listened, and since he couldn't get a word in, he nodded, even though Kay couldn't see him. 'I'm doing my best to get up there as soon as I can. Until then, what can I do to help?'

'Organise the funeral director. I'll email over the details. Other than that, I think the best thing you can do until you can get up here is talk to her, even if she pushes you away. She doesn't have any friends she can talk to. Never has had any real friends, just people who would flit in and out of her life as it suited them. I think they found her a bit too much.' She whispered the last sentence as if she was making an attempt to spare Beth's feelings. 'Try to get through to her. I've tried everything, but she just won't listen.'

Joe could hear the desperation in her voice.

'Sorry, I've just heard a beep,' she said. 'I have another call, so I'll have to go...'

Joe felt the weight of the responsibility on his shoulders, but he had to try. 'Of course, I'll call Beth's mobile now.' He got up and closed his office door.

For a moment, Joe thought about abandoning Tasker House to the care of his team and driving up to Leek so he was at Beth's side. All that stopped him from doing so was doubt about the reception he'd receive.

Chapter Five

BETH

'She hasn't stopped crying for days. She just sits in his chair, with that manky blanket of his wrapped around her, staring into space. We need to get everything sorted. People are asking about the funeral. Have you organised what we discussed? When are you going to get here? She needs you...'

Although she pretended to be asleep, Beth listened to every word her aunt relayed to Joe.

'Well, that's not good enough, Joe. She needs you now, not in a few days or a week's time. The shape she's in, she'll not be able to cope. Not with clearing this house, the funeral, all the organisation it will take...' Kay paused, and Beth could feel her jaw tighten as her aunt's fingernails tapped on the table. 'Fine. I'm getting the doctor in. He might be able to give her something, let her get some proper sleep.' Her aunt lowered her voice, but Beth was still able to hear the next damning words. 'I'm afraid you have no choice in the matter since you couldn't even be bothered to be here. I don't want to hear your excuses. I've got to go now. *Someone* needs to look after her.'

Beth jerked when Kay slammed down the handset. She wondered what exactly Joe had said. He had meetings that couldn't be moved. She knew that. She'd told him she understood, so maybe it was her fault he wasn't here. Her emotions were all over the place. Sometimes she thought she saw her father, but she knew that it was all down to the drink and her meds.

Joe loved her. Didn't he?

Of course he did. He'd proposed.

Kay came over and gave her hand a squeeze. 'Sorry 'bout that. I just want him... Never mind. Right. I'm calling Dr Griffin. He'll give you something to sleep … and stop all that nonsense'—Kay pointed to the dregs of vodka in the glass by Beth's side—'it's a slippery slope. You should know that, especially with your mother's history.'

Beth knew the comment was intended to be a reaction-provoking slap in the face, but she was too numb to care. If Kay only knew ... could only understand ... how hard it was for Beth to take that first sip. She'd been so angry with herself, but without it, she had other intrusive thoughts she didn't want to act on.

Beth's mother had left when she was seven years old. Kay meant well, but the last thing Beth wanted to do was deal with her father's death: dealing with family friends as they dropped in to offer their condolences, the funeral, clearing and then selling the house – it wasn't fair. She wasn't ready.

Why did he have to die and leave her alone like this?

'Call the doctor, you're right. I need sleep and the vodka

isn't helping anymore.' She swilled the glass and gulped the remainder down. 'After he's been, why don't you go home? I'll be okay. Sleep … hopefully. You've done so much already, and Uncle Frank will be wondering where you are.' Beth sat up and forced a smile.

'Let's just see how we go, love.' Kay picked up the bottle of vodka that was by Beth's feet. 'I'll make us some tea.'

Beth nodded. It would be no good arguing; it would only make her aunt want to stay. She could hear Kay on her mobile, talking to someone in the kitchen. Ten minutes later her aunt returned to the living room with two mugs and placed them on the table, her glass of vodka was gone for now.

'Doctor Griffin's on his way. I'll just wait till he goes and then I'll be out from under your feet. I'm worried about you, love. I know the house feels empty without your dad. I still can't believe it myself. He was my brother…' Her voice was cracking. 'But he wouldn't want this for you. I can help, there's no need for you to do it all on your own.'

'How many times do I have to say it's fine? In fact, you don't need to stay, I'm a grown woman and can see the doctor on my own. Give my love to Uncle Frank…' Beth took a sip of the tea and grimaced.

'Honestly, I don't mi—'

'Would you just go? Please,' she pleaded. 'I want to be on my own now.' Beth pulled the blanket tighter around her and turned her back to her aunt, staring at the flames as the last few logs burned in the fireplace. The blanket smelled of Dad's aftershave and the scent gave her far more warmth than the fabric.

Kay placed her mug on the table with a thump, and Beth waited until the front-door lock clicked before dumping the tea into the plant pot on the table – so unlike her. She pulled the other bottle of vodka out from the side pocket of the chair where she'd hidden it and filled the mug up.

If she missed the doctor's visit – she could always rearrange.

Chapter Six

JOE

Joe stopped at the corner shop and picked up some beers on his way home. He was exhausted. Once inside, he kicked his shoes off. If Beth were here, she'd have a fit. 'Everything has its place,' she'd say, but Joe wasn't bothered by a little untidiness.

After speaking to Beth and Kay, and overwhelmed with questions and accusations, he now had a headache. He went digging around for some ibuprofen, washing it down with a cold beer. Although Beth drank when they were out socially, she didn't like having any alcohol in the house unless people were coming around. Beth had told him that it triggered bad memories and she didn't want the temptation. She'd fought hard to beat her own problems with alcohol. From what Kay was telling him now, though, old habits had crept in.

He took his drink into the living room and flung himself down on the couch, placing his feet on the table as he flicked through the channels. Another thing Beth would cringe at if she were here.

He felt a buzz in his pocket and sighed. Looking at the screen he realised it was Kay.

'Hello?'

'Hi, Joe. I hope I'm not disturbing you.'

She was whispering and Joe sat up. 'Of course not. Is everything okay? How's Beth?'

'That's why I'm calling. She's in a bad way. Drinking, not eating... I'm really worried.'

This wasn't news. Joe wasn't sure whether Kay was exaggerating, since she said it every time she called. Beth had told him more than once her aunt was prone to histrionics.

'It's only been a few days since her father died,' he said. 'I'm sure it's nothing to worry about. Is she there? Can I speak with her?'

'I've just left. Doctor Griffin is on his way to see her and she wouldn't let me stay. I've had to chuck out her booze, but who knows what she does when I'm not around.'

'Beth can't really handle her drink, especially with the medication she's on. I'm not surprised she's overdone it. Who is Doctor Griffin?'

'The family GP and an old friend. I told him the situation and although he was hesitant at first, I think I convinced him to prescribe some sleeping tablets, and that way she—'

'Hang on. You know how Beth feels about that. I don't think it's a good idea.' Joe was standing now, looking out of the front window. While Kay was chattering in his ear, he was trying to work out a way he could get up to be with Beth.

'... Do you know what I mean?'

Joe hadn't heard a thing Kay had just said, too absorbed in his own thoughts. 'Sorry, could you repeat that, I was—'

'Too busy thinking of yourself? I mean, really Joe. Lisbeth

needs you. You should never have let her come up here on her own. I'll keep you posted on what Doctor Griffin says and sorry to have bothered you.'

The line went silent. Joe needed to speak to Beth, but her number just rang out to voicemail when he tried. After a third time attempt, he left a message.

'Hey, hon. I'm going to try and shift some things around so I can get myself up there as soon as possible. I love you.' He threw his phone on the couch and when he couldn't find his laptop, he went out to the car, the last place he remembered seeing it.

Looking through his work calendar, Joe's frustration grew. Two critical funding meetings loomed, both of which couldn't be moved – or trusted to anyone else's care. These weren't just routine check-ins; they were make-or-break moments for the charity, the last chance to secure the money that would keep everything afloat. If he lost this funding … well, that didn't bear thinking about. He couldn't afford another failure, not after the damage already done by his own bad decisions – decisions no one else could know about.

Maybe the second meeting could be done via Zoom, he thought, trying to find some flexibility in a situation that felt more and more like a noose tightening around his neck. But even that felt risky. He couldn't leave these meetings to chance, not now, not when everything was hanging by a thread. And yet, the weight of Beth's silence gnawed at him. He knew she needed him, but if he didn't secure this funding, there wouldn't *be* anything left for them to build a future on.

A knock on the door startled him to the extent he gave a small jump.

'Hi Joe. We heard Beth's father was unwell and we all

pitched in to get her some flowers.' Mrs Grenfell from next door handed him a bouquet, a small white envelope taped to the wrapping bore Beth's name. 'We were going to wait until she was back, but then saw your car and assumed…'

Word travelled fast in a village.

'Thanks so much. Beth's father unfortunately passed away a couple of days ago. I'm sure she'll love these, thank you.' He was about to close the door, but their neighbour had more to say.

'Oh, that's terrible. Why aren't you up there with her... It's Leek, right? Not that far. You could probably get there in—'

Joe felt his neck redden. 'Thanks for the advice. I'd better go.'

Who the hell does she think she is?

Joe chucked the flowers on the counter. No point putting them in water, they'd be dead before Beth saw them.

He took a picture on his phone and sent it to Beth with a message.

> From the neighbours, for you. X

He grabbed another beer, returned to the living room and drew the curtains, noticing Mrs Grenfell talking to Bob and his wife across the road. She looked over and gave him a wave.

She was right. He could've been in Leek this evening. Beth would never forgive him for this. She may even call off the wedding. If Joe didn't marry her, all his plans would crumble. His head throbbed as he thought about all the bad investments he'd made. He needed to make this right. To show Beth that it was just a stupid lapse of judgement. He needed to prove he'd be there when she needed him.

He could commute to and from work while staying with Beth. It would mean a lot of time on the road, but he could shift his more important meetings to the middle of the day to ease his workload; he'd be able to arrive late and leave early, and extra hours could be put in on his laptop while he was up there. It seemed like a decent plan until he thought of the M6. Did he really want to endure three to four hours of that every day? Wouldn't he just end up as frazzled as Beth was? They always fell out when under stress. He was damned if he did, and damned if he didn't.

And it took a lot less effort to be damned for what you didn't do.

Chapter Seven

BETH

Beth could feel her body shaking, a stern voice saying her name with each shake.

'Lisbeth! Wake up, come on now.' She felt herself being pulled forward and forced open her eyes. The stench of stale vomit hit her nostrils, making her gag.

'What ... huh...' A sharp pain pierced her skull. 'What the hell?' She pulled her arms away from the stranger in front of her.

'It's Doctor Griffin. You might not recognise me now that I've gone grey.' He laughed the genial laugh Beth had heard so often as a child, but she wasn't amused today. 'Your aunt left a key for me under the mat. Sorry if I frightened you.' He sat down in the chair opposite. 'Would you like to clean yourself up?' He pointed at the vomit on her shirt.

Beth wobbled as she stood to make her way to the kitchen and clean the mess as best she could. She grabbed a T-shirt from the laundry basket and changed before returning to the living room. She sat back down in her father's chair. 'I don't need a doctor. I'm fine.' She ran her fingers through her hair, a finger catching in the knots that had formed.

'No one's said anything is wrong with you, they're just concerned. Your aunt mentioned you haven't been eating or sleeping much.'

'No, not really. Every time I try to sleep, I see his face ... his jaw hanging open ... hear his last breath.' Beth covered her ears and closed her eyes to block out the memory.

It didn't work.

The doctor leaned closer. 'You've just lost your father, but that'—he pointed at the half-empty vodka bottle on the end table—'isn't going to help. With your drug hypersensitivity, the alcohol is going to cause problems. You need proper sleep and some food in your system.'

Beth didn't like the tone of his voice. 'Who do you think you are, coming in here and telling me what I should or shouldn't be doing? My dad is gone. Why didn't you catch the cancer sooner? I wouldn't be like this if you'd done your job properly!' Beth's shoulders shook and the tears came again. 'You should've saved him.' She leaned over, clutching her stomach. All she felt was pain in her limbs and organs, like a knife cutting through each slowly. Making her feel something when she just wanted to be numb again.

'Lisbeth.' His voice dropped, softer in tone and not as accusatory as before. 'I wish I had caught it sooner – but that's a conversation for another time? How about I make us a coffee, or maybe you'd like some water?'

Beth eyed the vodka. 'Water, please.'

Dr Griffin stood and reached across her, grabbing the vodka bottle and tucking it beneath his arm while he picked up the two mugs from the coffee table. Beth's arm shot out to grab the bottle back. The doctor put his hand over hers. 'I'll not dump it, just moving it out of here for now, okay?'

She wasn't sure if she should trust him. She wasn't sure of anything, but she let go of the bottle. If he dumped that one, she knew where she could find some more.

While the doctor was in the kitchen, Beth stood, looking at herself in the mirror hanging above the fireplace.

'Jesus.' No wonder he'd been concerned. Her eyes were red and puffy, and her nose matched. Her hair was matted, and her skin was pale and greyish in colour. She hadn't changed her clothes since leaving the hospital. She was so tired; she couldn't remember when she'd last had any meaningful sleep.

She heard a cough behind her and turned.

'I didn't want to frighten you again. I found some biscuits, not the healthiest of snacks but at least it's something.' He placed everything down on the coffee table and pushed the glass of water towards her.

'Thank you.' Beth took a sip of the bland liquid and winced.

'Did you want to talk about your father?'

'Not really. I'm sorry, you've probably wasted your time coming out here.'

'Against my better judgement, I've brought some sleeping tablets. I normally wouldn't do this, but...' He shook his head as if he'd already said too much and reached into his pocket and pulled out a prescription bottle, as if it had all been planned in advance. 'There's enough to last a week or so, and I've checked they shouldn't affect the medication you're already taking – but you have to promise, no alcohol when you take them. It could be dangerous.'

'Why are you giving them to me, then?' Her face was hot.

She hated having to take the medication she was already prescribed, so was wary of adding something new to the mix. She could feel her anger simmering beneath the surface as she realised he was treating her like she was an alcoholic and out of control. 'I'm not my mother, you know. I'm just stressed and low. And if you're so worried, don't bother leaving them. What kind of GP just drops by with drugs in his pocket, anyway?' She didn't want to snap at him, but the way he was looking at her made her feel like a child.

'No need to be defensive. I'm only trying to help, and have to warn you that mixing alcohol and this medication'—he shook the bottle—'may give you hallucinations, increase your anxiety and paranoia – or worse, it might kill you.'

Beth softened. 'I'm sorry. I know you're only doing this because you've known my family for so long. I obviously do need some proper sleep. I've been snapping at everyone and have a lot to sort out over this next week. I promise not to drink vodka with them, okay?' She knew he was only doing his job, and Dr Griffin had been a big help to her when she had gone through some dark times growing up.

The doctor finished the rest of his coffee and stood. 'Your aunt has my home number if you need anything else. I'll show myself out.'

Before he left, he turned back. 'I'll leave this with you.' He placed the spare key on the bookcase. 'Goodnight, Lisbeth.'

She heard the lock click as the door shut behind him. The silence pressed in, thick and suffocating as she walked over to her father's drinks cabinet, her hands trembling as memories from her past washed over her – nights she'd sworn she'd never repeat, promises she'd made to herself. She had fought so hard to manage her drinking, and for a while she had been winning. But tonight was different. The pull was too strong, and the need to numb the chaos in her head overwhelmed everything else. Beth told herself she was in control now; she wouldn't fall down that slippery slope. No one needed to know. She reached into the cabinet, finding the bottle of gin she'd been looking for, and opened it, pouring half a cup into the GP's empty mug. She hesitated for a second, a flicker of doubt in her mind, before brushing it aside. What did it matter? The doctor had prescribed the pills, hadn't he? What difference did it make how she took them? Opening the pills, she took one and gulped it down with a mouthful of liquid oblivion.

She returned to her dad's chair, pulling his blanket over her legs and staring at the floor. Her eyes already heavy.

'He said not to take it with vodka, he didn't mention anything about gin.'

She cried, the mug slipping from her grasp as sleep finally took over.

Chapter Eight

JOE

At work the next day, Joe's heart raced as he moved cash from one account to the other, he glanced up from the computer screen every now and again to ensure he wouldn't be interrupted or caught. A few months ago, he had made some bad investments and now his company and personal finances were taking the hit.

It was easy to do at first, and he felt no guilt at all, after all, the money was being reinvested into the charity and allowed him to keep existing staff as cuts from the government continued. But then, when he lost some of the money in bad investments, he had to use money from his and Beth's personal accounts. It was only small amounts each time, just ahead of potential partnership meetings, but now that the accounts were going to be audited, the panic set in. If he wasn't careful, mistakes would be made and mistakes are what would land him in a heap of trouble with the board … and the police.

'I brought you a coffee.'

Joe jumped. 'Shit. You shouldn't sneak up on people, AJ – but thanks.'

AJ sat opposite, placing the mug on Joe's desk. 'You're looking a little pale. Not nervous about the meeting, are you? Once they see how we can add value to their agency, I'm sure they'll want to work with us.'

Joe rubbed his eyes. 'Uh, yeah. Just going over everything. I know it's all part of the business, but I could do without it right now. Will you be okay covering the other stuff when I head up to Leek? You can do the additional days remotely, if need be, and I'll make sure you're paid for any extra overtime.'

AJ was only part-time because Joe couldn't afford or justify the additional costs and offer any more hours unless there were exceptional circumstances. Like now. With no reason or access to the financial accounts, Joe was confident that the rest could be handled by others on his team.

'I don't see why not. Unless something bad happens.' AJ laughed.

Joe didn't see the humour and scowled.

'Sorry, not the time, I guess. Speaking of which, do you have plans after work?'

'To be honest, I'll probably be here late. Why?' Joe's head began to throb. All the pressure was getting to him.

'A few of us are going to grab a bite and drinks at The Swan. Won't be a late one – you should come. You look wrecked and a couple of hours in the pub might be good for you. Plus, you've been a bit of an arse lately.' AJ had been with him since the beginning and they had enough of a friendship for her to get away with this sort of bluntness. Anyone else would have got a bollocking.

Joe sat back in his chair. He'd been irritable, but hadn't

realised it had been so obvious to his team. He was usually very good at hiding his feelings. 'Can I give you a provisional yes – if I can get through the bulk of this work before you all head out, then I'm in. Deal?' He shouldn't be spending any money at the moment, but one drink wouldn't break the bank.

AJ stood. 'Fair enough. Remember though, you've a whole team behind you – you don't have to do all of this yourself.'

Before Joe could reply, AJ was gone.

True. Joe did have a team, but if they knew what he'd been doing just to keep the charity going, he may not have them for long.

Joe spent the rest of the day looking over spreadsheets and reports, making sure that at least on paper, everything was accounted for. He looked up and noticed that everyone was packing up for the day, so he did the same. AJ had been right earlier, he did need to step away from things.

'First round is on me!' Joe called out as he walked into the open-plan office. He had to keep up appearances and they'd find it odd if he didn't at least offer

'Are you trying to bribe us? Because if you are, it'll take at least two rounds,' AJ said, and the staff remaining all laughed.

Joe must have looked confused, and a hand slapped his back.

'Relax. It was only a joke. When did you become so serious?'

On the short walk to the pub, everyone steered clear of asking about Beth, which made Joe feel a bit more comfortable. He didn't want to answer questions. Instead, talk revolved around recent books and TV shows that had caught their interest.

As they neared The Swan, a pub in the town centre, Joe was glad only four members of the team could make it as his bank balance was low and he didn't want to have to dip into the joint account again.

'I'm just going to grab some cash from the machine. Order me a pint of Stella and I'll be in to pay.' Joe left the group and headed to the cash machine. He pulled his debit card out of his wallet and his hands shook as he inserted the card into the machine. He hoped he wasn't overdrawn as it would be two more weeks before his salary was paid in. After punching in his PIN, and hitting £60 for withdrawal, his heart sank when the request was declined.

'Damn.'

He pulled out the card for the joint account. Beth had wanted him to keep hold of it because she said she'd be too tempted to use it. He would transfer it back from his work account first thing in the morning. Stuffing the bills into his wallet, he headed back towards the pub and walked in just in time to settle the drinks bill.

'There he is! We thought you'd stiffed us and snuck off home.' The group laughed.

Joe paid the tab and joined his colleagues at the table. He held up his pint glass. 'Here's to great colleagues, good friends and no talk about work this evening!' They all clinked glasses.

AJ leaned in and bumped his shoulder. 'Good to see you smiling. How's your missus? I meant to ask earlier.'

'She's coping. I'll definitely be heading up at the weekend and return by the end of next week, once the funeral and packing up her father's house is done.'

'Fuck cancer, eh?'

Joe pasted on a smile, looking down at the floor. 'Yeah, fuck it.' He wanted to change the subject. Spying the menu, he picked it up and began to browse the options, hoping AJ would take the hint. 'Looks good.' He wasn't hungry though so ordered a side of chips. They'd be enough to fill him up without emptying his wallet.

Later, he looked at his watch. Beth should still be up, and he was hoping to at least speak to her this evening before it got too late. 'Excuse me a minute, I just need to make a quick call.' He stood and headed to a quiet spot by the window. Although he hadn't been happy with Kay insisting Beth take sleeping pills, he hoped that she had managed to get some sleep.

He listened as the phone rang out. It was only 8pm, surely, she shouldn't be asleep yet. When he called a second time, and the answerphone kicked in, he left a message.

'Hey, hon.' He purposely tried to keep his tone light despite feeling slightly annoyed. 'Just checking to see how you are. Sorry I didn't call earlier. If you get this message tonight, give me a call. No matter the time. I miss you.' He hung up and played with the phone in his hand while staring out the window.

'You're miles away.' AJ slid into the booth seat across from him. 'You looked a little down over there and I thought you might like a chat away from the others. Save the rest of them asking you – I can spread the goss when you go.' AJ reached across and tapped his arm.

'Thanks. Just worried...'

'About Beth? She isn't coping as well as you've been telling us, is she?'

'No. Not even close. Her aunt has been at me daily for

being selfish. For not being there with Beth. As if I didn't feel guilty enough. Apparently, Beth's been drinking quite heavily, and I think she's been prescribed sleeping pills. I don't know if I ever told you, but Beth suffers bad with anxiety and has been on meds since her late teens. I'm not sure she should be mixing all this shit; she is hypersensitive to any sort of medication and her aunt knows this.' Joe looked up. 'Sorry, I don't mean to dump all this on you. Look'—he stood—'I think I'm going to go now.' He pulled out his wallet and handed over a twenty-pound note. 'That should cover my tab. Buy drinks with whatever is left.'

'Stay for just one more? Or at least eat your chips.'

'Nah, I need a clear head and I'm sure one of them will eat the food.' He pointed to the group.

AJ gave his arm a quick squeeze before they returned to the table.

'Right, you lot. Enjoy your night and I'll see you tomorrow.' Joe picked up his bag and waved to the group ignoring their shouts for him to stay.

Walking back to the office car park, he went through a mental checklist about what he needed to do before heading up to be with Beth. He was glad he hadn't carried on drinking as he wouldn't have to take the bus in the morning.

He didn't expect to see a scratch on the driver's door when he went to open it. 'Fucksake.' Joe looked around but there was no one in sight. He kicked the tire before driving off.

Chapter Nine

JOE

The next few days flew by without incident, though Beth still hadn't returned any of his calls. He'd left AJ in charge and emailed a list of things for the rest of the team to go through before loading his bag and funeral suit into the car. As he pulled out, he made a quick call to Kay. He wanted to know what he should expect.

'How she's doing?'

'Haven't you spoken to her yourself? Burying your head in the sand because you can't deal with—'

'Hang on a minute, Kay, before you carry on with whatever ridiculous scenario you've concocted in your head, I've tried calling her. She hasn't called me back.'

'Oh.'

'Exactly,' Joe continued while Kay stumbled about trying to make excuses. 'I'm on my way up and I don't want there to be any awkwardness between us. I think we both have her best interests at heart, and she won't need any additional stress, so can we just call a truce?'

'Of course. See you soon.'

The drive was uneventful, although the delays on the M6 did reinforce Joe's decision not to commute to work from Leek. Throughout the slog north, he listened to the radio and stared ahead, a conversation in his head about what he would say to Beth so she wouldn't be offended.

He wasn't sure that was even possible with the way she has been. He took a deep breath as he got off at the road heading to the Standford home and mentally braced himself for any surprises.

Chapter Ten

BETH

The week running up to the funeral had been a complete haze. Kay was in and out of the house like she owned the place and spent most of her time tutting or bossing Beth about. Beth was in no mood to see visitors, but Kay had gone behind her back and organised for people to call around today, especially if they couldn't make the funeral.

'Are you sure about cremation? Wouldn't it be nice to have somewhere to go and pay your respects?' Kay asked.

'Do you even know your brother?' Beth glared at her aunt, not waiting for an answer. 'Dad never wanted to be buried. He wants his ashes scattered by that tree in Rudyard Lake where we carved our names when I was a kid, just after *she* left.' Beth loved visiting the lake and fishing with her father. 'I'm keeping some back for a necklace. If you really want a memorial, you can do what you want with your portion of ashes.'

'A necklace? Isn't that a bit morbid? Never mind. You know best.' Kay backed down and started to sweep the floor, and Beth went upstairs to freshen up in her old room.

The pills Dr Griffin had left her were calling to her like a siren and she debated whether or not she should take one. Instead, she pulled the mini bottle of vodka from her pocket and stared at it. Her hand trembled as she twisted open the top and placed the opening to her lips. She fought hard not to take a sip, as once it touched the back of her throat and that feeling hit, she wouldn't want to stop.

Rather than fighting it, she downed it in one go. Anything to numb her feelings.

Joe was supposed to be arriving today. He'd be staying until everything was done and Beth was ready to go home. The intrusive thoughts returned, and all she could feel towards Joe was anger that he hadn't come with her when he knew how critical the situation was. She had *needed* him.

'Lisbeth! People are starting to arrive and I could use a hand.' Kay called up the stairs.

'On my way!' Beth pinched her cheeks and took one last look in the mirror. Her chest tightened and she held back the tears before making her way downstairs to greet her father's friends. It was Kay's idea to invite these people around, she didn't know why she cared.

Beth noticed Kay passing around a tray of sausage rolls and tried to avoid being seen, but it was too late.

'Ah, here she is. Lisbeth, come and meet Adam and his wife. Adam and your father used to play football together back in the day.'

'Hello...' Beth held out her hand, the name sounded familiar. 'Nice to see you both.' She couldn't bring herself to look at the couple and kept her eyes on their polished black shoes.

'We're sorry for your loss. Your father was such a character.'

Beth started to walk away. She didn't want or need complete strangers telling her how wonderful her father was. Her chest tightened.

The doorbell rang, and less than a second later she heard Kay's voice. 'Can you get that, Lisbeth?'

Anything to get away from Kay and having to pretend everything was normal. 'Of course.' Beth answered the door.

It was Joe.

'Beth, honey, I'm so sorry.' He pulled her into his chest and held her tight; she couldn't breathe. 'How are you?'

'I'm fine.' She pulled away from him. 'Follow me. I'll show you which room we're in.'

She waited for Joe to pick up his bag then she led him upstairs.

'Hon. Maybe you should have a lie down. You look wrecked. I mean of course you do with what's happened, but—'

Beth had only been half listening and held up her hand. 'Stop. I'm tired of people telling me what I should and shouldn't be doing. I just want to get the next few days over with. Then we'll go home, okay?'

Joe nodded. 'Sure. I'll just go to the loo and see you downstairs.'

As much as she would rather just curl up on the bed, Beth returned downstairs and saw the scowl on Kay's face as she waved her to come over.

Instead of going to see what her aunt wanted, Beth grabbed a drink from the buffet table and sat on the chair in the corner of the room. Every now and again, she'd get up for a refill to blur out the sea of sad faces and meaningless condolences. She wanted to be alone.

'We'll see you at the crematorium, then, Lisbeth.' A hand tapped her knee. She started awake, not realising she had even drifted off.

'Uh, yeah.' When she shifted in the chair, she felt something damp on her thigh, the glass in her hand empty – vodka on her trousers. 'Excuse me, I'd better sort this out.' She brushed by the next couple who'd come over to speak with her, and pushed her way through the remainder of guests. She'd had enough for the day and had no idea where Joe was.

Once she'd changed, she filled a glass with water from the bathroom and popped a sleeping pill, before tucking herself into bed.

'Night, Pops.' She closed her eyes. 'I'll see you in the...' She fell asleep, unable to complete the words she'd said every night she'd lived in this house.

Chapter Eleven

BETH

The alarm clock blared, and Beth felt something heavy pushing down on her. Her arms flailed and she hit something solid. 'What the fuck?'

'Hey, stop. It's just me. That alarm has been going off for ages.'

'I was just about to turn it off. No need to crush me.' She huffed.

Joe frowned. 'I know you're going through a tough time but...'

Beth sat up. 'But what? I'm not allowed to talk back? To stop you from crushing the life out of me. It's just a fricking alarm, Joe.' She flung the duvet off and stomped to the bathroom, ignoring Joe as he called after her. She didn't need this shit right now. What she needed was something to block out all the noise.

She jumped in the shower and turned the heat on full. The water burning her skin. After fifteen minutes, she got out and towel dried herself, brushed her teeth and then sat on the toilet, waiting in the bathroom until she heard Joe go downstairs.

She had just lost her father for fuck's sake.

It feels like everyone's just expecting me to get over it, like it's that easy. But why the hell should I?

Her hand ached. She'd been squeezing it so tight that her nails had broken the skin on her palm.

'For fuck's sake.' Beth rinsed her hand under the tap and dried it on the towel wrapped around her body.

She went back to the bedroom and dug through her case, looking for something clean to wear. Leggings and a hoodie seemed to be all she had left. She had been in such a rush to get here, she'd only packed a few things and forgot to ask Joe to bring her up some more clothes.

She looked around the room and noticed that Joe had tidied, placing all the dirty laundry in the basket by the window.

'Guess that's my hint to do the laundry, then.'

'What's that?'

Beth turned to see Joe in the doorway holding a mug of coffee out in her direction. Was he trying to make her feel bad?

'I said, I guess I'd better do some laundry, or I'll have nothing to wear for the funeral.'

'Here.' He handed her the mug. 'I'll do it.' Joe walked over and picked up the basket. 'You've enough to think about.'

'Jesus, Joe. I can do my own laundry.' She tried to grab the laundry basket back, but Joe ignored her and took it downstairs. She felt bad then. He was only trying to help and all she'd been doing was snapping at him.

Beth eyed the sleeping pills on the nightstand and then remembered she needed to take her anxiety medication. She had so much to get through today, and the mixing of pills made her feel worried; seeing shadows where there were none. A bit of a break from the medication might do her system good, but she'd need more before she went home.

She unplugged her mobile and googled Dr Griffin. She'd thought about asking her aunt for the number, but Kay would only give her grief since she was still drinking and she was getting enough side-eye from Joe, she didn't need any more.

She found a link and clicked on it to make the call.

'Wrenstone Surgery. How can we help?'

'Hi. I uh, wondered if there is a free appointment to see Doctor Griffin, today? I realise it's short notice, but my father has just died and—'

'Hold the line please.'

There was a clacking of keys, each tap pounding like a hammer in her head.

'No, unfortunately. We don't have any appointments for the next two weeks, but we do have drop-in hours tomorrow morning between eight and ten.'

Beth bit her lip. 'Okay, forget it.' If she went, Joe would ask too many questions. The sleeping tablets were only supposed to be a temporary fix. She'd just have to ration out what she had left and figure out something else later. The call ended and Beth's shoulders relaxed.

She gulped down her coffee, taking an ibuprofen to ease the pressure in her head. She had to speak to the funeral director today to get everything sorted for the cremation, but her head was pounding. She opened the top drawer of the dresser and reached inside, pulling out a few mini vodkas and placing them in her bag. They were for comfort; she wouldn't drink them.

Her hands shook from the anxiety, and she needed it to stop, or she'd have Joe and Kay on her back. *Fuck it. One won't hurt.* Beth uncapped a mini and chugged it back. She hid the empty bottle in a pillowcase that was thrown under the bed. She used to do this when she was a teenager, until her dad had caught her.

Pops…

She glanced out the door and down the hall. She had something she needed to do.

Beth walked down the corridor and stood outside her father's bedroom. She'd foolishly agreed to pick out his suit as well as the belongings she wished to keep.

Why?

Chapter Twelve

JOE

Joe thought back to earlier in the morning. He'd carefully leaned across Beth to shut off the alarm. He wasn't expecting a whack in his face for his efforts. Her eyes had been closed but her arms were flailing about. He regretted putting his hand gently around her wrist to hold her back.

He'd only wanted to calm her down, but it seemed to set her off.

Last night had been a disaster, with Beth hiding from the guests and leaving him and Kay to talk to all the visitors.

He went downstairs and opened the back door, walking over to the large bin to take out the rubbish. His eyes glanced over at the recycling bin. He needed to see for himself if Kay had been exaggerating about Beth's drinking. He slowly lifted the lid. *Jesus*. The bin was half full of vodka, gin, and wine bottles. He struggled to believe that Beth had drank that much alcohol on her own; she'd only been in Leek for a few weeks. He'd speak to Kay – this was getting out of hand.

Joe returned to the kitchen to make coffee. His stomach

grumbled and he thought about making some toast for himself, though Beth might feel more up to eating if they did it together, so he'd wait.

He loaded the washing machine and turned it on. His stomach grumbled again and once he realised Beth wasn't coming down to join him, he made himself some toast.

As he was about to begin eating, his mobile rang. It was an unknown number.

'Hello?'

'Why are you ignoring my calls?'

Joe's heart raced. *Why the hell is she calling me here?*

'I thought I'd made myself clear. This has got to stop.'

'Is she there? How is she? I'm just concerned about you both.'

Joe rolled his eyes. 'Look, I'll change my number if you don't stop calling me.' He ended the call and put his phone on silent. He was bluffing; he couldn't change his number as he used it for Tasker House, and all the partnerships and clients he'd dealt with over the years. But if she didn't get the message and continued to call, at least Beth wouldn't hear it ringing. He had to protect her. She wasn't ready for it. Not now.

Chapter Thirteen

BETH

She held open the door that led into her father's bedroom. The scent of Pop's aftershave hit her and Beth was dizzy. It brought back so many happy memories.

Weekends at the pub playing dominoes with the locals – his arms wrapped around her, hugging her whenever she needed it. His great belly laughs as he joked with her to 'fake smile' for the camera. It was amazing what a smell could do. She fought back the tears and got on with what she had come in there for.

Beth opened his wardrobe and breathed in. His smell was everywhere. She ran her hand along the hanging clothes. He didn't have many. She pictured him in one of the shirts she touched.

Two suits hung at the end of the rail, one navy and one black. She pulled them both out and held them out in front of her. She couldn't decide which to choose and staring at them wasn't going to help so she placed them on the bed. She could pick one later. Her next task was to go through his dress shirts, but a box on the top shelf of the wardrobe caught her eye.

Beth pulled down the box and walked over to the chair by the window. She rubbed her hand over the arm before sitting down. As a child, her dad would read her stories from this chair. It used to be in her bedroom, but when she'd grown out of the stories, she'd wanted it gone. Her father, however, couldn't bear to get rid of it and moved it into his room. She removed the lid from the box and her eyes were assaulted with the face of her mother. Bile rose in the back of her throat.

Memories of her mother sent hot blood pulsing around Beth's body. She didn't need more than two fingers to count the good memories. Beth picked up the photo, curious as to why her father ever kept any pictures of Mum, considering the way she'd treated him during all her alcohol-fuelled frenzies. She tossed the photo aside and rummaged through the remaining items in the box when she came across some letters.

Beth removed the rubber band that held the letters together and for a moment had second thoughts about reading them. They were addressed to her father and were private – if he had wanted her to know the contents he would have shared them with her.

'I'll just read the first one,' she whispered, as if her father might hear or catch her.

Beth's hands shook as she began to read the letter.

Kevin,

You've NO RIGHT to keep Lisbeth from me! She's mine. You don't even love her. You never did. One day she'll see what you're really like. How you crushed my dreams and made me feel worthless.

If you don't give me my money, I will spend the

rest of my life dragging you through court. Is that what you want for 'your' precious daughter?

It's your fault that I started to drink. Why did you make me have her? You knew how much I wanted to dance. It was criminal to hide my birth control — lower than low.

And when you saw how I couldn't cope, you left me to it. The constant crying and screaming ... who could put up with that? You spent all your time at work and then your nights trying to placate that demon child. I need compensation for all the years you took away from me. MAKING me give birth, you selfish piece of shit.

You deserve each other. Just send me my money and I'll be out of your life for good.

There was no signature at the end of the letter, but it did sound like every bit her mother. The woman was a walking contradiction, and the short note was practically incoherent. *What did she mean about Pops making her have me?* Probably drunk. Looking at the date on the envelope, 2002, Beth would've been twelve years old. Her mother had left when she was seven. She remembered the only time she had seen her mother in those years.

Her father had taken her to Brighton in 2000 as a surprise. She was ten at the time. They sat on the pier eating ice cream and her father was constantly checking his watch. Just when they were about to leave, her mother came stumbling down towards them.

'We're going now. You were supposed to be here three hours ago.' Her father had taken Beth's hand.

'Who the fuck do you think you are telling me when I can see my own child.' The words that flew from her mother's mouth were slurred, and spittle hit Beth's face, adding to her revulsion towards her mother, who lunged forward, pulling Beth towards her while Pops held tight to her hand.

'Let her go, Janis! Don't cause a scene.' He had peeled her mother's fingers from Beth's shoulder and she'd let out a jump-inducing scream. Beth hid behind her father and watched.

'He assaulted me! Did you see that? Someone call the police!' Her mother had waved to people passing by.

Beth didn't remember how long it was before a police officer approached but he took one look at her mother, spoke briefly to Pops and then he'd left, taking her mother with him.

After reading the letter, Beth wondered if her memories were lying to her. Was this real? Was that actually her mother? Or had she fabricated an image of her from pieces of conversations that she'd had with her father over the years.

One thing was certain, Beth never saw her mother after that incident.

Chapter Fourteen

JOE

Joe tried to put the call out of his mind. Beth would never speak to him again if she knew. He needed a distraction. A fire in the hearth would put a smile on her face. She always talked about the way her father had a fire going in the colder months, how Kevin would become sentimental, sharing stories about his own parents growing up.

'We used to have to walk miles to school and if we wanted to speak to someone, we'd go knocking on their door. There were no emails or mobiles back then,' Beth had told him, and laughed.

Joe could still hear Kevin's deep voice and his belly laugh.

After starting the fire, he ran the vacuum over the dining-room carpet and picked up some of the papers lying about. He'd been tempted to go through the post he'd seen piling up in case any bills were due, but that was perhaps a step too far. He'd speak to Kay and let her or Beth deal with it.

His mobile buzzed in his pocket. He could feel his neck

redden and was about to rage at the caller when he saw Kay's name. He counted to ten, attempting to calm himself, before he answered.

'Hi, Kay, what's up?'

'How's Lisbeth today?'

'Hmm. Quiet ... angry. I feel like I'm walking on eggshells, if I'm honest. I'm at a loss. I'm trying to help but…'

'Stop making this all about you.'

Joe bit his lip. His blood was boiling again. If Kay was calling to have a go at him, he was in the mood to give it right back to her. 'What do you want, Kay?'

'I didn't want to disturb Lisbeth. Today will be hard for her. Did she sleep okay last night, without any medication?'

'I don't know… wait, why is today hard for her?' Joe tried to think whether Beth had mentioned anything, but nothing came to mind.

'Really, Joe?' Kay tutted. 'She's sorting the suit for the funeral and going through her dad's things. Don't you listen to anything? I told you all this, did I not?'

'No, you didn't, but never mind. Look, I'd better go.' Joe didn't wait for a response, cutting Kay off before she could wind him up anymore. He was beginning to see why Beth got so frustrated with her aunt.

He stopped what he was doing and headed upstairs. The door to Kevin's bedroom was closed and he stood outside it, hand against the door, wondering whether it would be better to knock or just walk in. He chose the latter.

'Hey. Can I help?'

Beth pointed to the wardrobe. 'I need a tie and shoes. I ... I have no clue what he would choose.'

'Leave it with me. You must be exhausted. There's a fresh pot of coffee on. Why don't you grab a cup and sit by the fire.'

When Beth pushed past him, he had no idea what he'd done to piss her off. He'd finish up here and then perhaps suggest an early night. They had a lot to do tomorrow.

But he felt a storm coming for them.

Chapter Fifteen

BETH

Beth's stomach turned, the nausea was overwhelming. She'd only just made it downstairs to the kitchen sink before what little was in her stomach came frothing out from her mouth.

She wiped her mouth with the back of her sleeve.

'You okay?'

Beth jumped. 'Jesus, Joe. You could warn a person when you come into a room. I nearly pissed myself then.'

Joe cocked his head. 'Sorry. When you rushed out of your father's room, I was worried. Look, you need to get something in you. And I don't mean vodka or gin or whatever else you are hiding around this house.' He walked towards her, reached out and took her by the arm to the kitchen table. 'Just sit down. I'll make some toast and eggs.'

Another wave of nausea hit her. 'I'm not sure I could stomach the eggs, but I'll have the toast.'

Fifteen minutes later, the melted butter on her lips was

welcome. Her diet of late had consisted of various medications and alcohol. Not the food of champions, that's for sure. She hadn't realised how hungry she was. 'Thanks.' She waved a slice of toast in the air. 'I guess I needed this, but I really need to get over to the funeral home and sort...'

Joe stopped her mid-sentence. 'I was speaking with Kay before I came up and we thought it might be better to have a funeral director do all that stuff. It will save you the stress. I called and got that arranged...'

'You did what? Why is everyone treating me like I'm a child.' Beth pushed her chair back and leaned across the table. 'You had no right to do that!'

'Calm down. You're making a big deal out of nothing. He'll just do all the taxing work. It's what your father wanted, he had it covered. Kay checked. You have the final say on any plans, I made sure of that. Kay's going to go down to speak with the funeral director today.'

'Right, let's go then.'

'Go where?' Joe's face scrunched.

Beth was getting annoyed at his confusion.

'If you think I'm going to let Kay chat with the funeral director on her own, you clearly haven't been listening to me at all – she'll have my dad buried and not cremated.'

'She wouldn't do that. Please. You're scaring me now. Is it the meds? Might be wise to lay off the drink a bit.' He finished his toast. 'You've clearly got it in your head that you have to be there, so finish your breakfast and I'll take you around to Kay's.'

Beth forced the food down her throat to appease Joe. There was no way she would let Kay change everything Pops had wanted.

Beth was furious as they drove into town, when she learned that Kay had already made her way to the funeral home. Kay always had an agenda, and it was never about what was best for anyone else. It was always her way, her rules, as if no one else mattered. 'Didn't I tell you she had something up her sleeve. I can't believe she's doing this.' Beth couldn't shake the feeling that Kay was already making decisions behind her back, pushing her own beliefs onto the arrangements without a second thought.

'She's only trying to help, hon.'

His siding with her aunt was getting on her last nerve. 'Why are you taking her side? You don't even know her. You don't know what she's like. Really like.'

When he ignored her dig, that infuriated her even more. 'Are we nearly there yet?' She looked around, trying to spot the funeral home. So much had changed over the years, reminding her that had she visited her dad more often, she would've known this.

Joe turned sharply into a parking lot and Beth saw the funeral home across the street. 'You can wait here, I won't be long,' she said. Not waiting for an answer, she got out of the car and stomped over to the funeral home, flinging open the door. She had no idea where to go.

'Can I help you?' A small woman approached.

'I think my aunt, Kay, had an appointment with one of your funeral directors about my father, Kevin Stanford? Is she here?'

'We're so sorry for your loss.' The woman turned. 'If you'll follow me, I'll take you through.'

Beth took a deep breath and followed the woman into a small office.

'Oh, Lisbeth! I wasn't expecting you.' Kay stared at her, eyes wide.

'Yeah, I bet you weren't.' Beth put her hand out to the man. 'Hi. I'm Kevin Stanford's daughter, *Beth*, and you can direct any questions you might have in future to me. Thanks, Kay. I don't think you'll be needed now.' Beth made sure there was acid in her tone.

'I don't mind if your aunt stays, often it's good to have other family members around in case things get too...'

'I don't need her.' Beth shot Kay a look. 'I'll take over from here.'

Kay left the room in tears and Beth wasn't even bothered. 'Crocodile tears. She'll be doing that for your benefit. Now where did you get up to?'

'Your aunt was telling me your father wished to be cremated and that you'd like some of the ashes for a piece of jewellery, is that correct?'

Beth's body slumped in the chair. Kay had followed the instructions. For a moment, she felt bad – guilty, even – but the anger surged back almost instantly as the reality hit her again. Kay and Joe had gone behind her back and hired the funeral director, making decisions Beth should've been making herself. This was her responsibility, her way of honouring her father, and they had stripped that from her. Why did they think she needed someone else to take control? Her chest tightened with a bitterness she couldn't shake. Why did she feel so angry? Was it because Kay always took over, never trusting Beth to handle things on her own? Or was it because she had wanted this one last thing, the only thing left she could do, and now even that had been taken away from her? She clenched her fists, the frustration burning hotter. It wasn't just about the arrangements – it was about the loss of control, of her voice, of one final chance to say goodbye on her terms.

'Yes, that's exactly right.' Beth's mind switched off. She barely listened to what the director was saying. Her hands were shaking and she felt a bit faint.

'Are you okay? Would you like a glass of water?'

'No, thank you. It sounds like you have everything in hand. If you just call and let me know when we can do the cremation, so that I can tell people, that would be great.' Beth stood and shook the man's hand. He offered his condolences once again before leading her to the exit.

Outside, Beth could see Joe and Kay huddled together like conspirators. Probably whispering about how crazy she was acting. Neither would understand her grief, the hole in her heart and the loneliness that fogged her brain. Of course they were trying their best, but neither seemed to recognise that she could barely hold herself together. Were they blind? She just needed them to understand, to hear what she was saying instead of trying to take over.

'Having fun talking about me behind my back? What are you planning now? Going to get me committed, are you?' The snide remark rolled off her tongue with ease.

'I've heard enough from you, young lady! Your father would be appalled at your behaviour right now.' Kay started to walk away.

'How would you even know! You've lived in the same county for the last thirty years and have only seen him what –

once, maybe twice in the last twelve months? And how long before that? Why didn't you know he was sick?'

Kay spun around. 'Why didn't *you* know he was sick, you ungrateful little brat!' Beth didn't see the slap coming but the sting reminded her of all the times her mother had smacked her across the face. Kay stepped back. 'Oh, Lisbeth, I'm sorry.'

'You bitch!' Beth lunged forward but Joe jumped in between them. 'Let me go! She had no right!'

'Come on. Let's all calm down.' He dragged her towards the car and just about shoved her into the passenger seat. Beth's face still stung and when she looked into the rear-view mirror to assess the damage, there were red blotches on her cheek. Beth waited as Joe walked back to Kay, his arms animated as they spoke, and then Kay stomped off.

A sea of emotion came over Beth and she began to rock. *Why did you leave me, Pops? Why?* A tidal wave of tears crashed down her cheeks.

Joe slid into the driver's seat and wrapped his arms around her. 'Let it all out, Beth. I told Kay she was out of order, and she apologised again. Cry, scream, punch, whatever you need.'

Beth pulled away. 'Why would you say that? I don't want to hurt anyone. Is that what you think I'm doing?'

'You and Kay nearly came to blows. You both said things you shouldn't. Kay just wanted to help.'

'Just take me home.'

Beth stared out of the window as Joe drove them back to her father's house. They sat in silence, and her thoughts turned against her. In fact, everyone was turning against her. She had never felt so alone in her life. With Pops gone, there was nobody to console her. The emptiness threatened to pull her inside.

How much more of this could she take?

Chapter Sixteen

JOE

The funeral director worked quickly. Even on such short notice, the cremation went ahead a few days later. The ceremony had been a small event and thankfully Beth had remained sober.

Joe sat in the living room of Beth's childhood home, surrounded by memories of a man he had only met a few times. It was a sombre place, with old furniture, faded curtains, and a lingering sense of loss. They had been working for a few hours packing up the last bits and pieces of Kevin's possessions, and just as Joe was finishing with some old photo albums, his phone rang.

He looked at the caller ID. An unknown number. He hesitated before answering, it might have something to do with work. He accepted the call.

'Hello?' His voice was cautious.

'It's me.'

'I told you not to call me.'

'I'm her mother. I should be able to speak to my own child.'

Joe felt knots form in his stomach. He knew all about the kind of mother she was. The woman on the phone had only been a negative influence on Beth's life.

Joe remained guarded. 'What do you want?'

'You know what I want. I'm thinking about coming to visit.'

Joe felt a wave of panic. Beth wouldn't want to see her mother, especially after all these years. It was a mistake answering the phone. He shouldn't be talking to Janis behind Beth's back.

'I don't think that's a good idea.' Joe kept his voice even. 'Beth's not really coping right now, and she doesn't want to see you.'

There was a moment of silence on the other end of the line.

'She's not coping?' Janis' voice rose. 'What do you mean?'

Shit. He'd said too much.

'I just don't think it would be a good idea for you to come.'

Janis's voice grew more insistent. 'I've a right to see her. What about my grief? I also loved Kevin. I can be there for her just as much as anyone else.'

'I understand that.' Joe had to fight to maintain his composure. Janis would try the patience of the proverbial saint. 'But I also think that you should respect Beth's wishes. She's made it clear she doesn't want to see you.' Maybe if Janis thought he was taking her side into account, she'd drop this ridiculous idea.

'I don't believe that.' Janis's voice shook. 'I have a right to be in her life.'

Joe took a deep breath. It was like talking to a wall. She wasn't taking in anything he was saying. 'Look, I don't want to keep secrets from Beth, and I don't think it's right for me to be talking to you without her knowing. If you're that concerned, you should have called her directly.'

There was another moment of silence on the other end of the line.

'Give me her number, then.'

'I can't do that.'

Janis's voice was cold. 'You should know that you're making a mistake. Beth needs her mother right now, whether she realises it or not, and once I'm back in her life there may not be any room for you.'

And with that she hung up.

Joe sat there for a moment, feeling drained. He'd done the right thing, but it was still difficult. He didn't like keeping secrets from Beth, even if he had some of his own that he wasn't prepared to share.

Chapter Seventeen

BETH

Beth and Joe had done what they could to get the house ready for the sale, and Kay would do the rest. Today they'd be returning home to Gladstone. Beth wasn't sure she was ready. Leaving meant letting go of her grief, of him, and everything would feel more real. Not that reality hadn't already set in. A sense of gloom already followed her.

Beth was a paralegal and her firm had allowed her additional compassionate leave, more than was granted by its policy, though she still had a few days of annual leave remaining that she could use. Her boss had told her that she could work from home, and that they'd look into her return to the office when she felt better adjusted. But returning to work might be a welcome distraction.

'Let me know what time you want to set off. I think Kay said she and the estate agent are coming by to go through the house one last time. Letting her handle the sale was the right decision.' Joe squeezed her shoulder.

After the slapping incident, Kay had called to apologised

and Joe had encouraged Beth to accept it and move on. Right now, Beth didn't have the energy to reply to Joe. She nodded in agreement and finished packing her bag for him to take to the car. She needed him out of the room so she could remove all the mini bottles she had stashed. The last thing she wanted was for her aunt to find them and have another reason to pick on her. 'Right, my case is ready for the car. I'll just have another look around. Be on the road in an hour or so?'

Joe took the handle from her. 'Sounds like a plan.'

When Joe left, Beth grabbed a bin bag from under the bathroom sink and swept the upstairs, chucking in empty bottles. She ran downstairs to pop the bag in the bin when Joe appeared in the kitchen.

'I'll put the kettle on...' He looked at her longer than normal, glancing at the bin. She couldn't understand why, if it bothered him or he had something to say, that he didn't talk to her about it. She was only hiding them so that Joe and Kay didn't give her a hard time. But maybe he didn't care at all.

A knock on the door pulled them out of their staring competition. The noise echoed down the empty hallway. 'I'll get it.' Joe said, turning away.

'It's okay. I'll do it.' Beth needed to step away from the tension that was building in the room.

She opened the door to see her aunt standing on the step with a young man. He looked as if he was barely out of his teens.

'Geoff, this is my niece, Lisbeth. Although she's now the owner of the house, I'm the executor of the will and with her permission, I'll be handling all the ins and outs as she lives just over an hour away. It wouldn't be convenient to have her travelling back and forth, especially after just losing her father.'

Why was Kay giving this nobody their family history? Beth shook the man's hand and stepped aside to let them in. Although Beth and Kay had made up after the funeral-home fiasco, it was things like this that still niggled at her.

'Shall I make us some tea?' Kay avoided looking her directly in the eye.

'Joe's already in there.' Beth pointed towards the kitchen. 'Let him know what you're having and I'm sure he'd be more than happy to sort it.' She didn't feel like socialising, so she followed her aunt through to the kitchen, grabbed her coffee and went into the living room. She looked around, not ready to accept that this would soon no longer be her house – new memories for someone else when she wasn't ready to let go of her own.

No more Christmases with Pops. No more games nights. No more laughing as they sat around the fire and caught up on what was happening in their lives. Pops liked a bit of gossip now and again, even though he said he didn't. Beth smiled, holding onto the thought. She was so immersed in her memories she hadn't realised that someone else was there with her until there was a smash on the floor.

'What the—' She turned to see the young estate agent frantically trying to pick up the pieces of her dad's clay bowl. He'd been a collector of Stoke pottery since Beth could remember and she'd left that out for Kay to take.

'I'm so sorry. I'll get this replaced. I just thought it might look better over there.'

Kay came rushing into the room. 'What did you do, Lisbeth?'

Beth's eyes never left the estate agent. 'It wasn't me. Your incompetent agent here seems to have greasy fingers. You'd better watch what he touches, or you'll have nothing left for yourself.'

'Lisbeth Ciara Stanford! I've put up with your astonishing and frankly rude behaviour for the last couple of weeks because I know you are grieving, but enough is enough! You apologise right now. It was obviously an accident.'

Beth's eyes became slits. 'So, it's an accident when *he* does it, but you were quick to snap and point the finger with that whiny disappointment in your voice, when you thought it had been me.' Her words cut through the air, sharper than she intended, but she couldn't stop herself. She turned to the estate agent 'I sincerely apologise if I offended you.' She then turned to her aunt, her stomach knotting with a mix of guilt and fury. 'I think we need a bit of space. So the next time we speak, make sure it's to tell me the house is sold.' Beth pushed passed her aunt and went to see how long Joe was going to be. The sooner they left, the better.

'I'm ready to go any time you are.' She fought back tears, swallowing hard. But as she stood there, the weight of everything – her father's death, losing the home that had been her anchor, and the constant strain between her and Kay – threatened to overwhelm her. The sooner they left, the better, before she completely fell apart.

Joe was washing his mug in the sink, and he turned to face her. 'All done here. I'll say goodbye to Kay and meet you in the car.' He pulled the keys out from his front pocket and chucked them in Beth's direction. Beth ran a finger over the kitchen counter and whispered 'Bye, Pops.' She twirled the pendant her dad had given her for her twenty-first birthday between her fingers. At least she'd always have him with her.

Beth headed down the hallway and opened the door. A woman was standing in front of her. She looked familiar, and Beth cocked her head, trying to place the face.

When she realised who it was, her knees buckled.

'What the hell do you want?'

'Hello, Lisbeth. I'm so sorry about your father. Is it too much to ask that you give your mother a hug?'

Chapter Eighteen

JOE

What's happening now? Joe rolled his eyes. When the shouting got louder, he raced towards the front door with Kay not far behind him. He already knew what he'd find. He recognised the other voice from the calls.

Joe pulled Beth close and prayed that Janis wasn't going to reveal that they'd already been speaking. Based on her reaction, if Beth found out he'd taken calls from Janis and not told her, she'd kill him. Although, he had to admit she'd have good reason. Why hadn't he told her about the calls? Yes, she'd been through a rough time, but telling her quietly would have been far preferable to Janis throwing it in her face to cause trouble.

Joe's heart pounded, and for a moment, all he could think about was how much Janis looked like Beth. It unsettled him – like staring at a future version of the woman he was soon to marry, one shaped by different choices, harder years. They both wore their hair long, but Janis's had streaks of grey, and her face, lined and worn, told a story of years Beth hadn't lived.

But now wasn't the time to be focusing on their similarities. He clenched his fists, trying to steady his breathing. He was more afraid of what Janis might say, of what she might let slip. He needed to keep control of the situation before things spiralled out of his hands. Fear gnawed at him, but anger wasn't far behind. What the hell was she doing here now, of all times?

Janis made a sarcastic comment to Kay about going for younger men, eyeing up the estate agent and then Joe. He could see Beth was clearly uncomfortable, though he was relieved that she appeared to be sober.

Janis didn't *look* like the monster that Beth had portrayed her as, but this was his first time meeting her. He had no reason to disbelieve his fiancée. Looks, after all, can be deceiving.

'Why are you here?' said Beth. 'You've had nothing to do with me or Dad for over twenty-five years. Isn't there a bar stool with your name on it somewhere?'

Joe's eyes widened as he watched Janis take a step back and bite her lip. He needed to diffuse the situation before it got even worse. When she looked at him and smiled, he froze.

'This must be Joe.' She put out her hand and Joe didn't know how he should respond. When Beth pulled him away, his shoulders relaxed. The whole situation was awkward. Even Kay jumped in. There was no love lost between the sisters-in-law.

Before Joe could say anything, Beth tugged at him, her eyes still on her mother. 'Let's go Joe,' she said. 'And I think it's time for you to leave Janis.'

When her mother stood firm, Beth dragged Joe past her towards the car. He couldn't look Janis in the eye.

'I hope Kay will be all right,' he said. 'Maybe we should stay a bit longer.'

Beth snapped at him. 'Kay can look after herself. She's a grown bloody woman. She can always call the police if that parasite doesn't leave. I want to go now. I've had enough of this shit to last me a lifetime.'

Joe jumped in the car, reversed out of the driveway, and braced himself for whatever he'd have to face from Beth on the drive home.

More than he'd ever done before, he hoped that the M6 would be clear of delays.

Chapter Nineteen

BETH

The tension in the car could be cut with a knife. Joe tried to start a conversation, but Beth was having none of it. Her hands shook, and she didn't know whether it was from the fury she felt or from the fact that she could murder a vodka right now.

As they neared their village, Beth undid her seatbelt. 'Can you let me out here?'

Joe frowned. 'Why here?'

'I just want to pop to the shops. We'll need milk and other bits.'

'I can take you there, save you having to lug the bags home.'

'I want to walk, clear my head. Can you please just stop the car like I'm asking you to?' Beth's hand was on the door handle, ready to open it and jump if need be. She struggled to catch her breath in the stifling space of the car and Joe's company.

'Okay. Let me find somewhere safe to pull over.' Joe indicated and pulled into the bus lane.

Before he could say anything else, Beth jumped out. 'I won't be long.' She slammed the door and walked away.

Inside the corner shop, Beth grabbed a metal basket and walked up and down the cramped aisles.

'Hey, stranger, where've you been? Seems like ages since I last saw you,' Grace called after her. Grace owned the shop and had done so for about thirty years. At least that is what she'd tell everyone who'd give her the chance. 'Someone said your father passed. So sorry to hear that, love.'

If she already knew the answer, why did she bother asking?

Beth gave her a half smile and continued around the shop, grabbing some milk, bread, a bottle of gin and a few other bits. She let Grace chatter away as she rung in the items. Once they'd been bagged up, Beth paid and left the shop without saying a word.

Walking in the direction of home, she spied the pub and decided to go in. She'd just have the one.

That's all she needed.

Just the one.

One shot of vodka to take the edge off.

Chapter Twenty

JOE

Joe clenched the steering wheel, his knuckles turning white as he pulled away from the curb. He hated when Beth was like this. In her dark place. He never knew what to do or say. But how could he blame her? She'd just buried her father, and now she was being forced to sell her childhood home. Seeing her mother again after all these years, on top of everything else, had to be tearing her apart. And the drinking – he knew that wasn't helping. It was no wonder she was moody, uncomfortable, barely herself. He needed to be more understanding and stop taking things so personally.

Pulling into their drive, he was glad to be home. He took their luggage inside and turned the heating on. It was so cold; he could see his breath. Joe put the coffee machine on so there would be something hot for Beth's return.

He was shattered.

He went into the living room and turned on his PS5 to release some tension. He didn't want to start making dinner in case Beth wanted to order in.

After playing GTA for a while, he glanced at his phone. A few hours had passed already and he was surprised Beth wasn't back. She may have bumped into one of their neighbours and stopped in for a coffee. He rang her mobile, but it went straight to voicemail.

'Hey, hon. Call me back and let me know when you'll be home. I'm starving and I'm sure you must be, too. Should I order something in?'

When Beth hadn't responded after an hour, Joe called another couple of times and left more messages. He began pacing the room, wondering if he should go out and look for her. She hadn't been herself and there was no telling where she could've ended up.

It had now been a couple of hours since he'd last seen her and all sorts of thoughts were running through Joe's head. He grabbed his coat and headed towards the shops when he spotted her in the distance. She was unsteady on her feet, the bags pulling her from side to side.

'What are you doing out?'

Joe noticed the slur in her words. Eyes glazed over. She dropped the bags and flopped herself onto him.

'Jesus, Beth. Let me help you.' He removed her arms, taking the bags in one hand, he used his free arm to hold her up. 'Let's get you home.'

'I can walk on my own you know.'

'It's okay.' He was trying to focus on the path as the snow began to fall.

'Why don't you love me?'

Joe stopped in his tracks, and she pulled away from him. 'You know I love you. I wouldn't be out in this weather if I didn't,' he said. 'I can't help how you feel, but maybe you need to lay off the drink. You're stumbling about. I don't want you to get hurt.'

'Why do you always have to be an arse. If I'm such a burden, you can just fuck off. I don't need anybody.'

He wasn't expecting this sharp reply.

Beth stomped off, wobbling from side to side and began shouting in the direction of the neighbour's houses. Her arms were waving about. Joe came up behind her and lowered them as he led her back inside. He'd need to apologise to the neighbours in the morning after she shouted a few more insults as he closed the door.

'Enough! Why don't you change into some dry clothes, and I'll run a bath. We can chat then.' He'd need to keep an eye on her after all the drink she had.

He was about to go upstairs when he noticed her falling forward.

'Beth, watch out!'

Chapter Twenty-One

BETH

Dizzy, Beth reached out to steady herself but missed the doorframe. As she fell to the floor, she knocked over the glass vase that was on the small shelf by the doorway. Joe's warning had come too late, and her hand landed on a sharp piece of the broken vase.

She screamed.

There was blood everywhere.

Joe kneeled beside her. 'Here. Let me see.' He took her hand and examined the wound. 'Let's get this cleaned up. You may need stitches.' He picked her up by her functioning arm and they walked into the kitchen. 'Lean here.' He placed her by the table and went over to the sink, turning on the water and then calling her over.

'Run your hand under this.'

Beth lurched the two steps from table to sink and put her hand under the cold water.

'Ooh that hurts.'

'I'm not surprised. Though you're lucky, it doesn't look too deep. Keep your hand under the water and I'm going to get something to wrap around it.'

Beth stared out the back window. How had she ended up like this? Joe's words earlier had hit her hard. She wasn't an alcoholic. She wasn't her mother. But seeing her reflection in the glass made her wonder. She looked awful. It was a sobering reflection.

Joe was back within minutes and held her hand in his. He rubbed antiseptic cream on the wound before wrapping a cotton bandage around the palm of her hand. Taping the end of the bandage, he held her wrist and tugged gently, forcing her to look at him.

'Stop pushing me away, okay? Let's get to bed and we can talk more in the morning.'

Beth looked at the floor, finding it hard to keep eye contact, and nodded. 'I think I'll have that bath first.'

'You need to keep your hand dry and elevated. With all the drink, maybe a bath in the morning would be better?'

There it was. That whiny fuck-you-Beth tone in his voice.

'I'm not asking you to run it for me. I can do it myself.'

Joe huffed a short breath out. 'It's fine. I'll run the bath.'

Beth headed upstairs with Joe following close behind. She held on to the handrail with her good hand, to steady her steps. While Joe was filling the bath, Beth changed into her bathrobe, and then sat on the bed, staring at her hand.

Ten minutes later, Joe came into the bedroom. 'That's done. I'll sit in with you and keep you company.'

'No...' Beth got up and headed to the bathroom. 'Thanks.' She didn't need a babysitter.

Joe didn't reply. Before she closed the door to the bathroom, she saw him change into his PJ bottoms, mumbling something as he walked by and headed downstairs.

Beth sunk down into the warm water. Her left hand was hanging over the edge of the tub; the bandage was stained with a red patch of blood. She closed her eyes and relaxed as water mixed with lavender bubble bath lapped over her body. Her eyes felt heavy but a loud thump on the door woke her.

Chapter Twenty-Two

JOE

Joe got changed, pulling on a pair of checkered flannel pyjama bottoms. He was exhausted but he needed to do one more thing before going to sleep. As he passed the bathroom door he called out. 'I'll go and clear up that glass.'

He took the brush and tray out from under the stairs and began to sweep the shards when he heard a thump on the door. He looked at his watch. *Who the hell is calling round at this time?*

If it was Beth's mother, he'd tell her to fuck off. The woman couldn't take a hint. He yanked open the door. 'What is it?'

'Hi. Mr Travers, is it? I'm PC Richmond and this is my colleague PC Harper.'

What the hell were the police doing here?

'There's been a call out about some arguing. Do you mind if we come in?'

'Huh? Everything's fine. You've wasted your time. My fiancée is in the bath right now. I'd rather not bother her as her father has just died and she's, well, she had a drink and knocked over a vase.' Joe pointed to the glass on the floor.

The male officer pushed open the door and looked at where Joe was pointing.

'I see there's some blood. Please, sir, we won't be long.'

Joe stepped aside. 'Mind the glass.' An awkward laugh escaped his lips. 'Sorry, nerves I guess.'

The female officer brushed past him. 'Nothing to be nervous about. Can I speak to'—she looked at a notepad—'Lisbeth, is it?'

'Uh, yeah. She goes by Beth, though. She's upstairs in the bath. I'll go and get her.'

'I'll come with you if you don't mind.' PC Harper didn't wait for a reply. It wasn't a choice. Joe thumped on the bathroom door and before he could explain anything, Beth shouted.

'I'm okay. Would you just give me some peace for five minutes.'

Joe looked at the officer before opening the door a crack and putting his head into the bathroom. 'Can you get dressed? He was about to tell her the police were there when she kicked off.

'What the hell, Joe? I finally feel okay and now you want me to get out? I haven't even been in here for ten minutes.'

'Could you do as your partner asks, miss.'

Joe heard water splashing as Beth struggled to sit up.

'What? Who's that?'

Joe threw her towel. 'The police are here. Someone's called them.' Joe rolled his eyes so only Beth could see.

'We'll see you downstairs.'

Joe felt a tap on his shoulder and the female officer gestured for him to follow.

'Let's leave her to get dressed.'

He pulled the door shut and followed the officer downstairs. Her colleague, PC Richmond, if he remembered his name correctly, had been looking around the living room.

'Nice place.' He then headed into the kitchen and Joe didn't know what to do with himself.

A few minutes later Beth came down and Joe noticed her glazed eyes.

Had she taken something before coming down?

Chapter Twenty-Three

BETH

'What seems to be the problem, officer?' Beth smoothed her hair with her good hand, avoiding eye contact.

'Hi.' A male officer popped his head through to the living room and Beth jumped.

'Sorry. Didn't mean to frighten you. If you and my colleague, PC Harper, can chat in here, I'll go through to the kitchen with your husband.'

'Uh, he's not my husband, he's my fiancé.' That came out harsher than Beth intended, and Joe glared at her, a mix of hurt and anger in his eyes.

Beth remained with PC Harper in the living room.

'Your fiancé said you go by Beth, do you mind if I call you Beth?'

'That's fine.'

'We received a call from one of your neighbours.'

'Hmmph. Which one?' Beth went over to the window, looking out hoping to catch the traitor, sure they'd be watching.

'Can you come away from the window? Have a seat. We shouldn't be too long here.'

'I'd prefer to stand.' Beth moved away from the window. She didn't want to come across as difficult, but she felt her blood boil when she thought that some nosy arsehole had called the police. All she was doing was shouting in the street.

'Look this is all some sort of misunderstanding. I've been away dealing with the death of my father. I'd had a bit too much to drink and Joe came to collect me from down the road. I *may* have shouted at a neighbour who was staring out at me. It was stupid ... childish even, I know. Surely, it's not a crime, or enough of one for you to be wasting your time. I'm sorry.'

PC Harper tilted her head and scribbled some notes. 'We're not here because you were shouting in the street. A concerned neighbour heard some shouting from inside your house, and what they thought was glass shattering. They heard you scream. What happened to your hand?'

Beth held out her bandaged hand and then started to laugh. 'Oh this? I fell and knocked a vase over. My hand landed in glass, and I screamed because I cut it. Wait... Do you think Joe did this?' She started to laugh again. 'He wouldn't ... couldn't...' She shook her head as the thought was just ridiculous. 'We may have argued a bit, but what couple doesn't?'

'What were you arguing about?'

'I don't even know to be honest. Probably my drinking. His disappointment in me. Who knows.' Beth shrugged and sat down.

The officer frowned.

'Why are you looking at me like that? This really is a big misunderstanding.' Beth's leg shook.

'We have to take all suspected domestic abuse seriously. Do you need to go to the hospital and have someone look at that?'

'Domestic abuse? Oh my God, no.' Beth stood. This could affect Joe's job and maybe even her own at the law firm. 'You're taking this all out of context. I was drunk. I fell. Where's Joe? Joe! Come in here please. This is all wrong!'

'Please calm down, ma'am. We're just doing our job.'

'Joe! Please come in here.' Beth was screaming now.

Joe stormed into the room. 'What's wrong?' He jogged over to Beth's side. 'Are you okay?'

'They think you did this to me?' She held out her hand. 'Look at the way she's looking at me.'

'It's okay, hon. Sit down.' Joe helped Beth into a chair.

'Can we speak through here?' Joe nodded towards the hall and both officers followed.

Beth couldn't hear what was being said as they were whispering. Minutes seemed like hours and just as she stood to see what was happening, she heard the front door open and then close. She rushed into the hall.

'What's going on? They believed me, right?'

Joe's icy stare confused her.

'It's fine now. Do you see what happens when you get drunk? You scared me. You clearly upset and scared the neighbours, too. It's sorted now, but it's late, we can talk about this in the morning.'

Beth's hands shook, she needed something to calm her nerves but didn't want to upset Joe anymore tonight. She had stashed the sleeping tablets Dr Griffin had given her in her handbag. 'I'm just going to get a glass of water. Do you want one?' She didn't want to talk about this tomorrow or ever.

Joe's eyes said he didn't believe her. 'No. Please don't have any more to drink.'

'I promise. Just water.' She tried to smile, but it was a struggle.

Once she was sure that Joe was upstairs, Beth dug around in her handbag and found the prescription bottle. She took out a sleeping pill and grabbed a glass of water from the kitchen, swallowing the tablet.

She went up to bed, glad she wouldn't have to think about this evening.

Not waking up might be the best thing for everyone.

Chapter Twenty-Four

JOE

Joe ran his fingers through his hair as he lay awake watching Beth and recalling the events of the evening.

PC Richmond's eyes not giving anything away.

His throat tightened as he remembered the terse way Beth had corrected the officer when he'd called Joe her husband.

Joe had followed PC Richmond into the kitchen, feeling slightly dazed about the whole situation. Beth fell over – what was the big deal?

'Why do you think we're here?'

'Obviously someone heard Beth scream when she fell and knocked over the vase. I assume they rang you.' Joe shrugged, hoping it looked casual rather than uncaring. 'Bit over the top if you ask me, both Beth and I have worked with people who've suffered domestic abuse and I can assure you, this isn't what you think it is. Who made the call?'

'You'll know I can't disclose that.' The officer had smirked at Joe. 'Did you and Miss Stanford have an argument out in the street?' He'd tilted his head like he already knew the answer and what Joe said would make up his mind on where things would be going.

When Joe had explained about Beth's drinking that evening, the officer didn't look convinced. Joe didn't understand why he had found it so hard to explain the situation. It was the truth, but the officer's next question had thrown him.

'You didn't put your hands on her, then? Maybe push her? Only we were told that you were a little aggressive when you took your partner into the house.'

Joe had shook his head. 'You've got to be joking. I was embarrassed. She was drunk and making a show of herself. I just wanted to get inside.'

Now Joe looked over at Beth's chest, rising and falling – she looked so peaceful. He would never lay a hand on her.

The police had asked him if he had called an ambulance, but he didn't think the cut was deep enough to warrant a hospital visit. The he explained how he runs Travers House and works with the police and other agencies to help vulnerable people.

The officer shrugged.

The whole situation was a mess.

If he didn't have to move Beth and possibly wake her, he'd be looking for her stash of booze. He could do with a drink himself.

Chapter Twenty-Five

BETH

Weeks had passed since the police had come round, and although Beth couldn't confirm who'd called them in, she suspected it was the family next door. They lived in a semi-detached house and Beth had often heard their kids screaming through the walls. It didn't take a genius to work it out.

Since she'd run out of Dr Griffin's magic pills, her insomnia was intense, and her drinking increased. She hadn't wanted to rely on the sleeping pills, but they were the only thing that gave her a few hours of peace, and now, without them, her nights were endless. She'd been rationing them, trying to make the supply she'd been given in Leek stretch, but they'd been gone for weeks now. The restless nights only made her grief sharper. And then there was the drinking – she knew it wasn't helping, but it was easier than lying in the dark, staring at the ceiling, waiting for sleep that never came.

Not long after leaving her father's home, a withheld number had kept calling her but when she answered, all she

100

could hear was breathing. She suspected it was her mother but couldn't trace the number. Things were tense enough between her and Joe. If she mentioned it, there was the risk that he would make her feel like she was losing her mind. She'd find a way to deal with her mother.

Joe hadn't spoken to her about the police incident either, and Beth walked on eggshells, not wanting to upset him further. But her mind raced with different scenarios as to what he might be thinking.

My fiancé's a drunk.

She's losing the plot.

She's behaving irrationally...

Beth smacked the side of her head wanting to be rid of the intrusive thoughts. She wasn't any of those things.

Joe had already left for work, but Beth still had some time before she had to go in. She'd been working from home lately, and today was her first day back in the office. She played with her necklace, rubbing the mini urn that held her father's ashes. Kay had sent it to her when the funeral director had mistakenly posted it to her father's house.

Beth's boss had been very flexible. She'd been allowed to work from home, and was assigned the notes of a complicated case the firm was working on. Her boss had told her she could come back into the office when she felt ready to return. Last week they'd completed her return-to-work interview via a Zoom call and today she would be going back in, but on reduced hours.

In her role as a paralegal, she assisted a barrister and often helped out in the company's legal department. Occasionally, she'd be asked to conduct interviews, research, attend court, organise legal files but also had other general office duties.

Beth put on a black suit with a white blouse and black court shoes. As she applied makeup, she looked in the mirror and noticed the dark circles under her eyes. She hoped her boss wouldn't comment.

She grabbed her laptop bag and checked she had her meds with her, she didn't want to have a panic attack on her first day back in the office.

She double-checked if she had locked the front door, and then headed down the street to the bus stop with her head down, avoiding eye contact. She'd convinced herself they were all talking about her, and she wasn't in the mood for confrontation.

The bus ride into town was uneventful. She travelled in the opposite direction to Joe, which is why they never journeyed to work together. Beth stared out of the window, trying to manage her anxiety. Her fingers fidgeted with her handbag's tassels, and she forced herself to focus on her breathing to keep calm.

When she got off the bus nearly forty minutes later, she made a beeline for a café and picked up a cappuccino before heading into the office.

'Lisbeth, lovely to see you back. We're so sorry for your loss.' Glyn moved the headset away from her mouth and came over to give Beth a hug.

'Thanks. It has been quite difficult. Is Cassandra in?'

'She is. I'll just call ahead and let her know you're on your way up...'

Beth stood at the reception desk and listened to Glyn,

waiting for the thumbs-up. Once she got it, she waved at the receptionist and walked up to the second floor where the solicitor's offices were. She was also on the second floor, but the paralegals shared a large open-plan room in the far corner; it doubled as a meeting room if the space was needed. As they all worked from laptops, they often hot-desked.

Cassandra Lynch was one of the partners in the solicitor's firm, Lynch, Walker & Co, and was Beth's direct boss. She waved Beth over as soon as she saw her.

'Lisbeth. How are you? No bullshit, please.' Cassandra pointed to one of the chairs across from her. 'Take a seat.'

Beth did as she was asked. She wasn't normally nervous with Cassandra, but lack of sleep made her anxiety soar. 'I'm okay. I've good days and bad, but I guess that's to be expected.'

Cassandra pursed her lips and nodded. 'Yes. Absolutely. You're my top paralegal and I'm trusting you to keep me informed.' She paused. 'How are you getting on with that case I assigned you? It's a big one, with lots of public interest, so I need to know you're focused and capable. I may need you to attend court from time to time, along with your research and interviews. Are you up for that?'

Beth took a moment. Cassandra was blunt and wasn't normally concerned with people's feelings.

'Yes. I want to get back to some normality, and keeping myself busy will help me stop thinking about losing my father.'

'Hmm. Yes. And aren't you getting married soon or have I just made that up?'

Beth blinked at her boss's words, feeling caught off-guard. A wedding? Right now? It felt strange that her boss would bring it up, especially knowing she was grieving, as if somehow the idea of planning a wedding could smooth over the loss of her father. Did people really expect her to just ... move on? She wasn't sure if her boss was trying to distract her or if she was simply being thoughtless. Either way, the question left Beth feeling oddly disconnected, like the person her boss was talking about wasn't her.

She and Joe had wanted a spring wedding. They had decided on May 20th next year, but with Christmas coming up soon, she hadn't thought about the wedding for weeks now. 'Yeah, I think so. To be honest, I haven't really given it much thought.' The words felt hollow in her mouth, and now that it was in her head, she couldn't help but wonder if Joe had changed his mind, too. He'd been distant lately, like everything between them had shifted. Maybe he didn't want to talk about the wedding either. She'd speak to him about it after New Year's, as she had enough on her mind already.

'Of course you haven't.' Cassandra stood. 'Anyway. We've got a lot of work to do.' She snapped her fingers. 'I've emailed you the details of a bunch of documents I need, an interview that needs to be done and a bit of research, so why don't you get started on that.'

Beth picked up her bag and was heading out the door when Cassandra called out. 'Lisbeth, if you're struggling with anything I want you to let me know immediately. This is too important a case to screw up because you can't cope. Okay?'

'Of course.'

Cassandra really needed to work on her people skills. Her boss didn't become attached or invested in the people she worked with. Probably a good thing as the firm received a lot of hate mail and threats due to their clientele and her boss's high acquittal rate, many of whom she suspected to be guilty.

Her office area was quiet. Beth was the only one in, but the team was small with two others both of whom worked part-time. Brian was much younger than her and a bit of a know-it-all, but Beth rarely saw him. Then there was Rachel, who was a few years older than her and wrapped up in her kids, something Beth struggled to relate to.

She chose a seat with a view out the window; below her, she could see the fields and a canal where the boats were lined up. They looked so small, she often wondered how people could make them into homes.

Beth shook her head. 'Focus!' she mumbled to herself. Opening her laptop, she immediately logged in and went straight to her emails, reading the one marked URGENT from Cassandra. The email was long, and Beth scanned it, making a list on a yellow legal pad with her priority tasks.

Beth reread the details of the case. A man was charged with domestic abuse. Her stomach fluttered as she read what Cassandra had written.

Our position is this: we'll seek to make representations arguing that the charging standard as contained within the Code for Crown Prosecutors has not been met. Therefore, the CPS will be wasting taxpayers' money if they pursue, as there's not a realistic prospect of a conviction. It simply isn't in the interest of justice or the public.

Beth read on.

I didn't have an opportunity to fully review the CPS papers. But we need something that will be sufficient grounds to have the charges dropped – you'll need to find it. Make sure you consider 'pre-charge engagement' with the investigating officers, and find out if the charging standard has indeed been met. From what I've seen, it hasn't but I'd like your opinion. Bear all of this in mind, Lisbeth.

There were five people to be interviewed, but Beth was only tasked with interviewing one of the witnesses and liaising with the police. She pulled out her work mobile, organising for the individual to come in and speak with her. After that was booked in, she made herself a coffee. She felt tired.

As she sat back at her desk a call came in. 'Lisbeth. Do you have a moment?'

On autopilot, Beth headed towards Cassandra's office.

'Yes. Mr Brewer will be coming in today.' Cassandra was on speakerphone.

Beth recognised the name but couldn't place from where. Her boss must have spotted her confused look as she ended her call.

'Our client? The case I just sent you all the details on,' Cassandra huffed as she walked over to the bookshelf and retrieved a box. 'Here's more information I need you to go through. I'll say this one last time. If you're not up to it, tell me now and I'll get someone else on it. We can't afford to lose this case. The media are all over it and one wrong move could be devastating.' Cassandra placed the box down on the table in front of them. 'Can I trust you with this? Don't let me down.'

'I won't. I'm just a little tired, but this should help.' She raised her mug. 'I'll start on this now.' Beth placed the mug on top of the box and picked it up.

'I'd like you to interview Brewer. Tell me what your thoughts are after you speak with him.'

Although Beth had always been praised for her interview skills, after what Cassandra had just relayed, she was a little surprised she was allowed anywhere near the man. But she wanted to prove she was up to the task and that little niggle in the back of her head would just have to bugger off.

'No problem. Do I need to make an appointment, or does he already have one?'

'Haven't you been listening? He'll be here in two hours. So you'd best get through as much of that stuff as you can. There's a lot on the line, including your future here.'

Chapter Twenty-Six

JOE

Joe put the matter of the police call-out behind him. Beth *seemed* to be coping better and there was no point of dwelling on something that would only cause conflict. Work was stressful enough without all of this. He wondered whether she was still drinking as much because he thought he'd caught her slurring her words, but she'd sworn to him that the GP had increased her anxiety meds and he didn't want to argue with her anymore. With Beth finally back at work, things should return to normal. Right? She still struggled with sleep but had assured him that once the medication settled into her system, her insomnia would disappear. He had no reason not to believe her.

Besides Travers House, he kept thinking about money. The first time Joe had done it, everything was smooth. A quick exchange and no one noticed or suspected a thing. The only problem was the joint account had been hit, and if he didn't resolve things soon, there wouldn't be a wedding. He had made the mistake of investing the majority of his and some of

Beth's savings into a scheme that he thought would triple their income. He realised too late that it was a cleverly thought-out pyramid scheme and by that time, the company and their money was long gone.

Joe had hoped Beth's father's house would have sold much quicker, but months later and it was still on the market. When they had moved in together, Beth had asked Joe to manage their joint account because of her history with money. Although she'd worked hard to get out of debt, her finances were an area that always triggered bad memories for her. The last thing she needed was to find out about this.

Whenever Joe called Kay for an update on the sale, she said she'd speak to Beth when she had some news. It was as if she didn't trust him, and that put him on edge. Did she suspect something? Had she shared her suspicions with Beth?

Joe had to convince Kay that Beth wanted him to handle the sale because she was still struggling. This was just part of the truth. Eventually Kay told him that there hadn't been much interest in the house, but she promised to call if there were any offers. It didn't seem like Kay or Beth were pushing the sale either, but he supposed that was because of their shared grief. Selling the house would be a final goodbye.

Joe needed to focus on the positives, otherwise people would notice and when that happened, they'd ask questions he wouldn't be able to answer.

He had considered taking her for a psychological assessment at one point, as she seemed to be hallucinating, rambling things that didn't make sense and telling him her vision would go blurry from time to time as if she was going blind. Beth's GP, however. confirmed that the trauma of her father's death, self-medicating and mixing alcohol were just side effects and would ease once Beth stopped being so reliant on these artificial crutches. The GP's warning, that she wouldn't be signed fit for work if he didn't notice an improvement, was the one thing that had motivated her to ease back on the drink. It was the trump card he now used whenever he needed to limit her drinking. Was it all just wishful thinking?

'What do we have going on today?'

Joe looked up as AJ's voice carried into the office.

'We've got that domestic-abuse case. It's all over the papers at the moment. I told reception to signal us when they arrive.'

'The one where the husband claims she was making it all up?'

'That's the one.'

AJ sat down opposite him. 'There were some pretty graphic photos in the paper. Why would she make that up?'

Joe shrugged. 'He's obviously got a lot of money. Maybe he's going to try and buy his way out of this.' He'd seen it before. The power and control in abusive relationships often extends beyond the violence.

'If he has control over all the money, she'll have no hope to secure the same level of legal help if he pursues his own case, which is based on his defence that *she* is the violent one.'

But that's what Joe's charity was for, and he'd make sure this woman had all the resources she needed.

'Well, we'll try and help her as best we can. What's the plan?' AJ pulled a pocket notebook out ready to make some notes.

'An Independent Domestic Violence Advisor will be attending with her. She wants to get some things from the property. At the moment, she's staying with a friend, and I've contacted the police to arrange an escort. They'll meet her there.'

'You could have just said IDVA. I know what they are.' AJ laughed. 'That's a good start.'

'I guess housing, counselling and perhaps legal is what we can help her with? We'll know more when she arrives.' Joe couldn't think of anything else until they had more details from the client.

'Great. I'll get some numbers and leaflets together and set up the room.'

'Thanks.' Joe looked over AJ's shoulder and noticed the IDVA had arrived. 'I'll speak to her first.' He pointed. The receptionist brought the IDVA to his office and he stood, extending his hand. 'Hi, I'm the manager here at Tasker House, call me Joe. If you'd like to have a seat, we can talk through the strategy before Mrs Brewer arrives. Is her friend bringing her?'

The woman nodded. 'I'm Sharon. Nice offices here, I'm used to working in the Staffordshire area, but you know what it's like when there are staff shortages, we all rally round, eh? Normally I would've met her and brought her in with me, but she wanted her friend to drop her in, maybe stay, and I didn't think that would be an issue?'

'Not at all. As long as she's happy with discussing things openly, I can't see any issues. Do you have more background information? I know what's in the papers but not much else. I'd like to limit any trauma a meeting like this may inflict by going over what we can beforehand. Mrs Brewer can fill in the blanks if need be.'

'Aye. She told me that the relationship had been abusive for some time. Probably started seeing the red flags about a year after they were married. But she says she was too embarrassed to leave. Common in cases like this.'

Joe nodded. He'd seen it time and again: the abuser isolates the victim from family and friends, breaks their self-confidence, and makes the person feel as if no one would believe them. Gaslighting the shit out of the person until they don't want to ask for help.

'She did say she reached out to her mother-in-law after a particularly scary incident. She was hoping the woman might have some sway with her son. Instead, Mrs Brewer was basically told she was overreacting and would be left with nothing if she tried to pursue it. She had burnt bridges with her own family, thanks to Mr Brewer, so when she did try and reach out to them, they turned her away.'

Joe shook his head. 'Jeez. Nothing like protecting an abuser, eh? She's entitled to half of their assets, surely?'

'That's the thing. Mrs Brewer says she was tricked into signing something not long after they were married, but she wasn't allowed to read it. Apparently, he made a big song and dance about her not trusting him. If it's what I think, the mother-in-law could be right. I think she might have a case to contest it, though, if the criminal case sees him convicted.'

'The paper said she was doing this for the money. Her husband said the same and seems to have a lot of support on his side. Says she's been squirreling away money amounting to six figures or more.' Joe pulled out pages he'd highlighted and showed them to Sharon.

'I've seen that, too. And while she'll deny it to you, the truth of it is she's already told me that she *had* secretly stashed *some* money away, but it won't last too long. We see this all the time, and for me, I think it makes rather than breaks her position. People don't stash money away for a rainy day when they're happily married to someone rich.'

Joe raised an eyebrow and nodded. 'We'll need to find out more about that as it might mean she's not entitled to certain services.' He made a note. 'We've a counsellor here, which she'll have free access to...'

Sharon interrupted. 'Do they specialise in domestic abuse?'

'AJ's expertise is extensive. Bereavement, abuse, substance misuse, trauma and— Oh, I think Mrs Brewer has arrived. Let's continue the conversation in the conference room. My colleague will show Mrs Brewer through, if you'd like to follow me.'

Joe noticed that Mrs Brewer was wearing heavy make-up and dark glasses. She held her friend's arm tightly. Joe walked to the front of the conference room, noting that AJ had put out jugs of water and plastic cups on either end of the large table. She'd also set up a station for hot drinks and biscuits on the cabinet behind them. There were notepads and pencils spread out in case anyone wanted to take notes or doodle.

When Mrs Brewer walked into the room, she froze on the spot.

'No ... no... I can't do this with'—she pointed at Joe—'how can I after this...' She pulled her glasses off with a shaking hand and although they had faded, hints of bruising and scars were still visible. 'This is what he did to me, and you expect me to feel safe with a man in the room... He can feed lies to help my husband.' She began to back out of the door and Joe held his hands up.

'Hey, it's okay. You come through and I'll go.' Joe leaned down and whispered to his colleague, 'We'll speak after the meeting.' It wasn't the first time this had happened, and it wouldn't be the last. He should've done his checks beforehand. Rookie error. He realised that with everything happening at home his head hadn't been fully in his work.

Joe returned to his office and made a note on Mrs Brewer's file: *Female staff only.*

He had some time before the meeting was over. A sticky note stuck out of the corner of his bag, reminding him to grab some milk on the way home, and Beth popped into his head. He wondered how she was getting on. He couldn't call her, though, and risk an argument – she'd said she felt like he was constantly checking up on her and he'd promised to lay off. Instead, he called the one person he knew would tell him the truth and keep it confidential.

Chapter Twenty-Seven

BETH

B eth spent an hour or so going through the CPS papers and police and victim statements in relation to Jack Brewer. In the box given to her by Cassandra were some horrendous images relating to the wife's injuries: blackened eyes, fat lip, bruises on various parts of her torso, some already posted in the newspapers, but others had not been seen by the public. Bile rose in the back of Beth's throat as she flipped through the images. Additional backstory showed that the alleged abuse had taken place over a sustained period of time – eight years, in fact – though the wife had never reported it to the police. This was a common pattern Beth had come across in working cases of domestic abuse.

A statement caught her eye. It was a concerned friend who had contacted the police after receiving a phone call from Mrs Brewer.

Why did she call her friend first and not the police?

The notes showed the police had no records of any past call-outs to the couple's home, or any properties the couple owned, for that matter. Brewer had no previous convictions or history of violence, but Beth knew this meant nothing other than the fact he'd never been caught. Mrs Brewer's friend had applied online for a request of information under Clare's Law, also known as the Domestic Violence Disclosure Scheme (DVDS), which came into force in 2014. He'd applied for this information six weeks prior to the alleged assault under the 'right to know' protocol, but as there was nothing on Brewer, no risk identified, the matter was closed, and no information was provided.

What triggered the friend six weeks ago? There was nothing in the information to suggest a domestic-abuse incident had occurred. Did Mr Brewer think his wife was having an affair with this male friend? Most abusers isolate their victims, and a male friend would be like holding a red flag to a bull.

Beth would ask Cassandra.

Mr Brewer had been charged under the Offences Against the Person Act with Threats to Kill, and Wounding with Intent. The CPS believed they had a strong case based on the alleged victim's injuries, and a journal she'd kept recording the sustained abuse over a number of years. Brewer denied all charges, and in fact pointed the finger at his wife, saying she'd been planning to set him up for years. He also alleged that *she* was the abusive one in their marriage, but he never went to the police because he was embarrassed and thought he wouldn't be believed. Beth had seen this, too, in cases where a man was a victim of domestic abuse.

She pulled out a photo of Brewer. He was an unassuming male, average size, average height. She'd have to hear his story before she drew any further conclusions. Yawning, she looked at the time.

Shit. She had about fifteen minutes before he was due to arrive. Beth sprinted to the loo, and after washing her hands, she applied a little more concealer under her eyes to hide the dark circles. Her heart raced and she held onto the sink to calm herself down. A panic attack threatened to overwhelm her.

Not today. Not today. Not today...

She returned to her office and had just picked up the file and a legal pad with her notes when the desk phone rang.

'Hey, doll. There's a Mr Brewer here to see you.'

'Thanks, Glyn. I'm on my way.'

Beth took a deep breath. Her eye twitched and a headache began to form. She popped two ibuprofen which she washed down with the dregs of a now cold coffee before heading downstairs to reception.

Reaching her hand out, she walked over to Brewer and introduced herself. 'Hello, Mr Brewer?' He nodded. 'My name is Lisbeth Stanford. I've been asked to go through a few things with you, if you'd like to follow me.'

Beth noticed that Brewer followed close on her heels as she led him to one of the free interview rooms. 'Take a seat. Did you want anything to drink? There's water behind you, or I can ask Glyn to bring in some coffee, if you'd prefer?'

'Water is fine. I'm not sure why I'm here again, I've given a statement to the police and spoken to Mrs Lynch already.'

'I'm afraid you're probably going to have to speak to a lot of people, including me, multiple times while this is all going on. My job is to go through everything with a fine-tooth comb – that includes what's been said by the prosecution, the police, and you and your wife – and note any inconsistencies or irregularities and, bluntly, things that may come back and bite you on your backside. So it's best not to try and hide anything. What you say to me is strictly confidential.'

'Okay, but I've told the truth ... everything I remember.'

'My dad always had a saying about the truth.' Beth's eyes glistened and she fought hard to hide the tears. 'He said, if you tell the truth, you don't have to remember anything.'

'Hmm ... but her truth is different, how will anyone believe me?' His head fell into his hands.

'Mr Brewer. There's no such thing as his truth or her truth ... only *the* truth. And that's what we're going to focus on today.'

Chapter Twenty-Eight

JOE

'Hi, Cassandra. It's Joe Tasker here. I was wondering if I could have a few minutes of your time.'

'Joe? Oh, Lisbeth's Joe. Of course. Is everything okay?'

'Yeah, I don't want her to know I'm calling. She'll think I'm checking up on her and won't be happy.'

'Noted. But you are checking up on her. Right? Is there something I need to be aware of?'

Shit.

He hadn't thought this through. Joe didn't want to drop Beth in it or have her boss questioning whether she was ready to return, so he decided he'd be vague on what he said. 'No, nothing at all. She hasn't been sleeping very well. I wanted to make sure she isn't putting pressure on herself. You know what she's like.' He tried to sound casual, but his laugh came out awkward and croaky.

'Okay, I'll pretend I'm not going to read between the lines here. I've only given her one case. She's interviewing a client now and I haven't had any concerns, if that eases your mind?'

'Yes, yes, it does. Thanks.'

'I've got a meeting in about fifteen minutes, and I need to do some prep, so if there's nothing else.'

'Just one thing. If you could not mention I called.'

'Heard you the first time, Joe. Take care.'

Beth had told him about her boss's bluntness, and he thought she'd was exaggerating. She wasn't. He put his mobile back on the desk, and the tension in his shoulders eased. He felt foolish for calling. But at least now he could let it go and focus on his own job.

Joe looked at his watch, the meeting with Mrs Brewer would be wrapping up shortly. He was expecting someone from the paper to call to find out what the charity planned on doing. He wanted to be prepared, although he could only provide limited information. The charity would more than likely come under scrutiny by anyone who believed her husband. He started to formulate his press strategy, then he'd email it over to the comms manager before sending the statement to the media.

When his mobile rang half an hour later, he was almost glad to see it was Kay and not Beth. At least Cassandra had kept her word.

He ignored the call, letting it go to voicemail, but she wasn't going to let up as the phone rang again.

'Hello, Kay. How are you?' His jaw clenched. He'd enough people having a go at him and didn't fancy another.

'Why didn't you pick up the first time?'

'I'm at work. Can this wait until later?'

'No, no, it can't. I wouldn't be calling if it wasn't important.'

Joe bit his lip and waited.

'Hello. Are you still there?'

'Yes, I was waiting for you. What's so urgent?'

'Did you know Lisbeth has been having episodes?' The last word was whispered as if it was taboo. 'When I spoke to her the other day, and when I started asking for more information about what was happening, she gave me this song and dance about not wanting to be judged and then hung up on me.'

'What? By 'episodes' you mean the blurred vision and stuff?' Joe was surprised Beth had even said anything. Having no friends to call, Kay had always let Beth lean on her and she must have been concerned if she'd shared the episodes with her aunt.

'You knew?' There was a short disapproving pause. 'How could you let her go back to work, then? She deals with some really dangerous people. What if she faints ... or worse. Anything could happen! I expected more from you, Joe. Maybe I should come down for a few weeks. She's clearly not well.'

'Stop right there. Yes, I am concerned. But she's been in contact with her GP and he said these were all normal side effects of her medication. He increased her dosage after Kevin's death. I found that out by accident.' Joe had discovered a bottle in the bathroom and confronted Beth about it. She'd initially tried to play it down but then explained everything to him. 'Apparently, it's just the interactions and side effects from the meds, but this should ease soon. To be honest, getting back to work seems to be helping her.'

Joe kept his voice level. Although the anger was simmering beneath the surface, it would be wasted on Kay.

'Beth wouldn't appreciate you coming down,' he said. 'It could make matters worse. You two always end up fighting.' He regretted the words once they were out. It wasn't fair to lay blame on Kay, but meddling wouldn't be welcomed. Even though he didn't understand a lot of what was happening with Beth at the moment, he was sure about this.

'Well, I'm just trying to help, no need to be so rude.'

Kay was lucky he didn't say what he really felt.

Joe needed to end the call. He could feel his temper rising and was afraid he would snap if he didn't. He heard a sniff down the line and for a brief moment he felt guilty. 'Don't get upset. That wasn't my intention.' It was a good thing she couldn't see him right now. 'I'll keep a closer eye on Beth and if things get worse, we'll revisit this conversation, OK?'

'Fine... I guess that sounds reasonable. But there's also—'

Joe spotted AJ heading towards his office. The frown on his colleague's face wasn't what he was expecting. 'Sorry, Kay, I'm going to have to go. I'll try and call you later.'

Chapter Twenty-Nine

BETH

'I'm going to throw some facts about domestic abuse your way. Not because I want to catch you out, but because these are the things that Crown Prosecution is going to be focusing on to argue your wife's case, okay?'

'Sure. It can't be any worse than what is already being said.' Mr Brewer's shoulders slumped.

'They will throw stats at you, like'—Beth glanced down at her notes—'just over five per cent of adults experienced domestic abuse in 2023. I'm sure it won't surprise you to learn that more than two thirds of that percentage are females. The prosecution might then point out that domestic abuse is the leading cause of injury to women – more than car accidents, muggings and rapes combined.'

Brewer leaned over, combing his fingers through his hair. 'Jesus.'

'Your wife claims the abuse escalated during the pandemic... Physical abuse, and repeated patterns of abusive behaviours, which she said that you used so that you "could maintain power and control in your marriage". I found her wording to be curious.'

Brewer lifted his head. 'Why's that? I mean, it isn't true, but now you have me curious.'

'Because it is almost word for word the definition from the Office for National Statistics.'

'It was probably her solicitor who fed her that information.'

'Possibly. How long have you been having issues in your marriage?'

'That's the thing.' He looked out of the windows. 'As far as I knew, everything was fine. We had talked about having kids, we were looking at holidays ... and I had just bought her a new car which I was going to surprise her with at Christmas. She does have a fiery temper and could get aggressive at times, but I'd apologise for whatever she thought I'd done and we'd move on.'

Beth had seen in the notes that Brewer was not short of money. In fact, not only did he come from a wealthy family, he had also accrued a lot of personal wealth from his own IT business. He'd developed a new app that helped parents and police track missing children. This threw him into the spotlight on television and he was often featured in magazine spreads with interviews.

'I can't believe any of this is happening.' Brewer's voice cracked. 'I'm on one of those Domestic Abuse Protection Notices. I think I'm still in shock about the whole thing.'

Beth had done some research into DAPNs to make sure she had the facts right. They're similar to bail conditions but with a lean towards domestic abuse perpetrators. Brewer was told he couldn't make any contact with his wife unless it was through third parties, and he couldn't go within 500 meters of his wife. DAPNs can only be issued by police inspectors, and she'd made a note to tell Cassandra that someone would need to speak to the inspector. It was curious why normal bail conditions were not considered enough in this case, despite the nature of the injuries. Brewer also had no previous convictions for violence.

'Did you appear in court for a DAPN to be issued?'

'A what? Are you talking about the prevention order?'

Beth nodded.

'Yeah, I think the first one is only temporary. I'm scared shitless that she's going to make up more lies and say that I've breached the order, so I placed a tracker on my car and my phone to prove I'm sticking to the conditions.'

The more he spoke, the more Beth began to believe something more sinister was going on. *Was his wife setting him up?* She looked at her watch. 'We don't have much time left, can we run through exactly what happened that night?'

Brewer went on to explain everything, from the moment he got home to when he woke up in bed with the police standing over him. He said he was shocked when his wife had arrived home with marks on her face.

'So, there was no argument? How do you think your wife got her injuries?'

'I asked her about those, but she just brushed things off. She's quite clumsy. Always has been. And it wasn't the first time I'd seen her bruised. She swore it was an accident or'—he waved his hand—'something – I can't recall what she said specifically. She wasn't concerned, so neither was I. Obviously someone else is involved, because by the time the police arrived, her injuries looked worse. My family warned me that she was a gold-digger, but I refused to believe that. She didn't even know I was rich when we met.'

'Do you know if your wife was having an affair? Have you ever suspected her of having one?'

He shook his head. 'No. I mean I've never suspected her of anything like that. I guess she could be, but how or when or for how long – why would she let someone else do that to her? It couldn't be all about the money, could it?'

There were so many questions Beth needed to find answers for. 'I'm going to speak to Mrs Lynch, and she may want you to come back to discuss things further once she's had a chance to digest all of what you've shared with me today, okay?'

'Thank you, Ms Stanford. You believe me, don't you?'

Beth smiled at Brewer but didn't reply. She wasn't sure what she believed. Something about this case made her uncomfortable.

After walking Brewer out, Beth headed to Cassandra's office.

'So, now you've met him, what are your thoughts?' Her boss motioned for her to take a seat.

'We definitely need to find out whether the wife was or still is having an affair. Brewer's main defence is someone else caused those injuries, but would his wife really allow herself to get beaten up for the sake of money?' This was the bit that Beth struggled with.

'Lisbeth, money has an awful way of turning good people bad. Do some digging, use the firm's investigator to follow her if you need to. See what you can find out. I think we have a strong case, and with the right evidence we can show Brewer has been set up. One thing in his favour is the fact he has no history of abuse or violence. We have letters from his previous partners showing he has not so much as even shouted at them.' She took a sip of water. 'You look tired, and you've done a great job today. Go home and come back tomorrow with a fresh pair of eyes.'

Beth returned to her office and made a few notes before packing up for the day. She was exhausted. But there was something about this case that didn't make sense and Beth was determined to get to the bottom of it. Not just for Brewer's sake, but because of the synchronicity with her own life.

Chapter Thirty

JOE

Joe braced himself for more bad news as AJ stomped into his office.

'What happened in there?' Joe said and leaned forward.

'It was a strange one. She's not actually looking for our help. She only attended as she was advised to by her solicitor. Even the IDVA ended up looking uncomfortable.'

AJ's reaction seemed out of character to Joe. They'd seen this happen before and there could be a million reasons why Mrs Brewer was reluctant. 'That doesn't mean anything, though. She obviously has some existing support systems in place. What are you implying?'

'I really hate to say this, but I'm on the fence with this one.' AJ looked away. 'I know I shouldn't be thinking like this ... but something doesn't add up.'

'But the bruises ... they didn't look self-inflicted.' Joe rifled through the folder where the police photos were.

'Oh, I don't mean that. He definitely battered her ... or

someone has.' If AJ kept pacing around his office, the carpet would be worn out in no time.

In her description of events, it was telling that she'd used the word 'battered' rather than the official term 'assaulted'. That, more than anything, rang bells in Joe's mind.

'I'm sorry. I don't know what I'm thinking or saying.' AJ's head moved from side to side.

'Do you want to go and grab some lunch and we can talk about things?' He'd never seen AJ like this before.

AJ nodded. 'That would be great. I'll just get my things.'

Joe placed his mobile in his pocket and headed to the reception desk. After letting them know where they'd be, Joe waited outside. There was a café a hundred or so yards away and along with some excellent coffee, they made a great ham and cheese panini.

As they walker over, AJ looked deep in thought, and he didn't want to disturb her; she'd tell him whatever was on her mind when she was ready. The fresh air felt good, and he was pleased the café wasn't too busy when they arrived. They sat at a table that overlooked the park.

Joe stared ahead, unsure whether he should speak first or let AJ take the lead.

AJ's eyes darted around the place and then outside. Joe frowned.

'You going to share what's distracting you?'

He reached across and squeezed her hand but was surprised when she pulled away.

'Sorry. I didn't mean to make you feel uncomfortable.' Joe's neck was hot, and his cheeks flushed. He didn't think he'd done anything that could be considered inappropriate, had he?

AJ looked out of the window. Her eyes flitting around

quickly. 'It's not you. I've recently separated from my husband, and I think he's been following me.'

'Have you contacted the police?' Joe followed her eyeline but all he could see outside were a few kids messing about in the park.

'There's no point… He thinks I asked him to leave because I'm having an affair, but it's his paranoia and controlling behaviour that I've had enough of. Don't worry, I'm documenting everything. At the moment, we're sharing custody of our son, but I'm worried he's projecting his toxicity onto him – every time Nicky comes home from seeing his father, he's out of control and it takes ages for me to calm him down.' She pulled out a tissue and dabbed her eyes. 'I'm dealing with it.'

'I'm sorry you're having to go through this. You know that you can reach out to anyone in the team, including me, if you need help sorting things for you and your son. Okay?'

When the food arrived, they ate in silence. Joe didn't know why the atmosphere felt so awkward. He watched AJ pick at her salad, and although he was famished, his sandwich was unappealing.

AJ looked over. 'How are things with you?'

Joe took a gulp of water, and although he didn't really want to talk about his personal life, he couldn't ask AJ to share hers and not do the same. 'Beth started back at work today, and part of me thinks it's good for her, but I'm also worried it's too soon. She says she's coping, and I am torn as to whether I believe her or not. She's good at masking things. I think she's just burying her feelings about her father's death.'

'Maybe grief counselling will help.'

'I did think of that, but if I mention any sort of counselling, she snaps and misreads everything I say.'

'She's projecting, Joe. Give her time. Just be there for her.'

He nodded. 'I'm trying. Hopefully having a routine will help.'

'Oh, for fuck's sake.' AJ stood up so fast that her chair knocked over.

Joe looked around. 'What is it?'

'It's him! My ex... Pete. He was right there, but he's gone now. I'm sure I saw him.' She pointed to an alleyway just past the park entrance.

'Why don't we get back?' Joe looked at his watch.

'Uh...' AJ pulled some coins out of her purse. 'This should cover mine. I'm just going to pop over to the police station before I head back, this is getting ridiculous now. Maybe it is time I speak to them. That okay with you?'

'Sure, I'll see you back at the office. Unless you want to go straight home. I can write up our conversation about Mrs Brewer. You can check it over and fill in the blanks from home or when you're back tomorrow.'

'Really? Oh, thank you.' AJ left while Joe took the money to the till and paid. He'd never met Pete and didn't know much about him, either. He felt bad that he'd never asked any of his team about their families but his rule of keeping professional and personal lives separate was there so that lines didn't get blurred. His team worked with vulnerable individuals and bringing their own issues into the office wouldn't help anyone.

On the walk back to the office, Joe looked around for strange men that might pop out of alleyways and smiled to himself. He was probably being ridiculous. The smile was quickly wiped off his face when he scrolled through his phone and opened his emails, spying one from his accountant.

Hey Joe.

Just been going through the records again and have a few things I'd like to discuss. My address, which happens to double as my office these days, is at the bottom of this email. I'll see you at 7ish?

All the best,
Connor

This wasn't a request. Back in the office, Joe replied to the email and confirmed he'd be there, he then booked a taxi to pick him up from home as he knew a drink or two would be consumed. Before leaving the office, he updated Mrs Brewer's file with what little he knew.

If he was lucky, Beth wouldn't be back.

He wasn't sure she wouldn't see through his lies.

Chapter Thirty-One

BETH

Beth had only been home five minutes when Joe arrived. She wanted to tell him all about her day, at least what she could tell him without breaching confidentiality, but he raced by the living room and headed straight upstairs while shouting something about having to change.

Beth followed him upstairs to their room. 'You're going out now? I thought we'd have a nice dinner and chat since it was my first day back.'

'Oh, shit. Sorry, I hadn't even thought about it when I said yes. Taxi will be here in a minute. We can catch up when I'm back can't we? I won't be long.'

Beth didn't want to make a big deal of it and shrugged. 'Sure, I'll just have a long bath and see you when you get in.'

She left him to it and noticed he didn't bother saying goodbye as he rushed out the door ten minutes later. She hadn't even asked him where he was going or who with and he didn't offer the information either.

Just another excuse to stay away from me.

She smacked her head. *Why do I always jump to those conclusions. He loves me... I've been difficult ... distant. Of course, he just wants a break away.*

She opened the freezer and pulled out a ready meal, a lasagna. There was no point in making anything special if it was just going to be her.

She popped it into the microwave for ten minutes. She fought the urge to drink, but as she thought about Joe racing out, her anger took over and she poured herself a vodka and tonic, adding a slice of lemon. With Joe not here to criticise her, she may as well have one drink. He'd never know, and she had been good ... kind of.

Beth took a large gulp and savoured the feeling that washed over her. Relaxation, complete and utter relaxation. The microwave pinged and she popped the meal on a tray, taking it through to the living room with her drink. She plonked herself on the sofa and turned on the telly. The news coverage had Mr Brewer speaking about being wrongly accused and Beth wondered if the public would sympathise more with his wife given the images she'd seen earlier. He was well respected in the community – there was his obscene wealth and generous donations to charities, and then there was the Find My Child app.

She felt agitated and looked over at the bookcase, wondering if a true-crime novel would settle her. But she didn't have enough energy to focus on a book, and instead she returned her gaze to the telly and changed the channel, tucking her legs under her as she settled in to watch a repeat of *Criminal Minds* and eat the bland meal.

Once she finished eating, Beth chucked the plastic ready-meal container in the bin. Eyeing the cupboard where she hid the bottle of vodka, she figured one more wouldn't hurt. If Joe was much later, she may well be in bed before he came home.

He'd never know. She wasn't an alcoholic. She just had a taste for it now, and there was no reason to feel guilty. She pulled out her mobile to tell Pops about her day— And then it hit her. *He was gone.*

No more sharing her successes and hearing his pride when he cheered her on. No more calls to laugh about silly things they'd seen on TV.

She poured more vodka into her glass. *Fuck it.* She'd considered calling a friend except she didn't seem to have any left. They found her anxiety and moods 'too much'. Those that had stuck by her, she'd pushed away before they could leave her. She'd been doing it for so long, she no longer felt lonely. They would just think she was being dramatic. Who needed friends like that.

Beth sat on the couch, sipping the vodka as she stared at the telly. She couldn't stop thinking about Pops. The tears came suddenly and before she knew it, her face was soaked.

She rang Joe's mobile, but he didn't answer.

'So bloody selfish.' She dialled again and when it went straight to voicemail, she knew he was deliberately avoiding her calls. Her blood boiled.

'You don't even have the courtesy to answer when I call. When did you become such an arsehole? I felt good about things today until you said you were going out... Why do I even bother?' She hung up. Beth wasn't concerned with the fact that she was slurring her words. She had no reason to hide the fact that she'd had a few drinks after a hard day at work. If he'd been here to talk to her, she wouldn't have even wanted a drink.

It was *his* fault.

Every time she'd really needed him, Joe was busy. She finished what was left in her glass and poured another. She'd had a lot to process after what had happened at work today. The images of Brewer's wife flashed before her as she thought about how convincing Brewer was when he'd described what had happened.

The room seemed to close in on her. Earlier in the day she'd taken her medication, and now the effects of combining vodka with pills was making itself brutally apparent.

Her heart raced, and each thud echoed loudly in her ears, threatening to break free from her chest. The room seemed to tilt, and a cold sweat formed on her brow. A wave of nausea swept over her, and she swallowed hard, trying to keep her insides from turning out.

The air became thick, almost suffocating, and she found herself gasping for breath. Her hands trembled, and she gripped the couch, trying to ground herself. Shadows danced across the walls, as the lamp's light seemed to flicker, intensifying the surreal atmosphere.

As her mind raced with disjointed thoughts, Beth felt an overwhelming sense of doom. Every noise was amplified, from the ticking of the clock on the wall to the distant hum of the refrigerator, heightening her anxiety.

A silent scream built up inside her, wanting release. But all Beth could do was close her eyes, willing the overwhelming sensations to pass. She tried to remind herself that it was just a panic attack, but the toxic mix in her system made it harder to discern reality from the terrifying illusions of her mind.

As the evening wore on, more vodka slipped down her throat, and Beth moved on autopilot, repeating the process of filling up her glass, leaning back into the couch and staring past the telly and out the window, willing for her eyes to close.

Chapter Thirty-Two

JOE

Joe took a few deep breaths as he walked up the path and knocked on the door. A woman answered. The wife, he presumed.

'You must be Joe. He's in his office. I'll show you through.'

He followed the woman, noting the expensive décor.

'Joe!' Connor Walsh, his accountant, shook his hand. 'So good of you to come. Please have a seat. Can I get you anything to drink?'

Joe spied the whisky on the table. 'I'll have what you're having.' He knew Connor wouldn't take no for an answer. He could always just sip it.

Connor smiled. 'Good man. I'll just get another glass'.

When Connor left the room, Joe nipped around to look at the papers on the desk. Red marks everywhere, he felt like he was in school again.

'Here you go. Cardhu Gold Reserve, one of my favourites. Get that in you and I'll get my questions together. I'm sure you had a long day, so I won't keep you any longer than I have to.'

Joe didn't want to beat around the bush or waste time with small talk. 'Is there a problem?' He'd known Connor for years and he was always a straight talker.

'Well, there could be.' He looked over at Joe with a blank expression and Joe couldn't figure out whether he was playing with him or if he was screwed.

Joe shifted in his chair.

'There's a few transfers – rather large ones – as well as the odd payment that I can't account for.'

'Really?' Joe leaned in. 'If you could tell me which ones you mean, I'm sure I'll be able to explain them.'

The accountant shuffled through the printed pages and pointed out three transactions. Joe's shoulders loosened. 'Didn't you get the receipts for those?'

The accountant gave him a sideways look. 'If I did, we wouldn't be sitting here, would we.' Joe couldn't tell if the man was joking or not. 'These are quite substantial amounts, and they seem to have disappeared into the ether.'

Joe laughed, trying to keep the mood light, and not let Connor see how nervous he was. 'I can see why you'd think that but...' Joe pointed at the accountant's laptop screen. 'May I?'

Connor turned the screen towards Joe. 'Please do.'

Over the next fraught half hour, Joe explained to the accountant where the money moved to and where it came from ... for the most part. 'You see? We're invoiced for all of these and I can only apologise if the paperwork wasn't in the files and sent over. I've had a lot of stuff on.'

Joe's mobile rang and a quick glance at the screen told him it was Beth.

If he stopped and chatted, he may find himself having to

answer questions he couldn't – or more to the point, didn't – want to answer. He'd be home soon enough. He let it go to voicemail. If Beth got mad, he'd explain what he could to her when he got home.

As he was returning the phone to his pocket, Beth called again.

'If you need to take that I can step out.'

'No, no, it's fine.' Joe switched the phone to silent and carried on. 'As I was saying, those joint conferences are held three times a year. Each agency contributes an agreed amount which then allows us to approach the right partnerships for networking and all that fun stuff. These conferences ensure we get continued funding for our services.'

The accountant closed his laptop. 'Well, I'm glad we got that all cleared up. Be sure to get those invoices over to me. Right, I think that deserves another drink.'

Joe looked at his watch. 'I really should be getting back.'

'Come on, just one more. Think of it as networking. My wife can book your taxi.'

'Okay, thanks,' Joe agreed.

Connor left the room and Joe suspected evening drinks were a regular thing for him. His head was throbbing but Connor seemed as fresh as he had when Joe'd arrived an hour or so before.

Joe slumped into the chair, wanting to sink deep beneath the cushion and disappear. Although he hadn't lied, he also hadn't told the whole truth. Joe would have some work to do to get everything sorted and make it believable.

'That's the taxi booked. Here.' Connor handed him a larger measure of whisky, more than Joe was expecting. He lifted the glass, realising that if he drank it all in the twenty minutes before the taxi came, he'd feel the effects of every drop.

'Let's celebrate another successful year for Tasker House. Your grandfather would be proud.'

Chapter Thirty-Three

BETH

Beth didn't know how much time had passed when she'd startled awake, alone in the dark with a blanket over her and an empty glass knocked over on the floor.

She hadn't even heard Joe come in.

'Ah, shit.' She'd be in for a lecture in the morning. Then she remembered the message she'd left him.

Beth went to the kitchen and grabbed some ibuprofen, which she washed down with a glass of water. She had work in the morning and didn't want to have a hangover. She tiptoed up the stairs to the bedroom.

She could hear Joe's faint snores. The ones he got when he'd had just over his limit of pints. Well at least she could point that out to him if he made a big deal of things in the morning. She saw his mobile charging on the chest of drawers and went over to see if he had listened to her message. She covered the screen as she punched in his password, so as not to wake him when it lit up, and smiled when she saw that the message was still on his phone. She fumbled with the keypad to unlock it and deleted the message. No point in having a row over nothing.

She didn't bother to brush her teeth but changed into her pyjamas and slid in slowly next to Joe. He turned over with a grunt and wrapped his arm around her. She plucked it away carefully. His touch made her feel uncomfortable. Beth set the alarm on her phone and pulled the covers over herself and stared at the wall, waiting for morning to arrive.

After lying awake staring at the ceiling, Beth had come downstairs and scrolled through TikTok. She watched the sunrise through the large front window. When she heard Joe's alarm go off, she listened to his footsteps upstairs. He mustn't know she hadn't had a proper sleep; he'd only get angry. She ran into the kitchen to put the coffee on.

Joe already thought something was wrong with her and would make her go to the doctor again. It's like he'd forgotten her father died... Her fingers tapped the counter in a rhythmic beat.

Minutes later, Joe walked into the kitchen yawning and headed towards her.

Wrapping his arms around her shoulders he whispered. 'You're up early. I didn't hear you coming to bed.'

Why did he ask that? It was as if he knew something. Was he testing her? She couldn't work out his mood.

Beth pulled out of his grasp and poured the coffee. She'd give him a half truth. 'I woke up on the couch. Must have fallen asleep watching a film... I can't even remember what was on, but clearly it did me some good.' She stirred his coffee and handed it to him. He didn't need to know that she had barely slept, except for when she'd passed out before he came home. 'I didn't even hear you come in. Was it a late one?'

Joe was opening drawers and ignored her question. 'Where's the ibuprofen?'

She pointed to the small cabinet where they always were. *What is his game?*

'Ah, thanks.'

She watched as he popped two out of the blister pack and washed them down with his coffee.

'Sorry. Yeah, later than I was expecting. Connor, remember him? The accountant. Well, he was on whisky and wanted me to partake. You know how I am on the hard stuff, and he just wouldn't stop talking. I didn't want to be rude since he does the books on a discount.'

'Mmm-hmm.' Something they now have in common as Joe never shuts up about it. 'So, who else was there?'

'No one. Well ... his wife but she stayed in the other room.' Joe raised a brow. 'I'd wanted to be in and out but lost all track of time. He had some stuff to go through...'

'Did they ask about me?' Beth wondered what Joe was telling people about her. She was sure the neighbours were all gossiping about her, and assumed Joe's professional contacts would too.

'Huh? Why would he? It was whisky, work and a bit of bullshit.'

He was lying. She could tell because he wouldn't even look at her. He was playing the knight in shining armour, trying to protect her feelings as if she was a fragile piece of porcelain.

She'd let it slide, this wasn't the battle to focus on. If she didn't want him asking more questions about her, she'd better just leave it.

'Oh my God,' he said. 'How was your first day back? I can't believe I didn't even ask you.'

'It was fine. I was thrown into the deep end with that new case that I've been researching – should be an interesting one.' She looked at her watch. 'Speaking of work, I need to get a move on. I've so much to do today.' She skipped past him on her way up to the shower when Joe called out.

'I can give you a lift in, if you'd like?'

'Nah. I'll grab the bus, so that you don't have to go out of your way. Saves you having to weave your way back through school traffic.' She closed the bathroom door behind her and turned on the shower. She was out in less than ten minutes.

Joe was getting his clothes together as she entered their bedroom 'That was quick. I'll see you this evening.'

He gave her a peck on the cheek, like she was his friend and not his fiancé.

Beth put her hair in a bun and threw on the same suit as yesterday, only swapping the blouse for a light V-neck sweater.

Downstairs she pulled on a pair of low-heeled ankle boots and grabbed her coat. A reminder on her phone went off, prompting her to pick up the Christmas present she had ordered months ago for her father. It felt like she had been punched in the stomach. She leaned against the door and fought back tears. She hadn't got around to deleting all the reminders on her phone.

Everything would be different this year.

Shake it off, Beth.

She stepped outside and, in the distance, saw the bus

trundling along the road. She ran as fast as she could to the stop, the fresh air hitting the back of her throat like fire.

She'd made it.

She caught her breath on the bus, finding a seat in the back to avoid the stares. She pulled out her mobile, deleting all the reminders about her dad. Without the reminders, perhaps the significant dates – Christmas, his birthday – would pass without ripping her heart out.

When she finally got off the bus, Beth's chest felt tight. Just a few more steps to the office. She was struggling to breathe as she entered the building.

'You okay there, doll? You don't look too well.' Glyn stood behind the reception desk staring at her.

'I'm ... fine. Just a little ... out of breath.' Beth made her way to the toilets on the lower floor and locked herself in a cubicle. She had an overwhelming feeling of being trapped, and rocked back and forth, counting to ten, taking deep breaths. The feeling subsided.

What the hell was that?

Beth had never felt like this before. It felt different to her usual anxiety, although at times, that was equally debilitating.

It was probably a reaction to the reminder this morning. Although it had been months now since it happened, her father's death billowed over her every waking moment like a shroud.

She turned on the water and splashed her face, drying it off with a scratchy paper towel. She pulled out her foundation and reapplied the make-up that had been an effort to put on today.

Beth headed back towards reception and up to the

paralegal office, waving at Glyn, whose brows furrowed as she saw her. She was surprised when she saw Rachel in there. 'Have I missed a day?' Beth double-checked the diary. Rachel only worked two days a week and Beth was sure today wasn't one of them.

Her colleague laughed. 'Not at all. Cassandra has had me in for an extra day while you were off and decided to keep me on until you settled. Didn't she tell you?'

No, she hadn't told her. Another person talking behind her back. Did Cassandra think she wasn't up to her job?

'She probably did, I just forgot. It was a full-on day yesterday.' Beth didn't want Rachel to think she was incapable.

'I see you have a couple of interviews booked in. Why don't I help with those? We can split them up.'

'That's really kind of you.' Beth had to force herself to smile through gritted teeth. 'But I don't mind doing them, it's why I spread them out.'

'I insist.' Rachel stood and grabbed a notebook.

The woman's chirpiness was getting on Beth's nerves.

'I said, I can do it myself!' Beth hadn't realised how loud she'd raised her voice until she noticed Rachel had stepped back.

'Okay. I was only trying to help. I'll stay here and carry on with the research, shall I?'

Beth knew that the minute she was gone, Rachel would go running to Cassandra and tattle. She'd probably call her a bully and then a whole investigation would follow and that's the last thing she needed.

'Sorry.' She reached out and touched Rachel's arm. 'I didn't mean to shout. I didn't have much sleep last night. Actually, I could use your help so if you take the 10am appointment, I'll do the next one. Thanks.'

She might as well play the game. Although she was savvy enough to recognise she needed to play it better than she just had.

Chapter Thirty-Four

JOE

The whisky-induced sleep had Joe's head throbbing, though thankfully he didn't otherwise feel hungover. The ibuprofen was beginning to kick in.

Beth's paranoia seemed to be creeping back and he wondered how much she had to drink last night. She had lied to him about falling asleep watching telly because he'd found her passed out when he'd got home, and the telly was off.

On his drive to work, an unknown number called twice. He guessed who it was, and he'd be damned if he was going to give her the time of day anymore.

She was messing with the wrong person.

When Joe got into the office, he checked the appointment board and made sure that no one would disturb him. He pulled out his keys and unlocked the bottom drawer of his desk. Inside, he found the invoices that he had prepared for Conner but had 'forgotten' to pass on with everything else on. He smiled, pleased he'd been able to dodge at least one bullet for now.

Joe placed the papers in a brown envelope and walked over to the reception desk. 'Can you make sure these get posted today? First class.' The receptionist took the envelope and nodded.

'You've had a few calls from the same woman this morning. She said that it's very urgent she speak with you.' Molly, who had only been at Tasker House for a few months, passed him a Post-it with the details.

Joe took the messages, glanced at them and muttered under his breath. *Shit.* 'Thanks.' He went back to his office debating whether to ring her back or not. With the three calls at work, she'd rung five times in total and it seemed she wasn't going to relent.

He sent a text.

> Stop calling. I can't speak at the moment, but I will when I can. Joe

As he was putting his mobile on his desk a reply came through.

> You'd better or tomorrow Lisbeth will know everything.

He threw the phone down.
That bitch!

Joe had been so consumed with his thoughts, he only now realised he hadn't seen AJ in the office. After yesterday's conversation, he called to see how she was.

'Hey, hi. Everything okay today?'

'Yeah, nothing like possessive ex problems.' AJ's attempt at humour was poor.

'I've got some time if you want to talk about it? Just surprised you weren't in.'

'Oh, I have an appointment this morning. It's on the whiteboard. And as for the other bit, no need to chat. Like I said, just your typical ex-can't-get-it-through-his-thick-head-that-the-relationship-is-over. I mean the constant harassment and my response to that should be a big clue.'

Joe had looked at the whiteboard when he walked in and noticed it was wiped clean. He glanced at Molly and wondered if she had mistakenly removed the information. He didn't want to interrupt AJ, so kept the thought to himself as he waited through the awkward silence.

'Things are just really complicated because of our son, Nicky. I'm dealing with it, though, so no need to worry. How's your fiancée?'

Joe rubbed his temple. 'Unpredictable is a good way to describe her at the moment.' He was beginning to feel like a broken record.

'I don't want to overstep, but maybe you both need some time apart.'

Joe wasn't surprised by AJ's suggestion. He'd be lying if he said it wasn't something he thought about himself. 'Isn't that selfish, though? She's still grieving. And now I wonder if maybe going back to work so soon was a mistake. Plus, Christmas is around the corner. I can't let her be on her own. She and her dad always made a big deal about it.'

'Okay, now may not be the best time, but bottling up your feelings isn't going to help either. One of you will just explode. Oh, hang on. Pot-kettle-black comes to mind.'

It was good to hear her laugh.

'Thought I'd say it before you did. I should do as I say sometimes, eh?'

'Don't be so hard on yourself. It's always easier to give advice rather than take it.' Joe could relate.

'Yes, it is. Is that the time? Sorry to cut this short, but I need to get going. Another time, maybe.'

'See you tomorrow.' Joe ended the call. He hated to admit it but AJ was right. He and Beth had both been skirting around their feelings, and it was pushing them further apart. He didn't know what he could do to help her through this. In fact, he hadn't even taken the time to ask, but she must feel it, too. Was she hoping they'd split up? Is that what she wanted? He had to stop putting the conversation off.

He looked up.

The police officer he saw being led to his office meant the conversation would have to wait just a little while longer.

Chapter Thirty-Five

BETH

Beth needed to pull herself together, or she'd find herself in front of HR with her outbursts. The problem was, she wasn't even sure what was real anymore. The lack of sleep, the alcohol, and her meds – it was all starting to blur together, twisting her thoughts, making everything feel off. She could swear she heard whispers when she walked into the office, saw people exchanging glances when they thought she wasn't looking. If everyone would just stop lying about her and talking behind her back, there wouldn't be any problems. But then again, was that really happening? Or was it just her mind playing tricks on her? She couldn't tell anymore, and that terrified her. The paranoia hung over her like a haze, blurring the line between what she knew for sure and what her mind insisted was true.

She read through the evidence records, making notes until her phone rang; her appointment had arrived.

Rachel still wasn't back from the first meeting, so it was probably a good thing she'd offered to help.

She walked down to the reception area. 'PC Grover? If you'd like to follow me.'

The officer followed her into the interview room.

'I'm Lisbeth Stanford. I've been asked to go through a few things with you. It shouldn't take too much time.' She pointed to the chair. 'Please have a seat.'

'Is this recorded?'

'We do occasionally record the meetings but as this is more of a fact-finding exercise, I'll be taking notes. You're aware that I am a paralegal, correct?' She didn't want the officer to think she was the defence lawyer in this case.

'Yes.'

'My job is to gather your response to specific questions, so if you're comfortable with that, I'd like to make a start.'

Officer Grover pulled out his PNB – the pocket notebook the police carry to officially record details and incidents while on patrol. 'Do you mind if I refer back to my notes?'

'That's totally fine. I'd like to know what happened when you first arrived on the scene.' Beth positioned her pen on her legal pad, ready to jot down notes.

'A family friend had answered the door and told us that he'd separated Mr and Mrs Brewer. My colleague, who I guess you'll be speaking with separately...'

Beth nodded.

'He went and spoke to Mr Brewer. The friend took me through to the kitchen where Mrs Brewer was sitting having a cup of tea. She seemed to be calm until she saw me and then she got pretty agitated.'

'Can I just stop you there? When you say she got agitated, can you expand on that?'

'Well, I could see her on my way to the kitchen, before she

could see me. She was facing sideways and sipping her tea while going through a newspaper. When she turned towards the doorway, her eyes widened, like she hadn't been expecting me. Next thing I know, she is fidgeting and tearing at the newspaper. Then she started to cry.'

'Could that have been because now the police were there, she'd have to relive everything that had happened all over again? I understand she told you she'd been a victim of domestic abuse for about eight years and had never called the police, so what would that make you believe?' Beth wanted to find out whether he was reading the situation with Mrs Brewer subjectively instead of considering what he should know about domestic-abuse victims, and if it would impact on his testimony in court. It was his job to be objective, as he was trained to notice details that others might overlook, and this could be key for their client's version of events.

Officer Grover sat back in his chair and Beth could almost see the cogs turning as he recalled the night in question. 'I suppose she could've been afraid, I just found it odd as her mood was going up and down as I took her statement. When I asked her to describe what happened, she claimed that her husband had returned home from work in a foul mood. When she noticed this, she became nervous because she never knew how he would react to things. She claims she went into the living room and turned on the television. According to her, the next thing she knew was he was behind her, grabbing her throat. She scrambled off the couch, and he shouted at her about a burnt dinner. She said she tried to crawl away, but he grabbed her legs and pulled her back, flipping her over and punching her all over her body. She described him as a "mad man". Said this was the worst he'd ever been and for a moment, she thought that she was going to die.'

'Did you smell the burnt dinner or see anything in the bin? And can you describe the injuries you witnessed?'

'Yeah, the burnt remains of some sort of meal were on the counter. Just give me a second to find the injury.' He flipped through the pages of his PNB. 'She had a red mark on the left side of her neck. She had a fat lip and the inside of her mouth was cut. The right eye was puffy and swollen. She had a red mark on her cheekbone. Her arms were marked. I mean she was black and blue all over. You should have the photos and the video from my bodycam.' He shook his head.

Beth had seen it all. 'I understand she called a family friend first and not the police?'

She was curious about this.

'Yes, we see this all the time. She still wanted to protect her husband and needed someone to come over to get him out or take her away. It was actually the friend who contacted the police.'

'Who talked to him?'

'My colleague and I both spoke to him.'

'Okay. Your statements say he had nothing new to add as the argument had fizzled out by the time he arrived?'

'Yes, he seemed to be in shock, too.'

'Let's go back to Mrs Brewer. How long after the attack were you called?'

'I'm not sure. The friend had separated them and said he'd been there for two hours. The wife kept repeating how controlling her husband was and she was sick of it.'

'Can I ask one more thing?'

'Of course.'

'Do you think that Mrs Brewer could have caused those injuries herself or got someone else to do that to her?'

'You're referring to Mr Brewer's defence statement, aren't you?'

'Yes. He said she arrived home that way and brushed it off as an accident. He's very convincing.'

Beth hadn't decided whether she believed their client but that wasn't her job or this officer's business. She wanted to know what the officer thought in his professional capacity.

The police officer had sweat across his forehead and a thought came to Beth. One that no one else seemed to have taken into consideration. 'PC Grover'—she leaned forward and adopted a sympathetic tone—'exactly how much experience do you have when it comes to domestic abuse cases?'

Chapter Thirty-Six

BETH

The officer tilted his head and wiped his brow. 'Why are you asking me that?'

'It's my job. How many domestic abuse cases did you say you've dealt with in your career so far?' Beth started to shuffle through her paperwork to locate the information she was looking for.

'Enough. I don't know the exact number, but I'm sure you'll find it in those papers. Have you seen the pictures? What person would put themselves through that? You'd have to be pretty ... uh ... never mind.' He shook his head.

'Pretty what? Vindictive? Mentally unstable? A combination of both?'

'Well, yeah.'

Before he could finish Beth jumped in with one more question. 'Was Mrs Brewer under the influence of alcohol when you spoke to her?'

The officer shifted in his seat. 'She'd had a few drinks, according to her friend. She didn't try to hide it. Said she wanted to calm her nerves and take away the sting of her injuries. She wasn't intoxicated, if that's what you're suggesting?'

Wasn't intoxicated. Beth noted it down on her pad.

'I'm not suggesting anything.'

'You obviously have something to say, Miss Stanford, so why don't you just tell me?'

Beth held the officer's gaze and stayed silent while the cat-and-mouse game played out. If he thought she'd break first, he was mistaken.

The officer folded his hands on the table and leaned forward. 'Look, anything is possible, but when I interviewed her, she was coherent, focused and explained in full detail what had happened that evening. Sure, some of the injuries could've been self-inflicted, but not all of them. And yes, she could've had someone else do the rest, but we haven't found any evidence to support that theory – if you have, it's best you share it with me now or you could be arrested and charged with perverting the course of justice.'

Beth laughed.

'PC Grover, you need to rein yourself in. As you just pointed out, I'm asking you about *possibilities*. Our job is to defend our client, yours is to collect the evidence against him now that you've charged him.' If this officer thought he was going to use intimidation tactics against her he had another think coming.

'Okay. Just wanted to make my position clear. Are we nearly done?' He sat back in his chair and his shoulders relaxed.

Beth had all the information she needed for now but glanced at her notepad to remind the officer that she was in control of this interview and not the other way around. 'Yes, it looks like I've everything I need. I'll show you out.'

Once he'd left the building, Beth smiled as she returned upstairs.

'Looks like you had a good meeting. Come through and tell me all about it.' Cassandra waved her over.

Beth sat on the leather couch while her boss ate lunch.

'It was quite informative actually and possibly a way to substantiate Brewer's claim that his wife staged the whole thing.'

Her boss cleaned mayo from the corner of her mouth. 'Really? Continue.'

Beth explained the discussion and the officer's reaction to her challenge of the evidence. 'I'd like to speak to the family friend to see if I can get more information. Like, was Mrs Brewer having an affair? Maybe meet him in a less formal environment? I thought the coffee shop down the road would be good. His statement was quite vague, and I wonder if he knows more than he's saying?'

'Good work, you really should consider becoming a solicitor you know. I actually wondered the same thing about the family friend. Okay. Make it happen, sooner rather than later.' Cassandra waved her hand, dismissing Beth. As she left her boss's office Beth's stomach grumbled, reminding her she hadn't eaten anything herself.

On the way back to her desk she was caught by a dizzy spell and had to take a moment. Rachel was eating her lunch when Beth walked into the office. 'How'd your meeting go?'

Beth reached into her laptop bag and pulled out an energy bar, joining Rachel at the round table by the window where most of them ate their meals. 'I was just telling Cassandra about it. I think it went well, although PC Grover may think otherwise. How did yours go?'

Rachel had interviewed the other officer who had attended the incident. It would be interesting to compare notes. 'He was a right arsehole. PC Paul or Pe ... uh, whatever his name is, was very passive aggressive but very much on our client's side.'

'Well, that's curious. Tell me more.' Beth reached for her notepad.

'He thinks Mrs Brewer was having an affair. He wasn't very complimentary or professional when talking about her. Said she was obviously a gold-digger and probably hoping to cash in on the attention.'

'What?' That surprised Beth. This officer's attitude was something that should probably be reported, even if he was on their client's side. Beth glossed over that fact for the moment and would speak to Cassandra later. It would be up to the police to investigate. 'Did you record the conversation?'

'I wish I had. I mean it started off fairly tame, so I didn't think of it, and then when the attitude came in, I didn't want him to completely shut down. You know what I mean?'

'Yeah.' Beth scratched her head. 'I'll look through your notes when they're ready. His partner never mentioned anything about that and surely, they'd discuss it afterwards.'

'You'd think so. Unless he just hates women and thought he could intimidate me? He rushed out as he had another appointment. Might not be how he speaks to his colleagues... Damn, I wish I had recorded it now.'

Beth wished she had too, but as much as she wanted to criticise her colleague, she knew she needed to play the game. At least for the time being.

Chapter Thirty-Seven

JOE

'Do you have a brother you've been keeping secret from us? He's the spitting image of you.' Molly looked between them one more time before returning to her desk.

'Not sure about that, other than a beard.' The officer laughed. 'I'm just here to talk to you about the Brewer case if you have a few minutes?'

Joe noticed him looking around the open plan office. 'Sure, have a seat.' Joe's brows furrowed. He wasn't sure how he could help, or how the police even knew Mrs Brewer had been to the charity.

'Have you read about the case in the papers?'

'Yes, it's unusual, to say the least.'

The officer nodded. 'We wondered if either Mr or Mrs Brewer had been in contact? Perhaps to access some of your services?'

Joe shifted in his chair. 'Sorry, I really can't give out that information. Can you tell me why you need to know?'

The officer leaned forward, placing his hands on Joe's desk.

'Are you trying to obstruct an ongoing investigation Mr Tasker?'

What the hell was going on here?

Joe felt threatened. The charity worked in partnership with the police, but they'd never had any officers come around, unannounced, to ask questions in a domestic abuse case. He wondered if it was because of the high-profile nature of the case. Having never been involved in such a case before, maybe this was part of the procedure.

'I'm sorry, officer. I'm going to need a few more details from you before I can discuss anything further. Could I have the name of who's in charge of this investigation?'

The officer stood up abruptly. 'I'll email them over.' He grabbed a card from Joe's desk and pocketed it. 'I've another appointment to attend to now. Thanks for your time, and I'll be in touch.'

Joe watched, open-mouthed, as the officer left the building. He picked up the phone and dialled his contact in the domestic abuse team at Langley police station.

'DC Woodrow speaking, how can I help?'

'Hey, Scott. It's Joe from Tasker House.'

'Long time no speak, mate. What can I do for you?'

'I've just had an officer here asking questions about the Brewer case. He seemed quite angry when I said I couldn't disclose the information he asked for and wouldn't really explain the relevance. Then, when I challenged him, he got up and left. Do you know anything about this?' The more Joe thought about it, the stranger it seemed.

'Do you know the officer's name?'

It was then Joe realised he'd been so caught off guard that

he forgot to ask. 'Shit, I don't. He kind of just came in and started asking questions and I didn't think to ask.'

'That's not like you at all.'

Joe appreciated the concern but moved the conversation along. 'Busy time. Could you maybe look into it for me and find out if anyone was tasked to come and speak with us here. I mean, we could set up a meeting or something if there's info we have, and vice versa.'

'Leave it with me.' Woodrow ended the call and a bad feeling washed over Joe. He was about to make another call when AJ knocked on his door. He waved her in and put the receiver back on its base.

'Sorry, I wasn't interrupting, was I?'

Joe shook his head. 'Did you just get in? How did your appointment go?'

'Yeah, wanted to check in with you first. The appointment was okay. exhausting but fine in the end.'

Joe was curious but didn't want to overstep. 'Great. While I have you, has anyone from the police been in contact about the Brewer case?'

AJ looked up to the ceiling. 'Um... Not that I can think of. Why?'

Joe shook his head. 'It's nothing. I'm probably overthinking things. I'll speak to Molly. Maybe she forgot to pass on a message.'

AJ shifted one from one foot to the other.

'Are you sure you're okay?' He looked down at her feet. 'You seem a little on edge.'

AJ followed his eyeline and laughed. 'New shoes. Plus juggling a lot of balls at the moment. I have a few things to catch up on and not enough hours in the day.'

Joe didn't want to add further stress but if something was happening behind the scenes, he needed to make sure everything on his end was accurate. 'Can you make sure the Brewer record is up to date, as there may be a meeting about it.'

Joe followed AJ out and made a beeline for the reception desk. 'Hey, Molly. Did that officer have an appointment or leave his name?' He leaned against the counter.

Molly's face grew red. 'He didn't on both counts. I thought it might have been something you arranged and just forgot to put it in the diary.'

'Really?' Joe scratched his head. 'Why's that?'

'That's what he implied when he walked in. He looked over at your office and said, "Oh, good. He's here. Thought he'd forgotten about our meeting." So, I thought you'd just forgotten to mention it, too. I just... I'm really sorry, Joe.'

He could see Molly's discomfort. 'Okay, did he sign in?'

She shook her head. Her eyes glistened. Joe felt sorry for her as she was new and still in training.

'Look, it's a learning curve. You'll know for next time. Also, can you be sure not to wipe the whiteboard when you come in. It has everyone's whereabouts for the day. I'm just going to step out for a few minutes, ring my mobile if anything urgent comes up.' Joe left the building and walked towards the town centre. He sat on a bench and stared ahead until a figure blocked his view.

'I'd say this was a coincidence, but it really isn't. You ready to talk now?'

Chapter Thirty-Eight

BETH

'I'm off now, unless you need me to stay and help you?' Rachel stood over her.

'What is it with you? I'm perfectly capable of covering my own work. Are you after my job or something?' Beth looked up.

Rachel's jaw dropped and she stumbled with her words. 'Jesus, you're like Jekyll and Hyde. I'm only trying to help, but maybe I shouldn't bother.' She turned on her heels and headed directly for Cassandra's office.

'Fuck's sake.' Beth didn't know why she was so on edge. Everything seemed to be getting worse. It wasn't all her, though, if people would just stop blaming her and making her feel like she was the problem, she wouldn't snap back. Or was this all down to her pills? What was the point of her medication if it only heightened her anxiety rather than calming her down?

The desk phone beside her rang, pulling her out of her thoughts.

'Lisbeth Stanford speaking. How can I help?'

'My office. NOW!'

Beth's body began to shake and her chest constricted.

No. No. No... Not now, please!

The worst things about these damn panic attacks were their increasing frequency and Beth's powerlessness to thwart them. Tears were threatening to fall as she took a few deep breaths to calm herself down. She found the bottled water in her bag and took a few big gulps, before straightening her jumper and heading to Cassandra's office.

It will be okay.

'You wanted to see me?' Beth stood by the doorway.

Although her boss smiled, she didn't meet her eyes. Beth could see the red on Cassandra's neck rise to her cheeks. 'Have a seat.'

Beth did as she was asked and inhaled deeply, trying to focus but her eyes felt heavy, and she yawned.

'I'm sorry, am I boring you?'

Beth shook her head. 'Sorry. I haven't had much sleep lately.'

'And there lies the problem. Look, I don't want to be angry with you and I chose to ignore a few complaints when you initially returned because of your ... situation. But it's becoming a problem and after speaking to HR, I think you came back too soon and now everything is catching up with you. We should have formalised a back-to-work plan and for that, I hold my hands up. It was selfish of me to think that you'd be ready to return and if you're not sleeping, I'm guessing you haven't really dealt with everything at home yet.'

Beth was speechless. She struggled to get her words out and took some time as she didn't want to snap and prove her boss right. 'I'm okay to be here. I know I shouldn't have snapped at Rachel, and I promise, I'll apologise when I see her next but...' She choked on her words. She didn't want to be stuck at home with her thoughts. As she had no friends to share her feelings with, being at work gave her a distraction and made her feel less lonely. Joe was doing his best to avoid her. She was beginning to feel like they were roommates rather than a couple. She hadn't thought about the wedding for a while. Beth's face fell into her hands.

She felt a hand squeeze her shoulder.

'Lisbeth, grief isn't something you can just hide away for a few hours. I'm not saying that we don't want you back, but I'm suggesting that you look into speaking with a grief counsellor. While that's happening, you can continue to work from home. We have plenty of things to research. Since Covid, we have the flexibility to conduct interviews via Zoom, there really are a ton of possibilities – at reduced hours for the time being and we'll build it back up to your current hours. This isn't a punishment.'

'Then why does it feel like one?' She stood up and waited, hoping that Cassandra would change her mind, but she wasn't budging. 'Okay. If I speak to a counsellor and work from home for the next week or so, will you reconsider?'

'Let's chat next week. I'll book a call in the diary. Now get what you need together, and I'll get Glyn to book a taxi to take you home.'

She knew that was the final answer and stomped out of Cassandra's office. She packed up the notes and a few files, and it felt like all eyes were on her, staring through the glass walls. When she looked up, however, no one was paying her any attention.

Maybe Cassandra was right?

Beth took the lift down to reception and waited for what seemed like an eternity for the taxi to arrive. When it finally came, she was just heading out when Glyn called after her.

'Look after yourself, love. We're all rooting for you.'

Fuck off.

At least she kept that in her head. She nearly went back in to give the nosy cow a few choice words, but her eyes caught something in the distance, just past the taxi. She squinted.

Was that Mr Brewer watching her?

She bent over to tell the driver to hold on but when she looked up again, there was no one there. Brewer must have driven off. Goosebumps covered her forearms. Beth got into the back of the taxi and gave the driver her address before she sat back and closed her eyes. A bit of peace and quiet might actually do her some good.

Cassandra hadn't said she needed to physically attend counselling, Beth knew there were plenty online, and she'd prove to everyone that there was nothing wrong with her.

Yes, this could work out perfectly. She'd prove them all wrong. Every last one of them.

Chapter Thirty-Nine

JOE

Joe jumped up. 'Are you stalking me?'

A slight smile crept across the woman's face. 'Really? Is that any way to talk to your future mother-in-law?' She moved closer. 'Have you spoken to Lisbeth yet?'

Joe clenched his fists. 'You know damn well I haven't. I'm not going to either. She's made it clear that she wants nothing to do with you.' He leaned over, looking directly into her eyes. 'Why is it so important to you now? After all this time?'

Janis Stanford pushed her index finger so hard into his chest, he wouldn't be surprised if it left a bruise. 'Listen here. You do whatever it takes to reunite mother and daughter. You get me? I know things about you. I've been watching. I have my ear to the ground. You hear me? I have some favours owed to me and I can call them in at any time.'

Joe stumbled back. 'What are you talking about?' He wondered if Janis was delusional or if he should actually be worried. Janis must know some undesirable and unscrupulous people if what Beth had told him was true. She must be bluffing.

'You'll find out if you keep ignoring me.' The finger came out again. 'Now, you make sure'—she poked him—'that Lisbeth knows'—another hard poke to his chest—'how much I love her.' He moved out of the way, and she poked the air, 'You got that?'

'Are you threatening me?' Joe wasn't going to stand there and let this stranger dictate what he should and shouldn't be doing in his personal life. She didn't even know Beth. Just because she'd given birth to her, that didn't make her a mother.

'I don't make threats. I promise you Joe, you don't want to cross me.' She looked around and straightened her coat. 'Final thing. Next time I call, you'd better answer and have some good news.' She spat at his feet, turned and waggled her fingers over a shoulder.

Joe's body shook. *What the hell just happened?*

He couldn't understand Beth's mother's newfound family interest. It made no sense. According to Kay, she'd been sober for the last two years, so why had she waited until after Kevin had died to make contact. There was no way Beth would welcome this woman into her life now. And after what Joe had experienced today, her behaviour didn't show any growth. There was no trace of motherly love.

But she had managed to get under his skin. What could she possibly know about him and what would she do with that information?

Chapter Forty

BETH

When she heard the car pull into the drive, her body stiffened. She had come home to find a note through the door and wondered if it was worth an argument with Joe.

The note had said: *You should keep a closer eye on your boyfriend.*

There was no indication who had sent it. She crumpled up the note and chucked it in the bin before settling in the living room. She had enough to deal with.

She heard Joe close the door before he joined her in the living room. 'What are you doing home so early? I figured it'd be all late nights with the new case you are working on?'

Beth was silent. She didn't want his judgement.

He came over and sat down. 'Hey, everything okay?'

'Not really...' She turned and hugged him. She needed a partner. She needed Joe to be understanding. She needed him to prove that she had no reason not to trust him.

'What happened?' He rubbed her back. His voice was soft. Maybe he would understand.

How much could she tell him? Could she trust Joe to have her back? There was only one way to find out.

'They sent me home.' She was talking into his shoulder, afraid to look at him. 'Apparently, people have been complaining about me and they want me to go to counselling.'

Joe pulled away from her. 'Well, maybe that isn't such a bad idea.'

Her fists clenched. 'You think I'm losing my mind, too?'

'No one said you were losing your mind, hon. Stop being so defensive.'

'I'm not defensive.'

Joe's eyes flitted to her closed hands. 'Really? Look, you were so close to your father, losing him will take time to work through. That's natural. Normal even. Then with your mother showing up, you've had a lot to process in a short time. Maybe speaking to someone about it might not be so bad. You could always give it a shot and if it doesn't work out, no harm done, right?'

Beth hated the way he was looking at her. Hated that he felt she wasn't coping. Hated that a small part of her agreed with him.

'Fine. If I do it, will you get off my back?' She shuffled away from him and curled her legs up underneath herself. Despite understanding, her blood still boiled.

Joe shook his head.

'What? Now I can't even speak my mind without you criticising me?' She started to cry. 'I hate this, Joe. I hate how I feel. I've been—' She turned away from him.

'You've been what? Look at me. You're scaring me now, Beth.'

'I've been having panic attacks when I leave the house. I

feel like everyone is out to get me. Like people are watching me...' Relief washed over her as she said the words out loud, even though she hadn't told him she was still having dizzy spells and hallucinations. Joe would help her. She didn't need a counsellor. She needed her fiancé to listen, support her the way he had before. 'I feel like you're ignoring me. We're supposed to be getting married in a few months but there's this distance between us...'

Joe's eyes widened. 'I can't believe you're saying this. I've tried to get close to you, but *you* push *me* away. I ask you every day how you are, and you just give me a blank stare and walk into another room, and so I kind of stopped asking. And ... uh ... about the wedding...'

Beth's back stiffened. He was going to leave her, and then he would tell everyone she had lost her mind; he'd announce that he didn't love her. 'What about it?'

'I postponed it. I just pushed it back until September. You need time, and I thought a few extra months would help.'

'I can't believe you did that without even talking to me. So, it's all my fault?'

'That's not what I said at all.'

'Leave me alone. I need to find a counsellor.' She grabbed her laptop from the table and began searching. She needed to distract herself.

Beth could feel Joe's eyes on her before he stood up.

'I'm going out.'

'Yeah, just run away like you always do,' she mumbled, loud enough for him to hear.

She glanced up, watching as Joe grabbed his coat, and when he slammed the door behind him, her shoulders tightened.

Beth screamed as loud as she could.

It felt good to get it out and she screamed again. She couldn't understand why no one understood how she felt. Her world was coming apart and no one around her gave a damn.

How dare he postpone their wedding without discussing it with her first.

Screw them all.

———————

Beth looked down at the screen. The first person that popped up when she had searched for local grief counsellors was a woman. She'd feel more comfortable speaking to a woman.

She clicked the link, and the website was easy to follow. The woman, Alison Burgess, was offering online evening counselling. Beth didn't want Joe to be home and eavesdropping on their conversation, but he often worked late on a Tuesday and Thursday, so she hoped the counsellor had availability then.

Beth began filling in the contact form explaining what she was looking for and the evenings she was interested in booking. She then thought, as they were online, could they have the video off, at least for the first few sessions? She didn't want to see any blame or judgement in the counsellor's eyes.

Beth read over the contact form and hit send. If Alison Burgess wouldn't comply with her requests, there were others who would.

Beth closed the laptop and placed it on the table. She lay down on the couch and closed her eyes.

Chapter Forty-One

JOE

Joe put on his headphones and listened to a playlist on Spotify as he walked down the path; Beth's frustrated screams faded away. If the neighbours called the police this time, he wouldn't be there.

He walked through the park and considered his issues. If it wasn't the case he was working on, or his accountant, it was Beth and her mother. The other day, he'd overheard Beth telling Kay that she was receiving letters and now she was convinced that she was being followed. Yet, she hadn't said a word about the letters to him. Maybe they were another one of her secrets?

The chilly air nipped his ears and with the pub just ahead, he decided to step in for a few pints. He wasn't ready yet to face whatever Beth had in store for him.

Two hours later and a little tipsy, he stumbled through the front door of his house.

The lights were off in the living room, so when he heard a soft 'Hey,' as he locked the door behind him, it startled him.

'Sorry. I saw it was dark and I didn't want to wake you. Did you manage to get any sleep?'

'Uh huh.' Beth rubbed her eyes, and Joe could see they were swollen from crying.

He walked over and gave her a hug. 'I'm also sorry about earlier. Things got a little heated. I shouldn't have got so riled up, and I should've spoke to you about the wedding to see how you felt.'

When Beth didn't argue back. Joe took it that all was forgiven.

'Do you want some tea? I'm making myself a cup.'

Joe followed her into the kitchen and sat at the breakfast bar. He watched her mess about on her phone as she made the hot drinks. He pulled out his own mobile after hearing a beep. He caught Beth looking his way.

'Bit late for messages, isn't it?' She raised her eyebrows.

To Joe, it came across as accusatory and he bit his lip before responding. 'Just AJ reminding me to bring in some papers for tomorrow.'

'Show me...'

Joe held out his phone, he had nothing to hide. 'You don't trust me now?'

> Need all those forms for the housing department meeting at 11. Don't forget. AJ 😊

He watched as her face turned the colour of beetroot.

'Sorry.'

She didn't sound sorry at all. He gulped down the remainder of his tea and placed the mug in the dishwasher. 'It's fine. I'm off to bed. See you up there?'

The way the evening had turned out though, he knew he'd be sleeping alone.

Again.

But did he even care anymore?

Chapter Forty-Two

BETH

Christmas and New Year's had come and gone. Joe had understood how hard it was going to be and kept everything low-key. No presents or decorations. Just another day. She was glad that the year was over. Although she'd been angry at the time when she was forced to work from home, there was no denying that she was more productive.

Over the next few weeks, Beth did what she could to keep Joe onside. He seemed pleased she'd started her counselling and she kept everything else – the hang-up calls, feeling she was being watched, even the letters – to herself. No sense worrying him. He hadn't believed her when she first told him, and she wasn't sure he'd believe her now. When her head was cloudy, she wasn't sure if it was real or if she was imagining it. She was still debating whether to tell her counsellor. Alison was great in a lot of respects, but Beth was afraid of having yet another person think she was paranoid.

She opened the front curtains and caught movement in the bushes. What the hell was happening? Was she being watched at home? Whoever it was, maybe they were there getting ready to drop off another letter. Her hands formed tight fists.

That's it. I'm not going to be afraid in my own home!

She pulled on her trainers, picked up Joe's golf umbrella, and ran down the front path towards the neighbour's bush.

'Get out and show yourself!' She poked at the bush. 'You should be ashamed, trying to scare a person in their own home!'

The neighbour came running over. 'What are you doing?'

'I saw someone in your bush, staring at me ... trying to frighten me...' Beth held the umbrella tight, ready to poke it into the bush again if needed.

'There's no one there. I've been out here the whole time. Are you okay? Should I call your boyfriend?'

Beth looked over at the neighbour, whose face was full of pity. 'Well, whoever was here must have seen that I spotted them.' She walked over to the pavement and looked both ways down the street. 'Probably had a car nearby and took off as I was getting my trainers on.'

The neighbour shook her head and went back inside.

I know what I saw.

Beth's head was thumping. Guilt from shouting at their neighbour hung over her like a cloud. She needed something to calm her nerves but knew that it was a slippery slope if she gave into that need.

Once inside, her feet felt like weights as she dragged herself to the cupboard in the kitchen where she'd hidden a bottle of gin. She reached in but then pulled her hand out quickly. Alcohol wasn't the answer. But ... she needed *something* as her meds alone just weren't doing the trick.

Just the one.

Beth poured herself a glass of gin, mixing it with flavoured tonic.

'Better take my meds, too.' She mumbled to herself as she went to the living room and pulled out her medication from her bag, popping the required pills and washing them down with her gin and tonic.

Her shoulders relaxed.

When her mobile rang, she reached across the couch and picked it up.

Unknown Number.

What if it's another hang-up call?

The alcohol gave her courage.

'I don't know who the fuck this is, but I'm not in the mood to be messed with. Stop calling me or I'm calling the police!' She screamed down the line.

'Lisbeth? It's Cassandra. I'm just checking in to see if you have that paperwork ready to email over? We have a hearing this morning for the Brewer case.'

Shit.

'Sorry. When I saw unknown number I—'

'I'm using one of the duty phones. I left mine in my car. Can you email that stuff over now?' Cassandra sighed. 'Maybe you should take the rest of the day off ... sounds like you're stressed ... but make sure you send me that email before you clock off.'

'Of course. Has Mr Brewer been in the office?'

'Not yet. We're meeting at the Courts. Why?'

'I think...' Should she tell Cassandra that she'd seen him watching her?

'What is it, Lisbeth? I'm in a rush as it is.'

'Never mind. It's not important. I'll send those things over right now.' She ended the call and did as promised. She didn't need Cassandra thinking she was incompetent, or she may end up fired. She would need proof if she was going to accuse a client of stalking her.

She had a counselling session this evening, she'd speak to Alison about everything that had been happening.

She might even get away with a few white lies.

Chapter Forty-Three

BETH

Up until now, the counselling sessions with Alison had gone well, but they'd only scratched the surface. Beth had talked to her counsellor about her work, rather than any of the real issues she knew everyone wanted her to talk about. She wouldn't be able to put off what she had been avoiding any longer, though – her father, Joe ... and everything else that made her feel like she was losing control.

She wasn't sleeping any better, but she didn't want to go to her GP. She couldn't handle another lecture on how she shouldn't be mixing meds with alcohol and any more suggestions that she go for a bloody walk to ease her anxiety.

When Joe came home that evening, she did her best to keep the peace. 'Are you looking forward to your evening out?'

Joe looked up from the newspaper he'd been reading. 'I guess so... Hey, have you seen this?' He held the paper out towards her, and she saw a picture of Mrs Brewer's battered face on the front page.

'That's the case I'm working on... I told you that. Weren't you listening?' Beth couldn't believe he was asking.

'Did you?' He scratched his head. 'Of course, sorry. Just a bit distracted. So your firm is defending the husband, right?' Joe put the paper down.

'Yes... I can't really talk about it, but I'm sure the papers are trying to make him out to be a monster when in fact, it looks like she set him up.'

'Oh really? Does she have a history of that sort of behaviour? Sounds a bit controlling.'

She'd considered this herself, but was surprised that Joe was suspicious – after all, he worked with abused women all the time. And why was he so curious about the case? Was he working with the wife and using her to get some information? And the way he'd said it made her feel uncomfortable. As if he wasn't speaking about Mrs Brewer at all...

'What's with that tone?' she said.

'Well, I thought that's what you were trying to say. Why are you turning this into an argument?'

Beth hadn't realised she was. It was a discussion. Wasn't it?

'You're right. Sorry. Look it's a really tough case. I want to do my best.'

Joe came over and kissed her head. 'You don't have to prove anything to anyone. Why put so much pressure on yourself. I know you haven't been sleeping.' He cupped her chin and forced her to look at him. 'How is the counselling going?'

It felt like this was the first time Joe was even interested or took any notice of anything other than himself. Beth was caught off guard.

'It's fine.' She pulled away. 'Why don't you go and get

ready, I want to do a few things before my session and I'm sure you want to get over to the pub and away from your crazy fiancé.'

He grabbed her arm and squeezed it.

'Ouch! Let go of me.' Beth backed herself into a corner.

'I'm sorry, I didn't mean to hurt you. I don't think you're crazy, why do you keep saying that?' He walked towards her with his hands out and she didn't understand his intention.

Beth held her hands up, covering her face.

'Oh my God, Beth. What are you doing? Do you think I am going to hit you?'

She didn't answer.

'Fuck this shit.' Joe stormed off without saying goodbye and the front door slammed behind him.

Beth took a deep breath.

What was happening? Did she really think that he was going to hit her?

The way he'd walked towards her; his facial expression – mouth contorted, eyes slit, the creases on his forehead. He was angry and tried to turn it around. Made it seem like she was imagining things. He was turning on her.

Fifteen minutes before her appointment, Beth made a cup of tea with a drop of whisky and set her laptop up on the breakfast bar. She had to search around the house for Joe's secret stash as he hid all alcohol from her now.

She dimmed the lights and logged in to Zoom, waiting for Alison to join. When she saw Alison's face pop up, she felt unnerved. Her own camera was off, but she pulled her sweater around her, as if she needed to hide herself.

'Evening, Lisbeth. I thought we might try something different. I don't expect you to turn your camera on, though you can if you want.' Alison waited as Beth remained silent. 'Okay. Take a few deep breaths. In and out. Relax your shoulders. I thought that seeing my face might help you to open up a bit more.'

'I ... okay. What do you want to talk about?'

'Why don't we talk about your feelings in relation to your mother.'

Beth stiffened. She didn't want to talk about that woman just yet. 'I'll need something stronger than tea if we're going down that road.'

'I don't think that's a good idea, given what you've already told me about her.'

But it was too late, Beth had already poured herself a large vodka, pushing the tea aside and when the first sip slid down her throat she began to talk. 'Okay. My mother, the alcoholic. Wait, did you say I'm an alcoholic?'

'That's not what I said at all, but the way you described her sounds like she had her own demons to face and that she used alcohol as a coping mechanism. Do you see any parallels with yourself?'

'I thought you wanted me to open up? Calling me an alkie, saying I'm like my mother, that's not going to help. Maybe we should call it a night.'

'Hang on. I'm being led by you, Lisbeth. What would *you* like to talk about instead?'

Beth smiled. She was paying for the sessions, so she should be the one in control.

'I want to talk about my fiancé and the way he makes me feel. He belittles me, ignores me when I speak. Pushes me away when I need him... You know, tonight I thought he was going to hit me. I was actually cowering in the corner.'

'I'm so sorry. Has he hurt you before?'

'No, well, not physically, not yet...'

It seems she'd found something the counsellor was interested in speaking about that would keep her from having to talk about her parents. Beth wasn't ready to talk about either of them yet, and didn't know if she would ever be.

Chapter Forty-Four

BETH

Beth spent twenty minutes detailing to Alison the ways in which Joe belittled her. How he made her feel like she was slowly losing her mind. She'd never felt that way with him before, but everything had changed after her father died.

'That's fairly common in cases of domestic abuse.' Alison was nonchalant about her assessment.

'Whoa. My fiancé isn't abusive ... he just isn't around for me.' Beth rubbed her eyes. How did the conversation go from miscommunication to abuse. Did she do that?

'I don't mean to upset you, but you're describing gaslighting in my opinion. I work with a lot of people who've been emotionally abused by their partners.' Alison paused.

A noise caught Beth's attention. It was the front door closing. 'Oh, he's home... I should probably go now.'

Beth's eyes followed Joe as he stumbled into the kitchen. Arms outstretched, he came to hug her, but tripped over the laptop cord knocking the device off the counter. Beth cursed as it crashed on the kitchen floor.

'Oh shit. Sorry bout that.' He bent over – unsteady on his feet – to pick it up but it managed to slip out of his hands and fall to the floor again. 'Were you doing something important?' He knelt down and tried turning the device off and on.

Beth reached down and picked it up. 'Leave it. It's okay.'

'Only trying to help.' He used the countertop to pull himself up and walked over to the kitchen sink. He turned on the tap and filled a glass with some water.

Beth's mobile pinged. It was Alison.

> Are you okay? After you said your fiancé was home, the screen went black. A. Burgess

Damn. She didn't want to reply, but if she didn't she knew that the counsellor would phone the police for a safety check and that's the last thing she needed.

> All okay. Just an accident. Speak next week. L

Now she'd have more explaining to do. 'I can't seem to get this thing working.' She switched the laptop off and on and tapped the keys. 'I'll have to take it in somewhere and have it looked at.'

She didn't want to leave the house in case she was followed, but she needed the laptop, it had all her work files on it and she'd need access for her research, and more importantly, she needed Joe to think everything was okay.

'I can do that for you. It was my fault.'

'No, it's fine. Really. Might be good to get some fresh air.'

Beth didn't want Joe to make her feel bad again, and with a few drinks in him, he could go on and on. She didn't want to deal with that now.

He came over and gave her an awkward hug. 'I miss you. Come to bed so we can cuddle,' he whispered, and when he pulled his face away from her ear, he smiled.

Her skin crawled.

'I've got a few things to read first for an interview tomorrow. Shit, I'll have to set up Zoom on my iPad or phone.'

Truth was, she wasn't tired.

'Wake me when you come up, then.' A slobbery, wet kiss landed on her cheek as she turned away. She smiled, not wanting him moaning about how long it had been since they were intimate. Sex was the last thing on her mind.

Beth closed the laptop and waited for Joe to leave before she poured herself a measure of vodka and drank it neat.

She found her iPad and was downloading the apps and files she would need when a flash of light in the garden caught her eye.

She turned off the kitchen lights and peeked through the blinds. Who was doing this to her? Was that a person at the end of the garden? She was about to unlock the door and take a closer look when the neighbour's security light flashed and a cat scurried by.

Beth's heart was racing. Maybe Joe was right.

Chapter Forty-Five

BETH

Beth hadn't realised she had dozed off until her chin hit her chest and woke her up. She looked around, wondering how she got into the living room. The clock on the wall read 5:30am, and Joe wouldn't buy that she was up early again – he was already giving her the side eye on that. She picked up her mobile and set the alarm for 6am.

Beth crept up the carpeted stairs and headed to the bathroom. After brushing her teeth, she tiptoed into the bedroom and took off the clothes she'd been wearing, swapping them for a flannel PJ bottoms and a tank top. She inched her way into the bed next to Joe and held her breath, hoping she wouldn't disturb him.

When he didn't move, she turned over on her side and stared at the alarm clock.

At 6am, Beth stretched her arms just as the alarm started ringing. A groan from beside her signalled Joe was awake and he reached over, giving her a squeeze.

'Good morning. Sorry, I crashed.' He smacked his lips together and for some reason this annoyed her.

'Morning.' She tried her best to sound tired. 'I tried to wake you when I came up, but you were dead to the world.' She threw the duvet off and sat up.

Joe grabbed her around the waist. 'Where do you think you're going. We still have time.'

Beth wriggled out of his grasp and stood up. 'Heh-heh.' Her shoulders stiffened. 'As much as I'd love to, I've too many things going on and need to get in the shower so that I can be out the door at seven. I've got to catch the bus into town.'

Joe scratched his head. 'I thought you were still working from home?'

'Were you that pissed when you came in? You broke my laptop. Remember?'

'No need to snap. Jeez. It was an accident.' He turned over and pulled the duvet around his shoulder. 'Wake me up when you get out of the shower.'

'Fine.'

What was his problem? She hadn't snapped at him. Is this what Alison meant about gaslighting. Through her job, Beth had heard it used many times but had never experienced it herself.

Beth turned on the shower, letting the water heat up. She almost scared herself when she turned around and caught a glimpse of her face in the mirror. Her eyes were sunken with dark circles underneath. Had she lost weight? Her arms were like twigs. The mirror steamed up and Beth got in the shower, her shoulders relaxing as the hot water beat down on her back.

Twenty minutes later and feeling more awake, she wrapped herself in a robe and twirled a towel around her head. As she passed the bedroom she called in, 'I'm out of the shower now. I'll make the coffee.'

Joe mumbled a reply as Beth headed downstairs.

She put the coffee maker on and grabbed two Pro Plus pills out of her bag, along with her cocktail of medications, and washed them down with tap water.

Footsteps above caught her attention and once she heard the shower turn on, she returned to the bedroom to get dressed and put makeup on. Without it, Joe would comment on how tired she looked, and she didn't want to hear any more from him. She was just waiting to hear him say how thin she'd become. She was surprised at how much she had changed physically in the last few months. Her clothes were starting to hang off her.

But when Joe walked into the bedroom with only a towel around his waist, Beth got butterflies. She did miss being close, but the thought of sex was still a real turn-off. She smiled at him through the reflection in the mirror.

'Maybe we could do something this evening?' Joe pulled on his trousers and grabbed a white shirt from the wardrobe. 'We haven't really been doing anything together since... Well, you know.'

She did know.

If he said anything about it being months ago and that she should be over it by now she would lose it. 'Okay, sure. What did you have in mind.' Beth was struggling with going outside and wouldn't go into town, even though Joe would be with her. She also didn't want to stay at home, where he would probably try and initiate sex.

'We could go down the road. Grab a meal, then come back and watch a film. You can choose which one.' He smiled.

'Sounds good.' She plugged in the hairdryer. 'Shall I meet you there after work?' She could at least try and make an effort.

'Great. I should be finished around five so let's meet at six. Do you want your coffee brought up?' He draped a tie around his neck and stood in the doorway.

'No, thanks. I'll just dry my hair and come down after. If I don't see you, have a good day.' She turned the hairdryer on, its whirring buzz barred further conversation.

Beth wondered if maybe things were on the up. Joe might have been realising how awful he'd been and maybe connecting again was the solution. She could then stop the counselling and hopefully return to the office. They could return to their normal routines, and she could continue pretending.

Joe didn't need to know all her secrets.

Chapter Forty-Six

JOE

From a safe distance, Joe was trying to be supportive, and he was relieved to see that the counselling sessions were having a positive effect on Beth. She seemed to have cut back on the booze, though her lack of sleep, self-medicating, and paranoia hadn't disappeared.

He had to keep reminding himself it was still early days, and he couldn't force her to grieve quicker.

Janis continued to call him, and as far as he was aware, she hadn't acted on her threats to contact Beth. She was still pestering *him*, though, wanting to meet up, but he'd managed to put her off, mentioning meetings he couldn't reschedule. Joe hadn't figured out what she knew, and he wasn't going to give her any further ammo. It was evident that Janis had kept in contact with Beth's father, and he wondered whether Kevin said something to her. That she was twisting things around to make him paranoid. It seemed like something she might do. Could one of his clients at Tasker House be associated with Janis? He shook his head. She really had him on edge.

He was a little thrown – and wary – when Janis was understanding about being repeatedly brushed off, but he had too much to catch up on to worry about what she was playing at. She was already deep enough in his thoughts.

He was also relieved there had been no further visits from the mysterious police officer, so he left the matter alone. Nothing untoward had happened, and he guessed it might have been a rookie mistake. Once the copper had heard some buzz around the station and realised his error, he'd probably decided to keep his mouth shut, wanting to avoid any consequences. It was in their hands now.

If anything further was to emerge in relation to the Brewer case, he'd pass it over to AJ. The trial was beginning in a couple of weeks, and Joe would revisit the case with her, then.

He looked up when something, someone, caught his eye.

Speak of the devil.

'I've got a few meetings off-premises, and a parent-teacher meeting after that, so I probably won't be back until tomorrow.' AJ leaned against the doorframe.

'Thanks for keeping me posted. How are things?' Joe noticed the dark circles under her eyes and her sallow face.

'A little better, which is what worries me. He's ticking all the boxes in mediation, but I still feel like he's ... I dunno ... watching me all the time. You know as well as I do how some people can play the game when they have to, and then revert to type. That's exactly what he's doing.'

'And you had no luck with the police?'

'No. They're not interested. He's...' She waved her hand. 'You know what, forget about him. It'll get sorted.'

'Well, if you need anything, any time off, whatever, no need to even ask.'

'Thanks. How about things with you? Any better?'

'Actually, they are. Beth's taking some time off work and speaking with a counsellor. So, yeah, much better.' He wasn't sure what had compelled him to lie to AJ. He just didn't want her to feel like she had to be there for him when she had enough to deal with at home.

'That's good to hear. I'm so relieved for you, for both of you. I knew you'd get through it. Right, I best be off.'

Not too long ago, Joe had wondered whether his relationship would last much longer. The uncertainty had torn him apart – he couldn't imagine his life without Beth. The thought of losing her had once felt unbearable. But now, it didn't trouble him at all. In fact, the idea of them breaking up felt like a relief, like one less burden to carry. He loved her, he always would, but the constant mixed messages, the unpredictability, had worn him down. He had enough on his plate, and he couldn't keep pouring his energy into trying to fix her when he could barely manage his own life. He was no longer afraid of losing the relationship – he was more afraid of what staying in it was doing to him.

Chapter Forty-Seven

BETH

Beth nearly missed the bus. She checked her watch and reminded herself that she had to be back home by eleven for the Zoom call. She also had another meeting with the HR team this afternoon – they'd want to hear about the counselling and to see how she was getting on.

With the roadworks and diversions, it was an hour later when she finally got into the town centre. She grabbed a coffee at Costa and walked to the computer-repair shop. The bell jingled above the door to alert staff that someone had entered. It was a small, cramped space and Beth felt claustrophobic as she made her way to the counter. A middle-aged, bearded man came out eventually and looked at her.

'How can I help you?'

'I dropped this last night and now it won't work. Can you fix it?'

He nodded. 'What we'll do is take a look at it, find out what's wrong and then get in touch with an estimate.' He pulled a clipboard from under the counter, then took her contact details. His penmanship consisting of untidy block capitals that spilled across the lined pages.

'Thanks. How long will it take?'

'Depends on what's wrong with it. A few hours minimum. We've a few others ahead of you.'

'Okay.' As Beth trudged out of the shop, she couldn't escape the feeling that his eyes were focused on her, like a hawk watching its prey.

Her heart was thumping. She strode around a corner and leaned against a wall. She took a few deep breaths and decided to call her GP.

'Gladstone Surgery. How can I help.' A young woman answered.

'I wondered if there were any free appointments today. I'm feeling really ... anxious ... my father recently passed and—'

'Sorry. We've no appointments today. The soonest the doctor can see you is in two weeks' time.'

'Two weeks?' Beth's voice rose and passers-by looked her way. 'What if there is something seriously wrong with me? I don't think I can wait two weeks.'

'If it is an emergency you should go to A and E, or call nine-nine-nine for an ambulance. Did you want the appointment?'

The girl's tone was sharp. She probably had to deal with hysterical people all the time, but Beth wasn't hysterical, just desperate. 'Uh ... yes. But is there anything I can do to see if a space opens before then?'

'I'll note it down and we'll call if anything changes. Was there anything else?'

'No. Thank you.' The woman had ended the call before Beth could finish.

How rude!

She thought about calling Dr Griffin since he was aware of her history. She doubted he made house calls in other areas, but he could see to a prescription at her local pharmacy. She scrolled through her contacts and found the private number that he'd given Aunt Kay. She rang him.

'Hello?'

'Uh hi. Is that Dr Griffin?'

'Yes. To whom am I speaking?'

'It's Beth... Lisbeth Stanford.' Dr Griffin never got out of the habit of using her full name no matter how often she'd tried to correct him over the years.

'Ah. How are you? I saw your aunt the other day.'

Beth didn't want a run down of how her aunt was feeling. 'I'm not okay. I tried to get an appointment with my own GP, but they can't see me for weeks. I'm seeing a counsellor and I've been told that I need to work from home until they can assess that I'm better. I feel anxious all the time. I can't sleep.'

'Slow down. I can try and call your doctor.'

'Can't you just prescribe something? For my symptoms. I'm in town now.'

He hesitated. 'Normally, I would say no, but as I am your family's doctor, I will make an exception.'

'Thank you so much.' Her heart palpitations slowed.

'Before you go, can you email the details of your counsellor please and anything else from your HR department. I'll have a look at them.'

'Sure.' She ended the call. Why would he want that information? Did he want to have her sectioned?

Knowing that everything would soon be sorted, Beth felt her muscles relax as she walked over to the pharmacy, collected the prescription and made her way to the bus stop.

———————

At home, she popped two Pro Plus as her eyelids began to feel heavy. She checked her iPad to make sure that the Zoom connection was stable, then set up her workstation in the kitchen, carrying a box of notes and files over so that she could easily access the material. After receiving a text from the repair shop earlier with an estimate, she'd asked them to go ahead and do the work. She sent Joe a text asking him to collect her laptop on his way home and poured herself a tall glass of water. Her hands trembled and she wished it was a vodka.

What was wrong with her? She shook her head. It was her anxiety, nothing else.

If she repeated it enough times, she might begin believing it.

Chapter Forty-Eight

BETH

In a few moments, she'd be speaking with Mrs Brewer. Rachel was off sick, the other paralegal was on holiday and Cassandra had to be in Court. With Mrs Brewer requesting to speak to a female, there was no one else in the office available, and of the appropriate experience or gender. Beth had been given a list of questions she needed to go through. Cassandra had told her to tread carefully, advising that Beth try and come across as sympathetic so that Mrs Brewer would speak freely. Beth was surprised that she'd been trusted with this interview.

Two faces popped up on the screen. One, a man's – Beth assumed he was the solicitor – but it was the woman's face that surprised her.

Mrs Brewer looked broken. Beth began to wonder if her theories were wrong, or maybe this woman was a great actress. She'd soon find out.

'Good morning, Mrs Brewer. My name is Lisbeth Stanford. I'm a paralegal – do you know what that is?'

'Yes. My solicitor explained it all to me.' The solicitor

nodded and Mrs Brewer continued. 'You're going to ask me some questions about the incident and my statement.' She waved her hands around. 'All that stuff, correct?'

'Yes. That's right. Okay, shall we make a start?'

'Will you be recording this?'

'No. But I will be taking notes. Are you okay with that?'

'Yes.' Another nod from her solicitor. 'Okay. I'm ready.' The woman tucked a strand of hair behind an ear and then cleared her throat.

'Could you tell me about what you'd been doing prior to coming home on the night in question?'

'Yes, I was… Wait a minute. Are you trying to trick me? I was at home... If you—'

The solicitor jumped in. 'Miss Stanford. You have my client's statement in front of you, so please read it.'

'My apologies. I misspoke.' Beth had nearly caught her out. 'Could you tell me what you had been doing at home prior to the argument with your husband.'

Mrs Brewer proceeded to relay almost word for word what she'd told the police, and Beth sat back and listened waiting for the woman to stop. She wished she could point out that she knew she was lying, but she needed something that Cassandra could pick up when the time was right.

As Mrs Brewer recited her spiel, Beth's head started to spin and she held onto the table, closing her eyes until the panic that was surging through her body eased.

She needed a drink and badly.

When Beth next spoke, the words came out jumbled.

Wait. Was she slurring?

Mrs Brewer's face came closer to the screen. 'Are you drunk?'

'Absolutely not. I'm on medication.' Beth's eyes moved rapidly back and forth. 'It can have weird ... side-effects.' Beth shifted on the stool. Her head was spinning.

Mrs Brewer's solicitor pounced. 'I think we're done here. First you insinuate my client is being dishonest, and now you're drunk... We'll be putting in a complaint about you.'

Beth stared at the screen. Were they trying to deflect because Mrs Brewer had been caught out? She was about to respond when the screen went blank. She got up and made herself a coffee. Her head felt cloudy and as much as she wanted a drink, she had the HR call shortly.

A beep from the counter indicated the call was early, and when she saw the name on the screen, her chest tightened. How could Mrs Brewer have gotten to her boss so quickly?

Chapter Forty-Nine

BETH

Beth's heart was pounding as she answered the call. Cassandra's face appeared on the screen.

'I thought you were getting better? I've had multiple complaints come across my desk in the last two weeks about you, Lisbeth. Care to explain?' Other than Mrs Brewer, Beth had no idea what the other complaints were about or from whom – she had barely spoken to her colleagues, except over emails. The frown on Cassandra's face told her it wasn't going to be good.

Cassandra opened her screen wider, and Beth noticed she was sitting at the head of the conference table. A stern look piercing the screen. Next to her was a man Beth had never seen before. Beth moved her iPad back on the counter surface so that she could see everyone properly. Her vision was blurred and fuzzy. Some of them looked like blobs floating on the screen.

'Lisbeth, apologies for having to move the HR meeting sooner. I would've made arrangements for you to come in and do this face-to-face, but I didn't think we could or should wait any longer, you understand, don't you? You wouldn't want to drag this out any longer than needs be.'

Cassandra flipped through a notebook before continuing.

'I'm afraid we've received numerous complaints about your performance lately. It's alleged that you have been consistently failing to meet deadlines and you've been unresponsive to emails and phone calls.' Cassandra stared at her, and Beth wondered if she was expecting a response. 'There's also been some concerns you've been interviewing witnesses under the influence and at times have been accusatory and argumentative.'

Beth felt her face flush with embarrassment. Everyone knew she'd been going through a difficult time and although they may not have been aware of the situation at home, she had a lot going on in her personal life, too. She didn't feel she'd been struggling to keep up with her workload. She'd needed to think up an excuse, something that would allow them to see that she could cope and would change things.

'Cassandra, everyone, I'm sorry. I hadn't realised that I haven't been performing up to par lately. I've been going through some personal issues, as well as grieving the loss of my father. I'm on new meds, maybe that's having an effect as I have had moments where I haven't felt like myself. I've been—' She stopped herself before she admitted that she had been seeing things, hearing voices; they'd sack her for sure. 'I've been doing better. I swear, I haven't been drinking on the job. You know me, Cassandra. I wouldn't do that. I've done everything you asked. As you've suggested, I'm attending counselling. I've been to the doctor. I...' She shook her head. 'I love my job and if you think my work has been affected, I will do whatever it takes to get it sorted and do better.' Beth's voice trembled.

Cassandra nodded, but the man next to her spoke up. 'I'm sorry, Lisbeth, but this is a serious matter. We've statements that suggest this has been going on for quite some time. We'll need to investigate this further.'

Beth's heart sank. If an official investigation was launched, her job would be on the line. She prided herself on her work ethic, even with everything that she had been struggling with, and the thought of being accused of misconduct was almost too much to bear. If she didn't have work to focus on, she'd be consumed by her dark thoughts.

Her phone rang. She glanced at the screen and saw that it was her doctor's office and was in two minds whether to answer it. But maybe they could help her. Maybe they could make Cassandra see that it wasn't her fault. 'I need to take this.' She excused herself from the meeting, explaining that it was the GP surgery and once she'd finished, she'd return. She turned off the camera, put the mic on silent and answered the call.

'Hi, Lisbeth. We spoke to the doctor after you raised some concerns about your medication and wanted to talk you through the side-effects.' Beth wondered if there were listening devices in her home, as the timing of the call was impeccable.

'What's going on?' Beth looked around the kitchen and almost laughed. Why would the doctor be spying on her?

'We've received some reports from other patients that the medication can cause vision impairment and confusion. Have you experienced any of these side effects?' The nurse's voice was flat, uncaring.

Beth realised that this could help her case at work. She'd

been feeling extremely unfocused lately. 'Yes, I have. I thought it might be the meds, which is why I called. I'm on a conference call with my work now. Do you think you can relay what you've just said? It's really important. I don't want to lose my job,' Beth pleaded.

'I'm afraid I can't do that. Your employer will need to contact us. However, it's important that you let us know about any other side-effects you experience. We may need to adjust your dosage or switch you to a different medication. If there are no other questions, I need to go now.' Beth couldn't think clearly.

'Uh, I guess not.'

The nurse ended the call.

Beth took a moment, feeling relieved she may be able to get herself out of this situation at work. She'd have to explain what the nurse had told her and hoped that they'd understand and believe her.

When she returned to the conference, she noticed another person had joined. It was Mr Walker, the other partner in the law firm.

'Lisbeth, I want you to be aware that we all understand you're going through a lot of stress, but we've been talking while you were offline...' Walker's voice was serious and didn't sound understanding at all.

'Hang on. The call I just took – the nurse explained it all.' She held up her phone but everyone in the room shook their head. 'Don't you want to know?' A knot tightened in her stomach.

'Your phone never rang, Lisbeth. We're really concerned, and HR have been in contact to say that they're going to place you on enforced leave, paid, of course, while we investigate the complaints against you.' The look in Cassandra's eyes was one of pity.

Beth felt like the ground had been pulled out from under her. 'Maybe my phone was on silent and that's why you couldn't hear it?' She then checked her phone, but it wasn't on silent. 'I'm not lying. Cassandra, please. What does this mean? Will I lose my job?' Beth tried to keep her voice steady. She looked at her incoming calls, but the last one was Joe.

She must have deleted them. Damn.

'I don't know, Lisbeth. I'm sorry. You need to cooperate fully with the investigation, okay?' Cassandra turned away and the screen went blank.

Beth felt her knees buckle and she grabbed onto the stool as a debilitating numbness swept over her body. As if she didn't have enough to deal with, now this.

Joe would lose it.

Why was everyone against her?

Chapter Fifty

JOE

As he drove along the back roads into Langley town centre, Joe blared the Stereophonics' 'Have a Nice Day' and couldn't help singing along. It was one of those songs you could shout from the top of your lungs and feel good after.

He pulled his car into a free parking space behind the office and walked around to the front door. Nothing would ruin today.

At least, that's what he thought until he saw that police officer skulking around.

'Hey!' Joe started to sprint towards the building. 'Officer!' The man turned around. 'Yeah, you. Stop. I just want to talk.' The officer ran down the alley between the office and the building next to it. Joe followed, but lost him when he tripped over a homeless woman who shouted at him. 'I'm so sorry. I didn't see you there,' he said. His eyes had been trained on the fleeing cop.

'No one fucking sees us.'

Joe felt awful. He reached into his pocket and handed the

woman a few pound coins. 'If you need any help. I work on the corner at Tasker House.' Before he could finish the woman batted his hand away, scattering the coins onto the ground.

'Fuck off.' She carried on mumbling as she collected the coins.

Why was that cop hanging around his office? Joe needed to get to the bottom of this.

When Joe got back to the building, the front door was unlocked, and he noticed AJ.

'Another early bird.' He waved.

'So much to catch up on. You sure you don't need a full-time counsellor on board?' She raised a brow.

'You know if I had the funding, I'd snap you up in a second.' Joe wondered if there was any way he could secure a full-time position for her. She was a well-liked and respected member of his team.

'I know. I can't resist winding you up, sometimes. Probably for the best...'

'Yeah, I get it.' He smiled. 'Not that I want to change the subject, but did a cop pop in here about half an hour ago?'

AJ's face turned white. 'No. Why? Did you have an early meeting?' She shifted in her chair, and Joe thought her reaction was strange.

'No. I think it was the same cop who was asking about Mrs Brewer before, but when I called out to him, he ran off.'

The colour returned to her face. 'Nobody in the Domestic Abuse Unit that could help?'

Joe shook his head and shrugged. 'I'll call them again. I

wish I thought about taking a photo. Dumb-ass move. Next time.'

Joe left AJ, and when he was in his office he quickly went through his emails, relieved that there'd been no further queries from Connor. He had one final sum of money to move and that would be the end of that. As long as that wasn't questioned, he'd never have to worry about it again. If his financial manipulations were exposed, at the very least it would erode trust in him and Tasker House, at worst, he would be arrested. Everything would be ruined.

He needed to make sure he'd left enough money in the joint account so Beth didn't have any reason to get mad at him. If for any reason she needed to dip into it, there had to be sufficient funds for her not to notice, or shit would hit the fan.

He pulled out his mobile and noticed six missed calls, all from Janis. He now had her number stored as Colin, a fake friend, in case Beth went through his phone.

He scrolled to the contact he was looking for and clicked call.

'Kay, it's Joe. How are you?'

'We're well. In fact, Frank and I are just on our way out. So perhaps we can speak another time.'

Although her words were polite, he could sense from her tone she wasn't pleased to hear from him.

'This won't take long.' Joe wanted answers today. He needed to decide on his next steps with Janis Stanford. She was becoming a problem that needed solving, and quickly.

'Okay, what is it?' Kay's short answers told Joe he was pushing it.

'Has Beth's mother been in contact with you since you last saw her, after the funeral?'

'Please don't tell me that you've been speaking to her Joe.'

Was that fear he heard in her voice?

'No, I just wanted to check because I know it would upset Beth. I still don't understand why she appeared that day.'

'She's toxic, Joe. Always has been, always will be. And if she thinks she's entitled to something, she'll do whatever it takes to get it. Don't let Beth be fooled by any of her false promises, okay?'

Joe was confused. As far as he knew, Janis hadn't been mentioned in the will.

'That's what I can't figure out. What would she think is owed to her?'

'I'm sure Janis will tell you if she hasn't already.'

Was Kay trying to tease information out of him, or did she know he was lying.

'You should watch yourself, Joe. I hate to say it about my niece, but Lisbeth has that same toxic streak as her mother and she may be able to fool you, but not me.'

'Hang on. Beth has a lot going on right now, but she's not toxic, and as her family, you shouldn't be saying stuff like that. She's seeing a counsellor.' Joe regretted sharing that with Kay as soon as the words left his mouth. 'But you need to keep that to yourself.'

It wasn't as if Kay and Beth spoke regularly, but if she ever found out Joe was telling people... It wasn't his place or news to share, especially when she was already so paranoid. 'What am I missing, then?'

'Fine. You need to keep this to yourself. There was a provision in the will. My brother always hoped that Lisbeth and Janis would mend their relationship, if not in his lifetime, maybe when he was gone. Despite everything she'd done to him over the years, he still loved Janis. Anyway, when he was first diagnosed, he changed his will – I tried to stop him, but he wouldn't listen. Knowing what Janis is like, he put a provision in the will. I shouldn't be telling you this, but I need you to know how Janis manipulates things. If Lisbeth and her mother are to reconcile within six months of his passing, a third of the money from the sale of the house and his life insurance will go to Janis.'

Did Janis know this? Joe needed to find out.

Chapter Fifty-One

JOE

Joe felt like he had been sucker-punched by a professional boxer. After his call with Kay, he knew the real reason why Janis was trying to manipulate him to get to Beth. It finally made sense. Her motivations for reconciliation weren't driven by maternal feelings, which he suspected, but by greed. There were about half a million pounds' worth of reasons Janis wanted to be a mother again.

Joe didn't bother informing his team that he was leaving for the day. He headed towards the park, calling Beth's mother as he walked.

'This all needs to end. Meet me by the café in Langley Park.' He hung up the phone and now that he knew the truth, he no longer cared about her threats. He was going to take back control of the situation.

Joe wasn't sure where Janis had been staying, but suspected she'd probably found somewhere in Langley or one of the neighbouring villages. When he saw her waiting outside the café, his suspicions were confirmed.

'Joe. Are we going to do this the easy way or the hard way?' She tilted her head, her eyes dark and taunting.

Joe ignored her and sat down at one of the outdoor tables.

'Little chilly to be sitting outside, isn't it?'

Joe pointed to the chair across the room. 'Have a seat. This won't take long.'

Janis sat down. 'You haven't told Lisbeth we've been talking yet, have you?'

'Let's get one thing clear.' He pointed at her and then himself. '*We* haven't been talking. *You*'ve been harassing me, making threats and, based on our last conversation, stalking me, too. If you knew anything about your daughter, you'd know she only uses Lisbeth in a professional capacity. A mother would know that.'

'There's no law that says I can't see how my own child is doing.' Her face softened. 'Look, Joe, we shouldn't be arguing. We both want what's best for Lisb— for Beth.'

The shortened version of his fiancée's name coming from that woman's mouth, trickled ice water down Joe's spine. 'You might be interested to learn I spoke to Kay. I know what you're after. If, and I'm not saying I will, but if I do tell Beth you'd like to reconcile, I'll also be sure to add the reason for it.' Joe was taking a chance that Kevin had told Janis his plans and the scowl on her face confirmed it.

Janis pounded her fists on the table, causing Joe to jump in his seat. 'Who do you think you are to threaten me?' Janis leaned across the table, a snarl on her face. 'How do you think Beth would feel knowing you've been playing around with funds? Risking her financial future and keeping secrets of your own. I. See. You. Joe.' She pulled back slowly.

Joe was stunned. Was she bluffing? How could she even

know any of this? Before he could respond, he saw a figure approaching over Janis's shoulder. The person was waving. Janis turned and a sly smile crept over her face. 'Have I overstayed my welcome? I could make it look like that's your bit on the side, couldn't I.' She stood up. 'And make sure Beth knows about her.'

'Hey, Joe. Sorry, I didn't mean to interrupt.' AJ smiled at Janis.

'Not at all, darling. I was just leaving. You can have my seat.' Janis turned and started to walk away and Joe noticed that she had her phone in her hand. She stopped, turned back and looked at him, just as AJ gave him a hug.

Janis mouthed 'Gotcha!' before she carried on walking away.

Fuck.

AJ swivelled and looked in the direction of Beth's mother.

'What's the matter? What did I miss?' She waved over a waitress. 'Can I get a large black coffee?' She looked at Joe. 'My treat.'

'I'll have a large flat white, please. Thanks.'

'What's got your face all twisted?'

'That was Beth's mother.'

'You don't get along, I take it?'

'I don't even know her, and what I do know of her, I don't like.'

The coffee arrived.

'Do you want to talk about it? If you don't mind me saying you've been looking a bit worse for wear lately?' said AJ.

Joe looked down and noticed his shirt was out of his trousers, so he tucked it back in. He ran a hand across his cheek and felt his stubble. He hadn't been aware of how he looked to others. Beth had either not noticed, or not cared enough to comment on it – she was so focused on herself lately.

'You've enough on your plate,' he said. 'I've just been a bit lazy. I have a few personal things to deal with, but nothing that can't be sorted.' He took a sip of his coffee. 'How's things with your Pete?'

'Switching subjects? Smooth, Mr Tasker.' AJ laughed. 'Things have gone a bit quiet. I don't know whether to be relieved or worried.'

'How's your son handling it?'

'He has his moments, but kids are so bloody resilient. The school counsellor has been great. I just worry about all the bullshit his father says to him when I'm not around, but I can't really do anything about that.'

Joe didn't know what to say, and anything he did say would sound like something they'd say to their clients.

AJ looked at her watch. 'Nice chat. I promise it won't always be doom and gloom.' She reached across and squeezed his hand. 'If you ever need a sounding board, you know where I am. It's only fair.' She went inside and paid the bill before saying goodbye.

Joe had one more meeting before he could go home, and then he'd figure out what he'd tell Beth about her mother.

Chapter Fifty-Two

BETH

Beth had spent the last few hours after the call with HR, sitting on the couch, twirling her hair with one hand and sipping a drink with the other.

When Joe walked through the front door and into the living room, he looked exhausted. She noticed his face light up briefly, until he saw the drink in her hand and the expression on her face.

His smile faded. 'You didn't show up as we planned. Remember? The pub. What's wrong?'

Beth hesitated before answering. She didn't want an argument and he'd find out soon enough. 'I got suspended today.' She couldn't lift her voice above a whisper. 'They called it "enforced leave", but that's just HR speak for suspension.'

'What? Why?' Joe's eyes widened as he rushed over and sat beside Beth on the couch. His hands grasping hers in a gentle squeeze.

'Apparently, there were more complaints when I started

working from home. But it's the first I've heard of it. I thought I've been really good at getting back on track.' Beth's throat tightened with emotion. 'They're launching an investigation, and it feels like they're targeting me.' As Beth spoke, she saw Joe's expression grow more and more disappointed. It was clear that he was upset, but she didn't know if it was to do with her.

Joe was quiet. He just sat there, his arm around her, as she explained what had happened. Beth told him people had complained that she'd been difficult to work with and unprofessional. She told him about the call from the nurse, the side-effects she was experiencing and how no one believed her. 'Everyone is out to get me, Joe.'

There was a long silence until eventually, Joe spoke. 'Do you want me to call that nurse, get her to speak to Cassandra?'

'What's the point? They don't believe me and they think I'm shit at what I do.'

'I'm sorry this is happening to you.' He rubbed her shoulder. 'But remember, you're good at your job. You've never had any problems before. Cassandra has always sung your praises and encouraged you to progress. She wouldn't target you. This is just a blip, and they need to take that into consideration.'

Beth forced a smile. 'I hope you're right.'

Joe hugged her tightly. 'I am. And whatever happens, we'll get through it.'

Beth nodded, surprised but grateful for his support. Deep down, though, she couldn't shake the paranoia that had settled in her stomach.

What if this wasn't just a blip? What if the complaints had

some truth to them? What if she lost her job, and everything fell apart?

They sat in silence. Beth could hear the clock ticking on the wall, and cars pulling into their drives. Her world was crumbling around her, but everyone else's kept turning.

Chapter Fifty-Three

JOE

'You know what?' He stood up, 'I promised you a fun evening, so why don't I make my famous spag bol?' It was only famous in his mind, but always cheered Beth up when he made it.

And there it was – the smile he'd missed for so long.

When they sat at the table an hour later, Beth played with her food.

'Everything okay? I didn't put too much garlic in, did I?' He leaned down and smelled his own plate.

'I'm sure it's delicious. I just feel a little sick if I'm honest. You carry on, though.'

Joe shovelled a few forkfuls into his mouth, but he wasn't enjoying it either.

Another ten minutes passed in complete silence. His plan had backfired.

'I guess we weren't as hungry as we thought.' Joe took her plate and brought it to the sink, while Beth cleared the glasses and put the dishes in the dishwasher. 'Fancy a walk?

Remember when we first started dating ... those evening strolls?' Joe tugged her sleeve and smiled.

'Okay.'

They grabbed their jackets and headed outside. The air was crisp, and Joe inhaled deeply, the air biting his throat. He watched out of the corner of his eye as Beth pulled her coat tightly around her body. They were a couple of feet apart but were walking in synch, and he didn't want to ruin the peace between them by bringing up her mother now.

'We should go to the pub to warm up.' She was rubbing her hands together.

Joe stopped and turned to look at her. 'I don't think that's a good idea.' It was getting late; she'd already taken her meds, and God knows how many drinks she'd already had before he had come home.

She rolled her eyes at him. 'Oh, come on. Only a quick one. I'm not planning on getting drunk if that's what you're worried about.'

'That's not the point.' He paused, wondering whether he should give her a few home truths and potentially ruin the evening, or if he should give in like he always did just to avoid an argument. He chose the former. 'Your drinking has been pretty bad lately. It's never just one. Plus, you know that you shouldn't be mixing alcohol with your meds. You said so yourself. It's just not safe.'

Her face twisted and Joe took a step back.

'I can handle myself.' Her voice grew louder, and Joe looked around. 'I'm not a child, Joe, I know my limits.'

'It's not about that.' His voice was calm. 'I don't want you to do or say something that you'll regret in the morning. Why can't we carry on with our walk?' He reached for her hand, but

Beth turned and stormed off in the direction of the pub. Joe was stunned. He refused to follow her as she'd either make a scene in their local, or he'd be stuck at the pub waiting for her to decide when she was done. He turned down a lane and headed towards home.

Joe thought back to what AJ had said to him and was beginning to think maybe they needed some time apart. He could go and stay with his parents. He decided he'd call them when he got home, and then pack a bag for a week or two. He felt a sense of relief once he made the decision.

He'd tell Beth when she got home, provided she was sober enough to understand what he was saying without going ballistic.

Chapter Fifty-Four

BETH

As Beth walked towards the pub, she couldn't help but feel frustrated. Why did everyone think she was a failure? An alkie?

She'd worked so hard to get where she was, to be a good paralegal and a good partner to Joe. And yet, it seemed like nothing she did was ever good enough.

By the time she reached the pub, she was fuming. She pushed open the door, the warmth of the interior hitting her like a wave. But the sight of the patrons, laughing and drinking and having a good time, made her feel more isolated.

Despite knowing several people in the pub, she didn't want to socialise. Instead, she found a booth in the corner and ordered a drink to calm herself. With the drink in front of her, every sip made her feel worse, more alone, more like a failure.

Nursing her drink, the intrusive thoughts were back, and she wondered if Joe was right. Maybe she did have a problem. Maybe she was a let-down. She felt tears prick at the corners of her eyes, but she refused to let them fall. She was so confused.

When she finally left the pub, the night was taunting and cold. She wrapped her jacket around her body, warding away the chill, but the cold was nothing compared to the emptiness she felt inside. She had to figure out a way to prove to herself, to Joe, to everyone, that she wasn't the catastrophe everyone made her out to be. That she was capable of far more than they gave her credit for.

Chapter Fifty-Five

BETH

B eth had spent most of the night awake, and when Joe had ignored her when she had stumbled home, she vowed she would make positive changes to her life. Enough was enough, and she didn't want to think what Pops would say if he knew she was drifting back to a dark place. Her demons might now be interred in unmarked graves, but she'd always been afraid of the day she'd exhume them.

Was that day in her near future?

She hadn't had a nuisance call for a while, and she hoped that meant they had stopped. Just thinking of them was triggering. She didn't know who was calling or why, but the constant ringing had kept her anxious and on edge. It didn't seem to matter how many times she blocked a number; another call would come through and it was pushing her over the edge.

She needed to confide in someone. With her so-called friends abandoning her whenever she needed them, it would have to be her counsellor. She would tell her about the calls. If nothing else, Alison would be able to help her cope. Beth didn't want to call the police as there was no point, no threats had been made. They'd just tell her to log everything, and even then, without knowing who was making the calls, they wouldn't waste the resources to try and find out. The calls made Beth feel uneasy, but technically that wasn't against the law.

In the kitchen, Joe had set up her laptop, a kind gesture, a peace offering of sorts and for a moment she felt bad. Had she been too hard on him? Was she blaming him because she had no one else to blame? Maybe he was hiding something himself.

She smacked herself. Why did she think he was hiding something? The intrusive thoughts were returning and her need for a drink to drown them out was high.

But what if he did have secrets?

She dialled into the counselling session and let loose. As she talked about her concerns over Joe, she felt a sense of relief wash over her, and things suddenly became crystal clear. Then she dropped a bombshell.

'I think he's been cheating on me.' Beth could see Alison listening attentively as she shared her fears and concerns.

'It all makes sense. The hang-up calls ... feeling like I'm being watched. Either it's the partner of whoever he's cheating with, or maybe even the person themselves. Oh my God. I can't believe I didn't realise from the start. That's why he's always out, pushing me away. I'm right, aren't I!'

'Let's take a minute and talk it through. Are you sure you aren't jumping to conclusions?'

Alison gently probed her about her suspicions, but Beth didn't have any concrete evidence. She just had a gut feeling that something was off.

'You mentioned your medication was affecting you. Could it be that it's making you a little paranoid?'

Alison seemed to think she was grasping at straws, but Beth was now adamant something was going on. She couldn't shake the feeling Joe was hiding something from her, and the hang-up calls only added to her anxiety.

While Alison rambled on, Beth's anxiety piqued. She couldn't concentrate on the words the counsellor was saying, and instead found herself obsessing over every little detail of Joe's life since her father had died.

Give me a sign, Pops. Tell me I'm not losing my mind.

As the session drew to a close, Beth felt even more confused and alone. She wasn't sure if she could trust her own feelings anymore, and the suspicion Joe was cheating on her was eating away at her. She felt like she was trapped in a never-ending cycle of anxiety and fear.

'I need to go. Thanks for listening. You're right, I'm probably making something out of nothing.' Beth shut down the Zoom call before Alison could say anything else. She decided to find more evidence and then confront Joe.

Beth logged into her social-media accounts and checked Joe's Instagram and Facebook. He hadn't updated anything since last summer. She looked at his friends and followers, but there was no one out of the ordinary there.

Her jaw ached from the tight clenching as she paced the room.

As the day went on, she couldn't eat, and, as tired as she felt, when she went to lie down, to shut the world out with sleep, her mind raced even faster.

Maybe her meds did need to be adjusted.

The phone rang and Beth ignored it. When it rang a second time, she screamed down the line, 'What the hell do you want from me!'

'You should keep a close eye on him. He has a wandering eye. No surprise, though, considering the state of you.'

Beth dropped the phone. The voice was no more than a whisper and she couldn't tell whether it was male or female.

'No! No! No!'

She sat in the kitchen, staring at the laptop, her face as blank as the screen. The incessant ringing of her phone was boring into her head. She pulled at her hair willing for it to stop. She knew if she answered it, the caller would tell her more truths she wasn't ready to hear, and then abruptly disconnect with a click. She didn't want to listen anymore.

Was it just a cruel prank?

She needed to hear Pops's voice. He would fix everything if he was here. But he was not. Never would be again. Tears tumbled down her cheeks.

She poured herself a drink to take the edge off and collapsed onto the couch, huddling beneath a fleece blanket as if it was a shield protecting her from the world.

In that moment, all Beth wanted was to feel safe and loved. She longed for the comfort Pops had exuded with nothing more than a look or smile, and a partner who loved her unconditionally. Now she had neither and she didn't know what else she could do.

Screw it.

She scribbled a note for Joe and grabbed her coat. She needed to be where her thoughts didn't consume her, and she knew just the place.

Chapter Fifty-Six

JOE

Joe's morning at work had been a shitshow, and thanks to Beth's behaviour earlier distracting him, the meeting didn't go well.

'What's on your mind Joe? That was a disaster in there.' AJ looked back into the conference room. Joe had thrown some additional hours her way due to all the partnership meetings.

'Was it really that bad?' He gestured for AJ to follow him into his office and, once the door was closed, he told her about what had happened last night and Beth's outburst this morning.

'Ah, okay. That explains where your head's at. I'm sure we could smooth things over and—'

Joe interrupted her. 'All of a sudden, she's accusing me of cheating, saying she's been getting letters and calls. But I've not seen any letters. In fact, when she tried to show me photos she'd taken, one was a picture of a takeaway menu and the other a blank envelope. No nuisance calls either. Her phone log only shows calls incoming from me and her Aunt Kay. I'm really worried... But then I think she knows exactly what she's doing.'

AJ looked away.

'Am I the arsehole here?'

'Could anything have triggered these alcohol binges?' she asked. 'She shouldn't be mixing alcohol with her meds. You mentioned she'd stopped the booze for a bit. What happened to change that?'

AJ's response was odd, but as her boss he guessed she didn't want to deliver an uncomfortable truth.

He shook his head. 'She's just been really paranoid and jumpy. I wonder if she did ever stop. Maybe that's why—' He stopped himself mid-sentence. He didn't want to suggest his fiancée was suspended from work for drinking on the job, especially as there was no proof. Well, none that he was aware of anyway.

'You were about to say something. If I'm being too nosy, and you'd rather not talk to me about it, I get it.'

'It's not that.' Then it dawned on him. 'Fuck I really am the arsehole.'

AJ raised an eyebrow.

'Her father's birthday is coming up.' Joe smacked his head. 'I'm such a prick.'

'Well, that definitely could be a trigger. The *firsts* are always the worst after someone dies. Birthdays, special holidays. You said they were close, so this would definitely be something that's affecting her.'

'She hasn't mentioned it though.'

'Doesn't mean she hasn't been thinking about it.'

Joe held up his hands. 'Okay, okay. Total prick here. I need to make it up to her. Don't I?'

AJ nodded. 'I suggest that after the next meeting, you pick up some flowers and the biggest humble pie you can find and then head home.'

Joe flipped through his diary. 'Shite. I totally forgot about that other meeting.'

'There's still a bit of time if you need me to do anything.'

'It's just an update on the strategic plan. I should be okay.' He left his office and cracked on with going through the priorities. The only thing outstanding was the funding, but he knew what he could do if the application fell through.

Joe felt a pat on his back and was glad that everyone seemed to agree.

'Sounds like you have it all covered. Really impressed.' One of the suits whose name he'd forgotten, smiled.

'Thanks, and as long as the funding comes through, we should be good to go in the next few months.' Joe made a quick exit before the suit started talking again.

On his way to his car, he stopped in at the flower shop and picked up a mixed bouquet.

'Great choice. It'll get you out of the doghouse for sure.' The young woman behind the counter laughed as she wrapped the flowers.

Joe thanked her and left the shop. On the drive home, he thought of various things he could say but he knew that all Beth wanted to hear him say was that he was sorry. The house was lit up when he pulled into the drive; the front curtains were drawn, which was unusual. He hid the flowers behind his back as he stepped in the door.

'Hey hon! I've got a surprise for you.' He popped his head into the living room and spied an envelope on the table.

But no Beth. The note said she needed to clear her head which translated as she was getting shit-faced at the pub.

Joe scrunched the note up, went to the kitchen and grabbed a beer from the fridge. He threw the flowers on the counter by the sink and went to the living room where he searched around for the remote, then settled on the couch to watch a film.

Now who's the arsehole?

Chapter Fifty-Seven

BETH

After spending a few hours at the pub, Beth stumbled out of the door with the warm buzz of alcohol coursing through her veins. She'd sat by herself at a corner table with her back to the room, not trusting anyone to share her company. As Billy Joel sang 'Piano Man', she'd been drinking a drink they called loneliness. The singer had been wrong, though, it wasn't better than drinking alone.

The barmaid laid a hand on Beth's arm at closing time. 'Let me call Joe to come and get you. It's slippery out there.'

Beth shrugged the hand off and lurched into the night. She didn't need Joe. She didn't need anyone.

It was early February, and the pub was only a twenty-minute walk from her home. The streets were deserted, and the only sound came from the occasional rustling of leaves in the wind. The streetlights flickered overhead, casting eerie shadows across the pavement, and Beth's imagination began to run wild.

As she walked, Beth felt a sense of unease wash over her.

The feeling she was being watched or followed was the strongest she'd known it to be, but every time she turned around, there was no one there. The shadowy figures of the trees seemed to be closing in on her, and she quickened her pace, her heart pounding in her chest.

Her anxiety rose as she turned into a dimly lit alleyway, it was the quickest way home and the alcohol was beginning to make her feel sick. The creaking of old gates and doors made her jump at every sound.

She heard footsteps behind her, and her heart skipped a beat. She turned around, and there was nobody there. Was she being paranoid? Nothing bad ever happened in Gladstone. She lengthened her stride, each of her own footsteps echoing in the empty alley as her heeled boots encountered the concreted path.

As she came out the other end, Beth's thoughts were interrupted by a rustling sound in the bushes. She paused, her eyes widening as she stared into the distance. Her instincts told her to run, but her curiosity got the better of her, and she took a step closer to investigate. As afraid as she was, she needed to take control.

Her heart leapt into her throat, and Beth paused for a moment to catch her breath. She walked slowly towards the bushes; her eyes fixed on the shadow. Her nerves were frayed, and her hands trembled as she reached out to touch it. Just then, the ground beneath her feet gave way and she fell forward; something hit her head, and everything went black.

Chapter Fifty-Eight

JOE

Joe was even more determined to get away from Beth, but he wasn't sure how to tell her that he needed a break. Not a Ross and Rachel break, but one where they could really look at whether they had a future together. He had avoided calling his parents, too.

He needed to tell Beth first and she still hadn't returned.

His mother would fire questions at him like an AK47.

'What happened? Didn't I tell you that you were rushing into marriage? Is the wedding off? How long do you plan on staying with us?'

His head pounded as he thought about it. From the beginning, he should have insisted that Beth see a counsellor; have her deal with the grief at the time and be a supportive partner for her.

Wait. None of this was his fault. Dammit. Even when she wasn't here, she was in his head. Blaming him. Damn her.

Joe turned on his PS5 to play GTA. It was one way for him

to release tension and anger, so that he could focus on something other than the shitshow his life had become.

He'd been so immersed in his game that he was surprised when he looked up and noticed the time. Beth still wasn't home, and something stirred inside him. He was worried. He called her mobile twice but both times it rang out.

What if she'd got into an argument with someone at the pub? But the pub had closed over half an hour ago and she ought to be home by now.

He paced around the living room, looking out the window to see if he could spot her.

Fuuuuck.

Joe grabbed his coat, put on his trainers, wrapped a scarf around his neck and went to look for Beth. With each step, his worry faded, and his anger rose. He should be home in bed with Beth, not trawling the streets looking for her. He followed the route he thought she'd have taken, and when he turned down the lane – the shortcut through to the pub's car park – he saw a pair of legs.

His heart stopped before his brain kicked into gear, and he ran towards the person on the ground.

Oh my God, Beth!

He bent down and cradled her head in his lap.

How had this happened? Had she been mugged?

Various scenarios bombarded his thoughts. With his free hand, he was searching his pocket looking for his mobile, when he felt her move. Her eyes were blinking slowly as she came to.

Beth tried to sit up, but her face turned white, and Joe eased her back down.

'Don't move. I've got you.'

She groaned. Her arm raised slowly towards her head. 'What happened?'

'I was hoping you could tell me. You scared the shit out of me.' He gently moved hair out of her face.

'I ... I ... don't know. I think someone was following me. There was this noise in the bushes.' She touched the back of her head. 'Then pain... Then, well, I woke up and saw you.'

'Can you stand? No... Maybe you should stay lying down. I'll call an ambulance.' He rested her head in his lap and took out his phone.

Beth grabbed his hand. 'No... No ambulance. I'm okay. Just help me up.'

Joe stood and pulled Beth up from under her arms. She stumbled a bit before balancing on his arm.

'Well, we at least need to go to the police. Have you got your purse and mobile?'

Beth's hand shot into her pocket. 'Yeah, I've got them. No police. Please, Joe. I just want to go home and forget all about it.'

Joe was torn. Whoever did this to Beth needed to be caught. If they went on to hurt someone else, Joe would never forgive himself.

Then the strong smell of alcohol hit him, and then he realised – Beth thought the police wouldn't take her seriously, and she was probably right. Even Joe questioned what was real when she spoke to him lately.

He wrapped his arm around her shoulder, and they walked back to the house in silence.

At home, he sat her on the couch and made her some tea.

'I could do with something stronger.'

Joe turned his face away so she couldn't see his eyes rolling.

'I think tea is the better option here.' He handed her two ibuprofen. 'Take these.'

Beth rolled her eyes but swallowed the painkillers with a large gulp of tea. Her eyes widened and Joe followed her line of view, right to his packed bag by the living room door.

'You're leaving me?'

'Of course not. They're just some clothes I promised to bring over to the shelter tomorrow.' He hated lying, and cursed himself for not stashing the bag when he knew he wouldn't be heading to his parents tonight. Could she read the deception on his face?

'What's happening to me, Joe?' She rubbed her head.

'Let me have a look.' He walked around to the back of the couch and moved his hands over her head. He lifted her hair, searching for a cut or bump but couldn't find anything. Had she made up the story about being attacked? Was this one of her games? 'I can't see or feel anything.'

'Right. So, I guess I'm lying about this, too. Just crazy Beth, making things up so everyone feels sorry for her.' She stood, unsteady on her feet and Joe followed her to the kitchen.

'Stop putting words in my mouth.' He watched as she poured herself a large measure of gin. 'Come on, Beth'—he tried to take the glass out of her hand, but she pulled her arm away—'that's not a good idea.'

'I don't care what you think. Why don't you just fuck off, Joe, and leave me alone.'

And he did just that.

Chapter Fifty-Nine

JOE

Joe lay in bed, staring at the ceiling. His sleep had been restless, broken by the sound of Beth stumbling around downstairs, yelling at people who weren't there and then breaking into sobs. He refused to get up and comfort her. He didn't want to enable this behaviour, no matter how much it tore at him to hear her in pain. She'd pushed him away, made it clear she didn't want his help.

As much as he tried to distance himself, there was something holding him back from leaving her altogether. Yes, he had thought about walking away – God knew he'd considered it after everything – but now, after finding her unconscious on the ground and seeing her so vulnerable, he couldn't bring himself to abandon her. Leaving her now would feel like the coward's way out, and deep down, he still loved her. That was the one thing he knew for sure. As messed up as things were, as much as he didn't know if he believed her story about being attacked, he couldn't just leave her to fend for herself. Walking away would be easier, but he wasn't ready to take the easy way out – not yet.

He got up and had a shower, trying without success to wash away the anger and disappointment from a few hours before. When he dried off, got dressed and went downstairs, Beth was pacing up and down the hallway.

'We need to do something about them.' She pointed to the landline.

'Huh? About what?' He stood on the last step waiting for her answer, even though he knew he wouldn't like it.

'The hang-up calls. They kept me up all night, and they're increasing in frequency. How did you even sleep? The constant ringing.' Her eyes were wide.

'What the hell are you on about now? I was awake most of the night worried about you and I didn't hear the phone ring at all.'

'Oh my God. Why won't you believe me?' Beth screamed, grabbing him by the shoulders. When he smelled the alcohol on her breath, he turned his face away.

'What's wrong with you?' He pulled away from her grasp and Beth stumbled back. 'The state you're in. It's eight in the morning – have you been drinking all night?' Joe shook his head.

How could he leave her like this? But he had to. So much going on at work. He would check in with her later, after she crashed.

'I couldn't sleep. All the letters and the hang-up calls. Stop trying to change the subject. Is it true, Joe?'

What letters? What hang-up calls?

'Are you cheating on me?'

Where the fuck did that come from?

Joe rubbed his temples. She was drunk and he couldn't be around her like this. She just needed to sleep it off, and if he stayed home, she would just carry on. 'I can't believe you asked me that. I don't have time to get into this. I'm late as it is.' He pushed past her. 'Have you seen my laptop bag?' He looked around the living room.

'Have you checked in here?'

Joe accidentally bumped her shoulder as he looked around the hallway.

He found the bag in the cupboard under the stairs; he'd never left it there before. 'Got it. Right, I'm off now.' He made sure to pick up the bag of clothes from the living room in case Beth went through it and saw the things he'd never throw out. 'We'll speak tonight, and Beth...' He waited and as expected, he was just met with an icy stare. 'No more drinking today. Please? You need to get some rest.' He looked at his watch.

Shit.

He'd call on the drive in to let them know he'd be delayed. As he walked towards the car, Beth grabbed his arm.

'Please call in sick today. Don't do this to me. I don't want to be alone. I can't stand the calls ... the letters... They're driving me insane!'

Joe pried her fingers from his arm, one by one. 'You're making a scene. Get some sleep, lay off the booze and take your meds. I need to go. I have important meetings today.'

'Oh yeah, you and all those people you help. Where's my help? Just fuck off, Joe. It's clear everyone else is more important than me.' Beth stomped her feet like a petulant child and Joe caught sight of their neighbour, staring at them.

Joe saw Beth's lip curl.

'What the hell are you staring at? Can't I speak to my fiancé without you earwigging all the time? Do you put a glass up to your wall so you can listen when we're inside? I bet you do, nosy cow.'

Joe mouthed 'I'm sorry' to Mrs Grenfell. He hadn't seen Beth this bad and wondered if maybe she had hit her head last night. He almost changed his mind about leaving her alone but knew that once the alcohol wore off or when she woke up after passing out, she would be mortified by her own behaviour.

He jumped into the car, not waiting for it to warm up before he reversed out of the drive, and didn't look back. He could hear her shouting after him and turned up the radio to drown out her voice.

He knew from his years managing Tasker House, if Beth carried on like this, something terrible was going to happen.

Chapter Sixty

BETH

Beth pulled her robe tight around her and crossed her arms. The neighbour had distracted her and when she heard Joe's car-engine rev, her body began to shake. He reversed out of the drive and didn't even look back as he drove off.

Beth tossed the neighbour a glare as she threw her arms up in the air. 'You happy now?' She stomped back up the path and into her house, slamming the door with such force the windows shook.

She had half a mind to get dressed and confront Joe at his office. It was probably a colleague he was sleeping with. Or maybe someone at the pub, he had been spending more and more time out of the house with his 'mates'.

Then something struck her. What if it was a client? Joe had asked her to change the channel the other week when she was watching a true-crime show about a probation officer who had fallen in love and run off with an offender he was supervising.

She paced up and down the hall. A million awful scenarios flashed in her mind.

Beth had no close friends, no one she could speak to about what was happening. No one had contacted her after her dad died. Everyone had abandoned her. Screw them.

Was an affair the real reason Joe had delayed the wedding? Had he actually postponed it, or had he outright cancelled it? Should she call the venue to find out?

She needed to get a grip and think this through. A shower would clear her mind and maybe a few more pills would help her sleep. When Joe got back, her mind would be clear, and she'd get answers from him, one way or another. Whatever his answers turned out to be, she'd call their wedding venue herself. Either to cancel the wedding or postpone it again, until next year. Joe had a lot of trust to earn back before she'd take his name.

Beth felt like she was drowning. Water cascaded over her face and into the open corner of her mouth. She moved her arm and felt a sharp pain on her wrist. Opening her eyes she found herself lying in the tub with the shower spraying down on her. Her left wrist was sore. She must have fainted, but she couldn't recall anything since being downstairs and deciding to have a shower. She didn't remember coming upstairs or getting undressed.

'Ugh.' With her good arm, she pulled herself out of the tub and turned the shower off. Instead of feeling better, she felt worse, especially when she realised that she must have been lying there, out of it, for at least half an hour if not more; her wrinkly skin was evidence.

In her bedroom, she dropped her robe and stood in front of the full-length mirror Joe had fixed to the wall, looking over her shoulder she saw a large red spot on her lower back. That was going to bruise.

She pulled on a pair of black jeans and a T-shirt – both hung off her, and she needed a belt to keep the jeans on. Grabbing her oversized cardigan to keep warm, she headed downstairs. The cold seemed to affect her more than it used to, even when the heating was on. Beth rummaged through her handbag and found some ibuprofen which she swallowed dry to ease the ache.

She wanted to find that letter. Where the heck had she put it? She began shoving her hand between the couch cushions, reaching around to find only a few pound coins, which she placed on the coffee table. As she scanned the room, her eyes landed on the little side table by the chair. The small drawer beneath its top an ideal cache for an important document. 'It has to be there.'

Beth pulled open the drawer and took everything out, going through it all. Nothing.

Fuck. Fuck. Fuck!

She pushed her mind to recall the day the letter had arrived. What had she done that day? Where had she been when she'd read the letter?

Bits and pieces came back to Beth. She had been in the kitchen when she opened it, hadn't she? She ran towards the kitchen, her back aching with each step. Her head turned to the left and then the right... The bin.

She had torn the letter up in anger and chucked it in the bin. Right?

She opened the bin and dumped everything on the floor, rummaging through the trash, her nostrils crinkling at the smell. Nothing.

Beth screamed as loud as she could, an attempt to vent the frustration that had been building inside her. But the scream didn't begin to bring the release she needed. She threw everything back into the bin and was about to take it out, when a knock on the door surprised her. She pulled herself up and went to answer the door. When she opened it, no one was there.

Beth looked up and down the narrow road, flanked on either side by stone walls and hedgerows, but it was empty. Where were the nosy neighbours when she actually needed them? Maybe it was one of them, trying to mess with her head.

'Arseholes.'

She turned and was about to close the door when she saw it.

A cream envelope taped to the door with LISBETH STANDFORD handwritten in black ink on the front.

Chapter Sixty-One

BETH

Beth snatched the letter off the door and went back inside, clutching it close to her chest with two trembling hands. Whoever had written it, had come to her home again.

She locked the door behind her and then went around each room, checking windows and closing the curtains. Her hands shook as she tore open the envelope and removed the single sheet inside. The letter was typed and all in shouting capital letters.

HE'S CHEATING ON YOU!
WHY AREN'T YOU DOING ANYTHING ABOUT IT,
YOU SLAG.
DON'T MAKE ME HAVE TO DO SOMETHING FIRST.

Beth dropped the note to the floor. She ran up to the bedroom and grabbed her mobile, which was charging by the bedside. Returning downstairs, she picked up the letter and took a photo. If she lost it again, at least she'd have it to show Joe.

She needed to speak to him. She'd ask him outright and she'd be able to tell if he was lying. She held the phone to her ear, taking deep breaths to combat the anger and anxiety fighting to control her, constantly bubbling under the surface – and who would win? Joe's phone rang out to voicemail and Beth hung up. Calling again, she paced the room. Same thing happened, only this time, she left a message.

'Joe. Please call me back.' Beth winced at the pleading tone in her voice. 'I got another letter. There is a threat. I can't deal with all of this on my own anymore. Please ... call me.' She burst into tears and threw the phone on the couch. She'd had enough.

Beth's movements were uncoordinated as she headed downstairs, on the way she grabbed all the bottles of medications she could find, taking them into the kitchen and placing them on the counter while she poured herself a vodka mixed with a small dash of tonic in a pint glass. She'd been ordering the vodka online and stashing the bottles around the house. She took a large swig, staring out of the back window, contemplating what she would do.

Pops would've known exactly what she needed to do. He'd have believed her. He'd have listened. He'd have hugged her close and told her everything would be all right. She took another gulp as the alcohol hit the back of her raw throat, burning as it went down. The pain reminded her that she was living a nightmare.

Beth turned and looked over at the medications. The throb in her wrist dulled as the alcohol started to take effect. She refilled her drink, topping up what was already in the pint glass. She didn't refill the tonic.

Beth walked over to the pill bottles and ran her fingers over each one. She scooped them up and carried them with her drink into the living room. She threw the bottles onto one side of the couch and plonked herself on the opposite side.

She just wanted to sleep. She lay her head back and closed her eyes – her hand in reach of the glass. All she could think about was how her soon-to-be husband was having an affair, how her father was gone, and she was probably going to lose her job. Everything she'd worked for and wanted was leaving her, or soon would be. And the cherry on top of her disaster of a life was that everyone thought she was losing her mind.

Her eyes shot open. *I'm not fucking crazy!*

When Beth took another swig from her drink, it spilled down her chin and onto her shirt. She used the sleeve of her cardigan to wipe her mouth. Her head was spinning as an image of her mother flashed before her, like a reflection.

I'm not you! I feel love. I hurt. I would never leave my family for booze ... this? She held up the glass. *This is just helping me focus. I can stop any time.*

That's what I would tell myself. You're such a hypocrite...

Get out of my fucking head!

Beth took another large gulp and heard laughter. *You bitch! I can stop...* She threw the glass against the wall. *I'll show her. I'll show them all.*

She pushed herself up from the couch and sucked air between her teeth when a sharp pain shot up her arm. 'Dammit.' She held her wrist and rubbed it, tripping forward but managing to steady herself despite the vodka coursing through her veins. She went over to the bookcase to retrieve a notebook and a pen before returning to the couch.

She placed the book and pen beside her and popped three ibuprofens out of the blister pack. She leaned forward and pulled a mini bottle of vodka from her hiding place in the coffee table and washed down the pills with a few others from the collection beside her.

Time to sleep.

Chapter Sixty-Two

JOE

Joe was glad his day was filled with visits to other agencies. When Beth had accused him of having an affair, he'd wanted to grab her and shake some sense into her. He asked her again to show him the letters she'd received, but of course, she didn't know what she had done with them.

'Did you have any questions, Joe?' The woman chairing the meeting frowned at him.

'Sorry, no – it all sounds great. I think there's definitely some scope for a partnership. Do you attend the community safety meetings?'

The woman shook her head. 'Not yet. We've been trying to get an invite but we're not on the council's radar. It would be great if you could put in a word for us.'

'Of course.' He reached into his pocket and pulled out a card. 'Drop me an email and I'll be sure to get that sorted.'

The woman took the card and together they walked out of the meeting room. 'Ah, here's one of our residents now.' She waved. 'Come over and say hello.'

Joe turned to greet the resident, but when he saw her, he froze.

'Joe this is Janis Stanford. She's new to our facility and has been a real asset, given her two-years of sobriety.'

Janis held out her hand and Joe shook it reluctantly. 'Nice to meet you.' Her grip tightened. 'I need to be off now, but I'll be back in time for the group meeting later.'

Joe watched her leave. 'How long did you say she's been here?'

'Only a couple of weeks. Are you okay? You've gone awfully pale.'

'I'm fine. She just, er, looks like someone I know...'

The woman laughed. 'I've already taken up enough of your time, Joe. Thanks again.' She turned and started leading Joe to the exit.

'It's okay, I can find my own way. Actually, I'm just going to pop into the men's room, if that's okay?'

'Of course. Head straight down this hall towards the exit sign. The gents are on the left.' Joe jogged down the corridor to the toilets. Once inside he splashed some water on his face.

What the hell was Beth's mother doing here?

The facility was for recovered substance-misusers. Technically, Janis fell into that category. But it didn't make any sense to him. He dried his face and hands and then exited the building. He began walking to his next meeting when he felt a tap on his shoulder.

'Have you told her yet?'

Her voice was like nails on a chalkboard. He stopped and turned around to look Janis straight in the eyes. His jaw tightened and he leaned forward making sure he hissed his words. 'Beth is going through enough at the minute. The fact she hasn't reached out to you speaks volumes, doesn't it?'

'That's your fucking fault. Wait until she finds out you're lying. You're going to pay for this, you know!' She screamed so loudly that Joe had to cover his ears. Passers-by were gawping at them open-mouthed. The blame pointed in his direction.

His mobile rang. It was Beth. He started to walk away.

'Is that her? Give me your phone!' Janis lunged forward and tried to grab it from the mobile from his hands. He let the call go to voicemail – he couldn't risk being caught with Janis. He'd call Beth back as soon as he'd got rid of her mother. If this is what Janis was like sober, he could only imagine what Beth had had to deal with as a child. Joe quickened his pace to put some distance between them.

He needed to put an end to this. 'I know where you live now.' He called over his shoulder. 'And I'm going to ring the police. The way you've been acting, I'm worried what you'd do to Beth if she did meet up with you.'

'How dare you. How fucking dare you!'

Joe turned and was met with dead eyes. A chill came over him. Janis was unhinged, and he feared what she was capable of.

But then he noticed a subtle change in her demeanour, as if she realised how her behaviour would appear to onlookers. She smiled at him, but the smile didn't reach her eyes.

'I know things, too, Joe Tasker. I didn't want to go down this route, but you're leaving me no choice.' She turned and headed back towards the town centre.

Joe took a moment. Janis was unpredictable. He was sure that was a veiled threat. He needed to speak to Beth and warn her. Her mum was so manipulative, and he couldn't trust what she would say or do.

There were a few voicemail messages on his phone. He listened to them, and his heart raced.

He called Beth back but there was no answer.

Fuck.

He turned round and headed back to the office to pick up his car from the car park.

Joe was about to jump into his car when he heard AJ call out to him.

'Where are you off to? We had a situation here. There was a strange woman in the office about ten minutes ago shouting about you stealing money. Can you come in and speak to the team?' AJ kept looking at her watch.

Joe knew exactly who that was and was a little surprised at AJ's formal tone. Did she actually believe Janis?

'Ignore her,' he said. 'I'll explain everything tomorrow. Do you know where she went? If she comes back, call the police.'

Just as AJ opened her mouth to answer, his phone rang, and he held up a finger indicating for his colleague to hang on one minute.

'Beth, thank God, I've been trying to reach you.'

What Joe heard next made his blood run cold.

Chapter Sixty-Three

BETH

Beth woke up to a nudge in the leg. When she opened her eyes, her vision was blurry and Joe was standing over her. He must have rushed home after hearing her messages.

'How long have I been asleep?' She reached out, but Joe stepped back.

Beth rubbed her eyes but instead of clearing her vision, it seemed to make it worse. She shouldn't have mixed her meds.

'Can you help me? I can't see properly.' Joe grabbed her injured wrist and pulled her up off the couch.

'Owww.' Beth stumbled past him and felt her way to the kitchen. She thought if she ran some water over her eyes, it might help her sight return. But before she reached the sink, she felt a shove at her back.

'What the fuck is wrong with you?' Her words were slurred, and her tongue felt swollen. She turned around to face him and that's when she felt his fist collide with her jaw.

Stunned, Beth couldn't believe what was happening. She reached behind her and pulled a knife from the knife block.

'Stay the fuck away from me.' She waved the knife about. The blurry figure jumped to the left and laughed.

'What the—' Beth needed to call the police and remembered her phone was in the living room on the couch. She ran, bumping into walls and as she reached the couch, she felt a sharp pain on her arm.

Had Joe just sliced her arm? Beth backed away.

'Why are you doing this?' She waved the knife, unsure if she had hit him or not. 'Stop it, Joe. Stop!'

The door, if she could just reach the front door. Beth held the knife in front as she ran to the hall. Joe grabbed her by her hair, pushing her head down and stopping her dead in her tracks. He placed his body between her and the front door. She felt her hair tearing out of her head, but she got away and ran towards the kitchen, scrabbling to find her way to the back door. If she could get outside, she could call for help.

She felt a hand on her arm as her body was twisted around. A flash of silver catching the sun through the window and glinting in her eye as she held her hand up to protect herself. Her skin was punctured, blood dripping from the wound. She swiped the knife she held. Joe fell back but not before she felt something slice across her throat and she fell to the floor.

Chapter Sixty-Four

BETH

Beth could hear voices. Someone was touching her, and she tried to scream but no sound escaped.

'When's the ambulance arriving? We've got a pulse!'

There was more than one person. Beth wanted to ask where Joe was, had she hurt him? A sharp pain shot up her face as she moved her head. She could just about see Joe across from her, her vision still blurred. There was a lot of blood, and someone was with him. She tried to sit up.

'Stay still. My name is PC Bradshaw. We've called an ambulance.'

Beth closed her eyes. This couldn't be happening.

'Miss. Miss. Stay with me. Look at me, okay?'

She felt a pressure on her neck.

'Keep your eyes open, miss. I'm just pressing a cloth over the wound.'

How long had they been laying there on the floor?

'Faint pulse here, too.' Someone called out.

Joe! He was alive. Thank God. She needed to know what happened. Why he did this.

Beth tried to turn her head again, but it hurt too much. Her eyes took in what they could. The kitchen was a mess, with blood on the floor and the bin turned over. The once-white tiles on the backsplash were stained red, and a faint smell of burnt food lingered in the air.

She overheard one of the officers speaking into what looked like a walkie-talkie on his shoulder. 'There are signs of a heated argument. The stools surrounding the small dining table are toppled over. Smashed glass in the living room area, you can see it when you walk towards the kitchen, and an empty bottle of vodka here in the kitchen.'

Next thing she knew, the paramedics were lifting her onto a stretcher, gentle hands securing her head and neck while pressure was maintained on her throat. She winced in pain as they manoeuvred her through the door, her eyes darting around the room.

As they carried her outside to the ambulance, Beth wanted to ask the paramedics if Joe was okay, but she couldn't speak.

I need to make sure he's all right.

Her breathing was laboured as they loaded her into the ambulance.

He wouldn't hurt me intentionally. Something must have happened.

'You've been injured pretty badly, but we've got you now. Is it Lisbeth?'

Beth blinked.

'We're taking you to the hospital.'

'Mmm. Mmm.' She was trying to speak but she only heard noise.

'I'm going to give you something to calm down.'

Beth saw the needle as the EMT prepared to inject her and she moved her arm. She needed to stay awake. She needed to know what happened to Joe.

'Please, relax.' The EMT pinned her arm and stuck the needle in.

She started to feel woozy and fought to stay awake, but it was hard. Too hard.

Beth closed her eyes trying to piece together the events before the darkness took over.

Part II

Chapter Sixty-Five

BETH

B eth tried to lift her head, but it was like a weight was pulling her back down. Voices. She could hear voices whispering in the background. She forced her eyes open. Bright lights blinding her momentarily. Her heart raced.

Where was she? What had happened?

She moved her head from side to side. A window to the left and a long curtain to the right. Shadows in the background. Voices.

She was in the hospital. Memories came back to her like a tidal wave.

Blood. Joe. Fighting. Joe ... Joe... Where was Joe?

Beth lifted her arm and saw that her hand was bandaged. She tried using her other hand to grab the bars and pull herself up. It was bandaged, too.

The knife. She'd tried to deflect it coming towards her.

Why did Joe do this?

Beth wanted to get the attention of the people behind the curtain. She called out ... but no sound followed.

She could hear someone – a man – asking another person when it was 'likely they could question Miss Stanford about the incident.'

Question? Was she being blamed? Were they talking to Joe?

Her muscles tightened. She kicked the side of the bed and the bars rattled. The curtain was suddenly pulled aside, and Beth saw a doctor, a nurse and two men in suits one younger, one older. She assumed the men were police.

'You're awake.' The doctor came to her side and began checking her vitals. Prodding, staring. Making strange grunting noises.

Beth pulled back.

She used her hands to point at her mouth. Hoping the doctor would understand.

'You can't speak?' The doctor – she glanced at his badge, Dr Harris – tilted his head before writing something down. 'Could be temporary because of the injuries you sustained, but we'll keep an eye on that.'

Beth caught him looking at the police officers.

Did they think she was faking it?

Beth tried to sit up again. The people hovering over her were making her feel uncomfortable. The doctor placed a hand on her shoulder and eased her back down. 'Rest.' He smiled and turned to the suits. 'I'm afraid you won't be able to ask her anything today. Let's see how she is tomorrow, okay?'

The police officers both scowled, as if she was avoiding them on purpose. Screw them, she had her own questions.

The older one spoke first. 'We'll call back in the morning.' Then he looked at Beth. 'The sooner we have answers, the sooner we can clarify what happened, Miss Stanford. We know you'll want to help us any way you can. Your partner is in a bad way.'

Beth's eyes widened. She struggled to pull herself up, fighting against the nurse who held her down.

'That's enough! I'm afraid you're going to have to leave, officers. Be sure to call before you return as I wouldn't want you to have wasted a trip.' The doctor nodded to the nurse and Beth felt woozy. The injected medicine was taking effect. She watched as Dr Harris escorted the police out of the room and she could see his hand waving about, pointing down the hall as he said something to them but too quietly for her to hear. Her eyelids went heavy, and then she couldn't see anyone anymore.

Chapter Sixty-Six

BETH

Beth lay in the sterile hospital bed, her body aching and bruised, her mind clouded with fear and confusion. She had no idea how much time had passed. The white walls surrounding her seemed to close in, trapping her in a suffocating silence. She cast her eyes around the room, searching for a sign of familiarity or solace, but all she found was the impersonal atmosphere of the room. No one had told her anything about what had happened or where Joe was. Had he been arrested? Brief flashes of the attack haunted her dreams and sent shivers up her spine.

Why did he do this?

Dr Harris entered the room. He approached her bed, the sound of his footsteps echoing through the emptiness. His eyes betrayed a sense of concern.

'Good morning.' His voice was laced with compassion. 'How are you feeling today?'

Beth's lips trembled, her voice a mere whisper that refused to escape her throat. She felt a surge of anxiety and panic as she tried to speak, but no sound emerged. She attempted again, the injury on her throat had stolen her voice, leaving her trapped in a silent prison.

The doctor's brows furrowed as he noticed her distress. He pulled up a chair and sat by her bedside, his eyes fixed on her face. 'Beth, I understand this must be frightening for you. Your injuries, both physical and emotional, are severe. The larynx, your voice box, has been damaged, and that's why you're unable to speak at the moment. Luckily, it wasn't cut but there's quite extensive trauma. You suffered multiple contusions and lacerations on your face. The injuries on your body show signs of a struggle, indicating a violent altercation. Do you remember anything?'

Beth's eyes widened and she shook her head, tears welling up as the reality of her situation sank in. She tried to convey her frustration through gestures and facial expressions, but it was a poor substitute.

'I know it's hard,' his voice was full of empathy, 'but I assure you, with time and proper treatment, you'll recover. We have a specialist who will be assessing your condition in the coming days, and trauma support. In the meantime, we'll provide you with something to aid in communication.' He gently patted her bandaged hand. He looked at the nurse and she left the room only to return a few moments later with a pen and notepad.

Beth nodded, her eyes locked onto the doctor, searching for reassurance that he wasn't just trying to placate her. She felt vulnerable and powerless.

Tears cascaded down her cheeks as a mixture of relief and despair washed over her. She attempted to squeeze the doctor's hand, but the bandages prevented anything other than an awkward punch.

The doctor stood. 'I'll be back soon.'

As the doctor exited the room, Beth was left alone with her thoughts.

Time passed in a blur, until the door opened again and Dr Harris had returned with the two officers from before, their faces etched with determination. They introduced themselves but Beth wasn't paying attention.

'Ms Stanford. Please, if you can, tell us what you remember.' The detective sounded sincere.

She stared at them, her eyes still heavy with tears.

They needed her voice, but even if she could speak, she didn't know what she would say.

Chapter Sixty-Seven

BETH

Images bombarded her mind – darkness, a blur of movement, and the sound of her own muffled screams. But nothing was clear, nothing made sense.

Detective Thompson was leaning forward, his eyes locked with hers, as if he could read her mind. Goosebumps formed on her arms.

She tried to convince herself that Joe *wasn't* the one who had hurt her – her mind couldn't cope with the thought that the man she'd planned to marry would do this to her.

The hospital staff remained tight-lipped. They spoke in hushed tones when they thought she couldn't hear, their eyes avoiding hers as they scurried past her room. Why were they keeping her in the dark? Panic swelled within her, clawing at her chest. Beth's eyes darted anxiously between the detectives, her body trembling with unease.

'Do you remember what happened to you?' The doctor's tone was tinged with caution.

Flashes of distorted images darted through Beth's mind –

her futile attempts to defend herself, Joe's anger spiralling out of control, and the overwhelming sense of fear that had consumed her. Pain coursed through her body, a stark reminder of the violence she had endured. But the details remained out of reach, hidden in the depths of her injured mind.

She blinked once, her only way of responding until her hand healed enough to write.

The doctor's expression softened. 'It's okay. It's not uncommon for memories to be fragmented after such a traumatic event. Give it time.'

Time? She didn't have time. Tears welled up in her eyes again, then cascaded down her cheeks.

The doctor's face turned solemn. 'You're probably wondering about Joe.' He turned and looked at the officers behind him. 'I'm limited in what information I can share, but ... I can tell you that he's also sustained serious injuries. He's in a critical condition, but we're doing everything we can to stabilise him.'

Her breath caught in her throat as she heard the words 'serious injuries' and 'critical condition'. She wanted to see Joe, to look at him and get answers.

Just as her despair threatened to consume her, a single thought broke through the haze – a fleeting image of a birthmark on the attacker's face. Just above his right cheek – not a mark Joe had... Or was it? Was she just trying to excuse Joe for his actions?

Beth couldn't rely on others to piece together her memories, but she questioned whether she could trust what she remembered seeing. Since being in hospital, she had been weaned off the cocktail of meds and alcohol that had clouded her mind and the paranoia had eased.

'So can we speak to her?'

Dr Harris looked at Beth and then back at the officers. 'Don't push her. I'll be back shortly.'

Beth silently pleaded with the doctor to stay but it was too late. She could see the police were not going to listen. They'd already made up their minds and she needed to know why.

Chapter Sixty-Eight

BETH

Beth's eyes darted anxiously between the two police officers standing before her, their grave expressions making her feel small, intimidated.

Detective Johnson, a middle-aged man with greying hair, with the more sympathetic demeanour of the two, approached Beth with caution. He seemed to understand the delicacy of the situation and his voice gave her the impression that he was trying to ensure Beth felt comfortable enough to share her side of the story. Beside him, Detective Thompson, the younger officer, had an air of arrogance about him. He leaned against the wall; his eyes fixed on Beth with an unsettling intensity.

'Hello, Beth,' Detective Johnson began, his voice gentle. 'I know this is a difficult time for you, but we need to understand what happened that night. Can you tell us anything about the attack in your home?'

Beth opened her mouth to speak, then remembered her voice had been stolen. She pushed the bandage down on her right hand, so that she could hold the pen, and her trembling hands struggled to form legible words on the notepad resting on the tray.

Detective Thompson scoffed. 'Still can't talk, huh? Convenient.'

Detective Johnson shot him a warning glance before turning back to Beth. 'It's okay, Beth. Take your time.'

Beth scribbled down her response, her penmanship shaky.

I don't remember much. Everything is blurry.

Detective Thompson snorted, crossing his arms. 'Really? Blurry, huh? Must have been quite the party.' His hand mimicked taking a drink.

Beth's heart sank as the officer's sarcastic tone further diminished her already fragile confidence. She tried to shake her head, but the movement only aggravated her injuries. How could he speak to her like that? Like she was a suspect.

Detective Johnson spoke up, his voice tinged with irritation, as he eye-balled his colleague. 'Enough. We're here to get the facts.'

DC Thompson shrugged, a smirk playing at the corner of his lips.

Beth's hand held down the notepad. She needed them to understand, to believe her. She wrote again, her pen pressing hard against the paper.

I wasn't myself that day. My meds. I had too much to drink. But I would never hurt Joe.

Detective Johnson nodded. 'No one is accusing you, Beth. We're just trying to piece everything together. Can you remember anything at all? Anything that might help us work out what happened?'

Beth furrowed her brow, her mind struggling to recall the events of that fateful night. Flashes of images, fragments of memories danced in her mind, but they were hazy and elusive. The way Officer Johnson was talking, she couldn't work out if he thought Joe was responsible for her injuries or not.

But if it wasn't Joe, who was it?

Detective Thompson came forward then, his eyes narrowing. 'Come on, Beth. Surely you remember something. Did you get into an argument with Joe? Did things turn violent?'

Beth's heart raced, panic seizing her. She scribbled her response, her handwriting barely legible.

No. We were working through things. I would never hurt him.

Detective Johnson intervened, his voice calm but firm. 'Hey, ease up.'

Thompson reluctantly took a step back.

Johnson resumed his gentle tone. 'Did you see anyone in your home that night? Did you hear or notice anything out of the ordinary?'

Beth's mind swirled with frustration as she struggled to remember.

I don't know. I was disoriented. Scared.

Thompson rolled his eyes, unable to hide his impatience. 'Disoriented? Scared? Sounds like a convenient excuse to me.'

Johnson shot him a stern look. 'Last warning. Show some respect.'

Ignoring the warning, Thompson turned to Beth, his voice dripping with accusation. 'Did you intend to kill Joe, Beth? Is that what happened?'

Beth's breath caught in her throat, her eyes widening with shock and disbelief. The words hung heavily in the air, leaving a trail of tension in their wake. She stared at the two officers before her, her heart pounding, desperate to make them understand the truth.

The room fell into a deafening silence as the question lingered, unanswered. Johnson apologised and pushed Thompson out of the door, telling Beth they'd be back in a few days. Beth grappled with the weight of their suspicions. Her paranoia, the hallucinations. Her lapses of memories.

I didn't do this … did I?

Chapter Sixty-Nine

BETH

A heavy cloud of suspicion clung to Beth like a second skin. She couldn't bear the thought of anyone believing she had harmed Joe. She was the victim.

Her head pounded. The person she trusted most, the one who had promised to protect her, had turned into a monster, shattering her world.

It had to have been Joe. She'd seen him with her own eyes. But how had the fight started? They'd been arguing a lot. She'd been drunk a lot of the time. Had she flipped and attacked him? And what about the birthmark. Was her imagination, or her memory, playing tricks on her because she couldn't face the truth?

She was torn, unsure what to believe.

The hospital staff whispered things behind her back. Did they fear for her safety? Or were they protecting Joe from her?

It didn't matter what their reasons were. Until she could speak again, there was no point.

A mixture of emotions swirled within Beth, anger and

betrayal mingled with confusion and doubt. How could she have been so blind? Had she missed the warning signs? And most importantly, did she truly remember the events accurately?

Images flashed before her eyes, disjointed and fragmented. The darkness of their home, the glimmer of a knife, and Joe's menacing face twisted with rage. But how much of it was real? How much was a manifestation of her intoxicated mind?

Beth reached for the notepad lying on the bedside table, her trembling fingers grasping the pen. She wrote in hurried, desperate strokes, hoping that by transferring her thoughts onto paper, she could make sense of everything.

What really happened?

She stared at the words on the page. The bruises, the marks on her body, she had felt the searing pain and the terror that gripped her. But with each passing moment, the memories seemed to blur, fade away like smoke dissipating in the wind.

The door to her hospital room creaked open, interrupting Beth's turmoil. A nurse walked in. 'How are you holding up?'

Beth looked up, her voice still imprisoned in her throat.

The nurse approached, placing a gentle hand on her shoulder. 'I know it's difficult, but you've had a few people asking after you. Do you still not want any visitors or calls? And don't worry about the press, we're under strict instructions not to speak to them or let them anywhere near you.'

Beth shook her head. If her so-called friends were interested now, it would be because of the press coverage, and she wasn't ready to see Aunt Kay just yet. She started writing on her notepad, passing the paper to the nurse.

The nurse shook her head with a soft smile. 'I'm sorry. It's not safe for you to have contact with Joe right now. The police are conducting their investigation and we've been told that under no circumstances can you visit him, but we'll continue to screen calls and visitors until you feel better.'

As the nurse left the room, Beth traced the bruises on her body, the physical reminders of the attack, and a shiver ran down her spine.

She had no choice but to confront the chilling possibility that she might never know the whole truth.

What if Joe wasn't the one responsible for the attack? What if the injuries I've sustained were him defending himself against me? Am I truly my mother's daughter?

Chapter Seventy

BETH

The days turned into an agonising blur, restlessness gnawing at Beth's bones, each moment stretching like an eternity.

Her frustration boiled beneath the surface as she lay in her bed, the silence punctuated only by the monotonous beeping of machines. Just as her patience reached its breaking point, a knock on the door interrupted her spiralling thoughts. Startled, Beth turned her gaze towards the entrance. The door creaked open, revealing Joe's parents, with Dr Harris behind them.

Joe's mother stepped forward with tears glistening in her eyes, her voice trembling. 'Oh, Beth, we're so sorry. We had no idea what was happening. We were away with no signal and couldn't check our messages.'

Beth looked at the doctor, angry that her instructions to keep everyone away had been ignored.

Joe's father stood beside his wife, his face lined with worry and uncertainty. 'The police think it's possible that you hurt

Joe. We need to understand what happened. We want answers.'

Joe's mother hit his thigh, a warning that now was not the time.

Beth's hands trembled as she grasped the notepad, her eyes welling with unshed tears. The police were using Joe's parents to bait her.

Please, you have to believe me. I didn't hurt him. I was only defending myself.

'From whom?'

JOE

Joe's mother reached out her hand, clasping Beth's gently. 'Beth, we're so sorry for what happened, but you must be confused. Probably all that … drinking. Joe's always been so kind to you. The police think *you* hurt *him*. We need answers, Beth. We need to know what *really* happened. The news people keep hounding us. Just tell us the truth.'

Beth scribbled her response again, her pen pressing deep into the paper.

I would never hurt Joe. He attacked me. I had to defend myself.

The doctor, who had been silently observing, stepped

forward, his expression grave. 'Mr and Mrs Tasker, I understand your concern, but pushing Beth for answers, is not helping the situation.'

Mrs Tasker's voice wavered, her eyes pleading for understanding. 'But how can we know what really happened to our son?'

Her husband ran a hand through his thinning hair, his face etched with worry. 'Will she remember what happened?' he asked the doctor.

Beth's heart sank as her future in-laws grappled with their own doubts, their hidden judgment hovering like a spectre in the room. She needed them to believe her, to see the truth etched across her face. Her strokes were sharp and desperate as she wrote.

Please, you have to believe me. I love Joe. I didn't do this. He did.

Mr Tasker's voice trembled with a mix of pain and uncertainty. 'Beth, Joe's our son. He's not a violent person. You must be wrong.'

Beth's vision blurred by the weight of her emotions. Faced with his parents' plea, she didn't want to hurt them, but they had to understand that Joe had fooled them all.

Joe attacked me. I had no choice. He must have snapped.

The room fell into a heavy silence, tension thickening the air. Beth's breaths came in shallow gasps. A nurse entered the room, and her grave expression made Beth's pulse quicken, her heart hammering in her chest. Something was wrong.

The nurse whispered into Dr Harris's ear.

'Mr and Mrs Tasker, can we step outside for a moment,' he said. 'I've some news I need to share.'

Beth's eyes widened and Joe's mum looked at her and then the doctor. 'Tell us here, tell us now.'

No. Don't say it. Don't say it.

The doctor sighed and nodded. 'I'm sorry to inform you that Joe's condition has worsened, and he's slipped into a coma. As you know, his injuries were severe, and we're unsure of his future prognosis. It's touch and go at the moment.'

The words sent shockwaves through the room.

Mr Tasker collapsed into a nearby chair, his face buried in his hands, while Joe's mum crumbled beside Beth's bed, their distress mingling with her own.

Her hands trembled uncontrollably and her vision was blurred by a flood of tears. She longed to scream, to turn back time and go back to their happy lives before all this.

What have I done?

Chapter Seventy-One

BETH

The Taskers left to see their son and Beth's frustration grew as she spilled her feelings on paper to the doctor, her eyes pleading for understanding.

Why won't they let me see Joe? It's been over a week, and I need to see him. I need to make sense of all of this.

She hadn't been charged with anything and couldn't understand why the police were being so obstructive.

The doctor sighed, he was empathetic yet firm. 'I understand your frustration. I've spoken to the police. They've finally agreed to allow you a visit, on the provision that you'll be accompanied by an officer.'

Beth's eyes widened with relief. Finally, a chance to see him. She nodded eagerly.

I need to know what he remembers. Maybe he'll wake up and clear this whole mess up.

'It's unlikely that Joe will wake up just because you're there,' the doctor told her. 'You must prepare yourself for that—'

He was interrupted by the door opening, and the detectives appeared in the room. Detective Thompson approached Beth.

'You should count your lucky stars we're even considering letting you in to see Joe,' he said, his eyes cold. 'And we're only permitting it on the slim chance that either one of you recalls the truth. The press has been on our backs to release a statement but we're keeping them at bay for now.'

Beth's eyes blazed as she reached for the pen.

I didn't do anything to him! Some part of you must believe that because you've not mentioned a thing about charging me!

She shoved the notepad at him.

Detective Johnson now stepped forward. 'Beth, we're here to gather all the facts. To see where the *evidence* takes us. We have to consider all angles. I understand this is difficult for you, but please try to cooperate.'

Beth nodded. She had no choice but to accept what they said. And though she was certain she had not tried to hurt Joe, seeing him might jog her memory and bring back her voice. And it might supply the missing pieces of that terrifying night.

As the nurse approached with a wheelchair, Beth glanced at

the IV line attached to her arm and she shook her head. No, she wouldn't be wheeled in like a fragile patient. She needed to stand on her own two feet. She grasped the IV pole, pulling it alongside her as she walked past the wheelchair.

Johnson exchanged a glance with the nurse and dipped his head in agreement. 'All right. We'll walk together. Just take it slow.'

Beth's heart pounded with anticipation as they made their way through the sterile corridors. Approaching Joe's room, her steps faltered, her breath hitching in her throat.

A police officer sat outside the room, his presence catching her off-guard. Detective Johnson instructed the guard to take a break, obviously sensing Beth's unease, and Detective Thompson moved forward, ready to escort her in. Beth shook her head, nodding at Johnson, something about him instilled trust within her.

Johnson raised an eyebrow but understood her unspoken plea. As they neared the room, he hesitated, glancing through the partially open door. 'Hold on. Joe has a visitor. We'll have to wait a moment.'

Beth's heart sank as she peered into the room, her breath catching in her chest. A woman was holding Joe's hand; their connection palpable even from a distance. Recognition struck her like lightning, causing her knees to buckle.

It can't be true.

She knew that woman.

It was her counsellor, Alison – the one she had confided in, trusted with her deepest fears and insecurities. But what was she doing here, by Joe's side, holding his hand?

Alison turned then, and as their eyes met, a jolt of

recognition flickered in her counsellor's eyes. A scream built in Beth's throat, clawing to be set free. Her surroundings spun, as the ground beneath her seemed to crumble.

Was it true?

Had her fiancé been cheating on her all along?

Chapter Seventy-Two

BETH

The sight of Alison sitting at Joe's bedside made Beth's chest constrict. It was a sucker punch to her heart. She felt Detective Johnson's hand on her arm, offering support, but she shrugged him away, clinging to the IV pole for stability. Tears welled up in her eyes, a mix of shock, hurt, and betrayal flooding her.

Johnson's voice held a note of concern. 'Do you know this woman?'

Beth's throat tightened, and it was the first time she was glad her voice was gone as all she wanted to do was scream until all the pain and humiliation was gone from her body. She didn't want to admit that she knew Alison but that might reinforce to the police that she had something to hide. She looked across at Johnson and nodded.

Officer Thompson's gaze intensified, searching for answers she was not ready to provide. Her silence prompted him to give her a strange look, his eyes accusatory with suspicion. 'Was your fiancé having an affair? Is that why you're so upset?'

Beth's eyes widened. Thompson's words raised doubts and questions that she had been grappling with. Had Joe been seeing Alison behind her back? Had their conversations in therapy somehow reached his ears?

The officers exchanged bewildered glances as Alison stared at Beth through the glass panel in the door and then got up and headed towards them. A tremor of panic shot through Beth and she backed away. She couldn't face Alison, not now.

Beth started to walk away, as fast as her weakened body would allow, ignoring the shouts behind her, and didn't stop until she reached her own room, the door swinging closed behind her, providing a barrier of solitude, though she could hear Alison's voice coming from outside.

'Lisbeth. I can explain!'

Beth's heart pounded as she leant back against her closed door, one hand lingering on the door handle, a pull of curiosity battling against the overwhelming betrayal she felt. But she still couldn't face this, whatever Alison was going to tell her, not now.

Eventually, Alison's voice disappeared and Beth hobbled over to her bed. She lay down with her back to the door, facing the window, and closed her eyes. She felt her heart rate slowing down. But her respite was short-lived, as both detectives entered her room.

Beth turned and glared at them.

Detective Johnson's voice was level and calm. 'We want to help you, Beth. We've seen how much you've been trying. Please, use the notepad. We're here to read, if not listen.'

Beth sat up, her eyes flickering to the notepad. An internal battle raged within her – should she tell the officers, and confront the accusations she knew would follow, head-on? It was a motive, wasn't it? She'd suspected Joe of having an affair and now that it seemed it was true, she'd be blamed.

Her fingers hovered above the notepad as she wavered, ready to disclose her thoughts. But then she caught sight of Alison who'd appeared behind the police officers, an enigmatic expression on her face. Her presence was a glaring reminder of Joe's betrayal.

Alison's voice cut through the tense silence, her tone laced with both remorse and determination. 'Officers, please, let me talk to Beth.'

Beth's breath hitched in her throat.

What is Alison going to tell me?

As Detective Johnson exchanged a glance with Thompson, Beth placed her hands over her ears, like a child. She knew that she stood on the edge of a revelation, one that could shatter everything she thought she knew about her relationship with Joe, and she wasn't sure she was ready to hear what was coming next.

Chapter Seventy-Three

BETH

The atmosphere in the small room was heavy as the two police officers fixed their eyes on Alison, who took a deep breath and addressed Beth.

'I need to explain. I work part-time with Joe. In fact, he's my boss. I've been off dealing with some personal matters of my own and then I saw the news about the attack and rushed here to see him. I didn't realise that you were his fiancée. Not until now. You told me your name was Lisbeth and I never put two and two together when Joe spoke of you. He always called you Beth. When I saw your full name in the newspaper and the look on your face a moment ago… Well, it all made sense.'

Confusion etched across Beth's face, she grabbed the notepad and scribbled.

Joe has never mentioned anyone called Alison working with him. How do I know you're telling the truth?

Alison's gaze was sincere. 'I go by the name of AJ, mainly. My real name is Alison-Jane but that can be a mouthful. I use just Alison as my professional name for my online-therapy sessions, but otherwise most people know me as AJ – just like I assume most people know you as Beth?'

Beth's mind reeled as she tried to process the information.

Officer Johnson, intervened. 'We'll need to speak with you later, Alison, but for now, if the two of you need some time alone, we can accommodate that.'

Alison nodded, her eyes still on Beth. 'Can I stay and speak with you?' she asked her. 'I want to explain everything.'

'We'll leave you to it.' Detective Thompson nodded at Johnson, who looked reluctant to leave. 'But we'll be right outside.'

After both officers had left, Beth looked expectantly at Alison. This was her chance to see if Joe had been gaslighting her all along, making her feel like she was unhinged, when all along he had been making a fool of her.

Alison sat down next to Beth's bed. 'Maybe I should have realised when you spoke of your father, but I honestly didn't make the connection. I deal with a lot of clients who are grieving.' She shook her head. 'I can assure you, I'm not, and have never had, an affair with Joe. He's my boss and I'd never do anything to jeopardise my job.'

Beth's eyes searched Alison's face, before she wrote down her thoughts.

Did he tell you my father died? Did he say I was losing my mind? How could you not realise?

Alison sighed; her eyes filled with regret. 'I can't really talk about that. I was told things in confidence, yes ... but honest to God, I didn't make the connection with you. I don't know if you'll ever believe that but please try. Joe loves you very much. He only ever wanted to help you through your grief and problems.'

Beth was torn between disbelief and a desperate desire to trust the woman in front of her.

Did Joe know about our conversations?

Alison's shook her head vehemently. 'No. Absolutely not. I'm going through a tough time with my estranged husband, and Joe has been a source of support. I never discussed our sessions with him or anyone. I would never break that confidentiality. And Joe kept a lot of things to himself.'

Beth's heart twisted with relief, although she still couldn't help but feel some doubt.

Alison leaned forward. 'I need to understand. What happened. Did you attack Joe?'

The question again struck Beth like a blow, her body recoiling as though she'd been hit.

He attacked me.

She scribbled furiously on the page.

He became violent, and I had to defend myself.

Alison's brow furrowed; confusion evident in her eyes. 'In all the years I've known Joe,' she said carefully, 'he's never so much as raised his voice, let alone put his hands on anyone. Are you sure it was Joe?' She paused, adding gently, 'Had you been drinking?'

Beth's frustration grew and pain bubbled to the surface.

I loved him. I still love him. Why would I lie? I didn't do this damage to myself.

She threw the notepad down and pointed the injuries on her body.

Alison tried to calm her, her hands reaching out in a placating gesture. 'Okay. Okay. Please, let's talk through this.'

But anguish and frustration exploded within Beth, and she began to pound her fists loudly against the bedrails, her throat choking with tears. All she wanted was to speak, to be heard and believed.

The next thing Beth knew, Thompson and Johnson were back in the room with a couple of nurses.

'Perhaps best if you leave now, Alison,' said Detective Johnson kindly, signalling to one of the nurses to take her out.

'Of course,' said Alison, getting up and nodding at Beth, who watched her being led away.

But just as she reached the door, Alison paused and looked

back at Detective Johnson – and her next words sent a chill of fear through Beth.

'I need to speak with you, officer,' she said. 'And as soon as possible.'

Chapter Seventy-Four

BETH

Writing had become Beth's lifeline. Her right hand had healed enough for her to hold a pen for longer periods and better communicate with others. But she feared her voice would never return, despite the hours of therapy she had already received, and she yearned for her father's presence, his reassuring voice and unwavering belief in her. The memory of his death tore at her, leaving an empty ache that gnawed at her soul. She needed someone to believe her truth.

Beth had overheard fragments of conversations between the doctor and nurses, catching snippets of discussions about her potential discharge. The idea both excited and terrified her. Leaving the hospital meant facing a world that had turned against her, a world that painted her as the villain in a toxic relationship. She was told that some reporters still hung around outside, hoping to get a story from anyone who knew her or had crossed her path.

Under the guise of building her strength, she roamed the

hospital corridors, her footsteps echoing in the sterile environment. The officer stationed outside Joe's room would give her odd looks, but she paid him no mind. It wasn't Joe who needed protection. At least not from her.

The news flickered on the TV screen in her room, and Beth watched herself on the screen, her image distorted and twisted by the media's portrayal of her. She was being cast as a person of interest in a toxic relationship, which could end in murder if Joe didn't survive his injuries. Beth was angry, frustrated, scared. They knew nothing, and yet they passed judgment with ease. She now understood how Mr Brewer had felt – perhaps he *was* innocent after all.

She had to stop herself from speaking again to the police without advice from a solicitor, though the urgency to set the record straight clawed at her. But anyway, could she trust them to listen? And if she got a solicitor involved, would they see that as a sign of guilt?

Fragments of memory were beginning to resurface and Beth needed them to be clear before she spoke to anyone. She couldn't allow the authorities to twist her words, to manipulate her narrative into something unrecognisable.

Alison was due to come and see her again today. Beth had no idea if her counsellor had spoken to the police, or what about, but she had spoken to Beth on the phone, and advised her not to speak to anyone else until they had a chance to go over things in person.

Though she still felt a little wary of her, Beth at least no longer believed that Alison was having an affair with Joe. That was something. Maybe Alison could be her voice and advocate; it was best she start trusting someone.

Turning onto her side, Beth stared out the window,

yearning to feel fresh air against her skin; a brief respite from the sterile walls that held her captive. She was too afraid to venture out with all the reporters camped outside. News must be slow if she was their main story.

As she began to close her eyes, the whoosh of the door opening shattered the silence. Expecting to see Alison, her heart froze in her chest. It wasn't her therapist who stood before her – it was someone entirely different, someone unexpected.

'Hello, Lisbeth,' The woman's voice was over-familiar. 'You need your mother now.'

Beth's breath caught in her throat, her eyes widening with shock. After her father's funeral, she thought she had made it clear – she didn't want to see Janis. The woman was not now, and never had been any sort of mother to her.

What did she want? Why had she come now?

Chapter Seventy-Five

BETH

The fact that Janis was so audaciously trying to insert herself back into Beth's life, made her blood boil.

How dare you!

She scribbled, her hand aching from how hard she pressed as she wrote.

Where were you when I needed you? Now you show up, calling me Lisbeth as if you have any right to use that name.

Her mother looked down at the floor. 'You need a solicitor. Don't speak to the police until you have proper legal representation. I've seen the news and you're in a lot of trouble, but I can help you, even take power of attorney to assist with the costs while you're incapacitated. I want your forgiveness. I want to show you I can be the mother I should have been all your life.' Janis made to wipe her eyes, but Beth noticed there were no tears there to wipe. 'Your father wasn't who you thought he was. Sure, he may have been nice to you, but he stole my dreams – and if it wasn't for him, you and I could have had a good life together.'

Beth glowered at her, though her heart wavered, just a little, torn between scepticism and a tiny flicker of hope. When she'd showed up after the funeral, her mother swore she had been sober for two years and vowed to make amends for her past mistakes. But there was something in her eyes now that told Beth not to trust Janis. She picked up her pen again.

Easy to knock Dad down when he's not here to defend himself. You were an adult, you can't carry on blaming others for your mistakes.

Janis was right about one thing, though: Beth needed a lawyer. The police had been circling like vultures, hinting at the possibility, but lacking enough evidence, to make an arrest. If she wanted to safeguard her future, perhaps Beth had to heed her mother's advice, as reluctant as she was to trust her.

Janis was still talking, but Beth through the torrent of promises and apologies, she only heard one thing. Her mother was claiming to have been in contact with Joe ever since the funeral.

You're lying.

Janis went through her texts and phone logs to show Beth Joe's number, and then she scrolled to her camera roll, found a photo and held it up to Beth's face. It was a picture of Joe, hugging a woman. Beth felt her breath catch in her throat, and her stomach plummeted.

Who the hell is that?

'Just thought you should know,' said Janis.

Beth searched her mother's face for any sign of deception, any flicker of manipulation that might betray her true intentions.

And there it was.

A chill scraped Beth's spine. That familiar glimmer in Janis's eyes, the subtle smirk that passed too quickly to be noticed.

The room felt suffocating, the air thick with tension. Beth wouldn't allow her mother to poison her thoughts, to dictate her actions.

'I have the relevant paperwork here. All you need to do is sign.' Janis waved the papers in front of her before placing them on the bed.

As if I'd let you have any control over me. Ever again.

This time Beth looked at Janis and gave her mother a sly smile. She picked up the paperwork and tore it to shreds.

'You'll regret that,' said Janis. 'Silly girl'.

Beth picked up her pen again and wrote.

Never try to contact me again.

Chapter Seventy-Six

BETH

A few minutes after Janis had left, the door to Beth's room creaked open and she turned to see Aunt Kay enter.

'Lisbeth. Oh, my goodness, I didn't expect to find you out of bed. How are you?'

Beth gave a small smile and wrote a few words on the notepad.

I'm doing better, thank you.

Kay settled into a chair and Beth noticed her lip twitch. 'I saw your mother leaving. She came to visit you?'

Beth gave the thumbs-up.

Kay's eyes narrowed slightly. 'What did she want?'

Beth shrugged. She didn't want to share any more with Kay. Apart from anything else, she wasn't prepared to listen to the lecture that would inevitably follow.

Kay's gaze softened. 'She hasn't been the best mother to

you. She wasn't there when you needed her most, and her drinking...'

The memories of her mother's alcohol binges resurfaced like a tidal wave. Beth remembered the tumultuous teenage years after her mother had abandoned her and Pops, the times she, Beth, had gone off the rails, searching for an escape from the chaos. She didn't need Kay to remind her, she had lived it. Spending so much time alone in bed made her reflective: hanging onto all that anger had held her back, and she finally needed to heal those wounds to move forward.

'I just worry that she'll hurt you again,' Kay went on. 'Janis will never change, and I don't want to see you spiral again. Look at where you are.'

Kay was right but why did she always have to have that little dig? Beth changed the subject, picking up her pen again.

How's Frank? Why didn't he come?

Kay's face darkened. 'He's not well at the moment and this whole situation has upset him terribly.'

Was Kay blaming her for the stress her uncle was experiencing?

It's not my fault! I didn't ask for any of this to happen.

She threw the notepad on the table.

Kay reached out, placing a comforting hand on Beth's

shoulder. 'I know, sweetheart. I'm not blaming you. I'm just worried about you both.'

It felt like everyone was gaslighting her. Beth wanted to lash out, to push everyone away. As if sensing her mood, Kay's tone softened slightly. 'I went to see Joe. He's not doing well. The doctors aren't sure when or even if he'll wake up.'

This news hit Beth like a punch.

'The news is saying the police have enough evidence to arrest someone. Forensics had a field day, apparently.'

Beth's body stiffened, her mind racing as she tried to piece together the fragments of her memory. She had flashes of that afternoon, but they were disjointed, hazy, clouded by the effects of the drugs and alcohol in her body when it had happened.

'The police have been in touch with me, too.' Kay's gaze locking with Beth's. 'They want to know what's really been going on.'

Beth's heart raced.

What are you going to tell them?

'I'll tell them the truth, of course.' Kay's head tilted. 'Whatever I know, whatever I've seen, I'll tell them the truth.'

Chapter Seventy-Seven

BETH

Beth ran her fingers through her hair, which was still damp from the shower she had taken earlier. As her attendant nurse changed her bedlinen, Beth's eyes darted to the clock on the wall, counting down the seconds until her discharge. She still wasn't able to speak, although every now and again a small whisper would escape; she had practised on those nights she was unable to sleep.

She was not being told anything about Joe, and still unable to fully recall the details of the attack, she wondered if she had escalated an argument that led to the attack. There was a part of her that wanted to blame herself, because it was just so out of character for Joe. But then in those flashbacks, she was sure it was Joe's face she saw, his twisted mouth and his narrowed eyes as he'd plunged the knife into her body.

The nurse glanced at her. 'I suppose you're looking forward to getting out of here,' she said. 'Your voice will recover fully with time. Just make sure you don't strain it too much.'

Beth gave a weak smile and shrugged.

'I think a police escort has been arranged to take you to visit Joe before you go,' the nurse added.

Beth felt her body stiffen at the mention of the police escort. She wanted to see Joe, hoping against hope that he would wake up and tell her the truth: that it wasn't her who'd hurt him, that he knew she'd never do that.

A few hours later, as Beth sat in the waiting room reading, she looked up and saw Alison walking towards her. Her hands trembled as she clutched her book, anxiety mounting as Alison drew closer.

'Are you ready to go?'

Beth hesitated; her brows furrowed. She reached into her bag and pulled out the notepad.

I'm supposed to wait for the police to take me to see Joe. Why are you here?

She held up the notepad and watched as Alison's eyes ran over the words.

'Detective Johnson contacted me. He asked if I would accompany you to visit Joe and said he would let you know, but clearly, he hasn't. I understand Joe's parents have been told and they are going to grab some dinner. I'm afraid the police guard may also be in the room with you. Should we go now?' Alison reached down and picked up Beth's bag.

Beth pushed herself up out of the chair and followed behind Alison. As they passed the nurses station, she felt like they were all whispering about her. She kept her eyes on Alison's back.

The fluorescent lights flickered above, casting an eerie glow in the corridor. When they reached Joe's room, Alison spoke to the police officer stationed outside the door. Beth couldn't hear what they were saying as they spoke in hushed tones. She looked into the room. The sight of him lying there, unconscious and vulnerable, sent a burning lance through her chest.

Alison tapped her shoulder. 'The guard said it would be all right if I stood a bit away from you once we go inside, he'll remain outside, but with the door open. At least you can have a bit of privacy.'

Beth nodded, appreciating the gesture of trust, as they stepped inside and she walked over to Joe's bedside. Her hand reached out to touch his, hoping for some kind of connection, but she pulled back at the last moment. The fear of what she might remember overwhelmed her, leaving her paralysed.

Joe, please wake up.

Beth's body trembled as she tried to project her thoughts into words. *I need to know what happened that night.*

He wasn't going to wake up.

Unable to bear the weight of her own thoughts any longer, Beth turned and walked out of the room with Alison following close behind.

'Do you want to leave him a note? I'm sure the officer will pass it on.'

Beth shook her head. What was the point. He may never wake up and she was sure the police would only try and use whatever she wrote against her. Maybe that was Alison's plan. Was she working with the police?

'Okay. I'll take you home? Do you want to go back to your house?'

Beth nodded. She had nowhere else to go. Although her aunt had offered her a room at their home in Leek, she could only stand Kay in small doses.

After finding Alison's car, they drove in silence, the tension in the car palpable. Beth couldn't bear the quiet, and yet she couldn't say the words to break it. She wondered if she could trust Alison completely. She needed someone she could rely on; someone she could talk to. Finally, a friend. Maybe if she lowered her walls, they'd stick around longer than five minutes.

As they arrived at the house, Beth got out of the car and felt a knot in her stomach. The sight of it brought a flood of memories, but they were tainted and blurry. Beth turned away, unable to cope with the flashbacks. Her neighbours were outside, talking in hushed tones, and it felt like their eyes were on her, judging. She glared at them, tempted to give them the middle finger, but that would only fuel their gossip. A few journalists must have caught wind of her discharge, but Beth ignored them as Alison pushed by to clear the way for her.

Beth let Alison help her inside, and her heart sank at the sight before her. The house was a mess, washed bloodstains still visible on the walls and floor. Images of the violent altercation came rushing back to her, making her knees weak and her breath shallow.

Oh, God. Tears welled up in Beth's eyes. *Why can't I remember what happened?*

Alison looked uneasy, glancing away for a moment before meeting Beth's gaze. 'I don't think you should stay here, especially with those vultures outside.'

She had no family nearby, and none of her so-called friends had visited her or offered any help after what had happened. She had nowhere to turn.

'I have nowhere else to go,' Beth stammered, the words tearing at her throat despite being only a whisper. Desperation crept into her voice.

Alison's eyes widened. 'Your voice, it's back! This is great!' She squeezed her arm. 'But also worrying. I'd hate to see it disappear again if something in this house triggers you. I know we don't really know each other well, but why don't you stay with me for a little while. I can organise for a deep clean here, so it's ready for you when you feel up to coming back. My place isn't big, and my son will be there, but he keeps to himself most of the time. It's just until you figure things out.'

Faced with no other option, Beth knew she should be grateful for the lifeline being thrown her way. 'Okay.'

'Great. Grab anything you think you might need, and we'll get going. I'm not too far from here, actually.'

Beth was sure she saw a slight smile creep across Alison's face, and she wondered whether she was making a huge mistake.

Chapter Seventy-Eight

BETH

Inside her modest but welcoming home, Alison showed Beth to the spare room, providing her with fresh towels and a warm blanket. Beth looked around. She didn't like staying in other people's houses at the best of times, but something about this felt wrong.

'You're being so kind to me?' Beth turned to Alison. 'You barely know me.'

'We're both going through tough times. I feel like Joe would want me to do this. I'm no longer your therapist, so maybe we can just be friends?'

Beth nodded and placed her travel bag on the chair by the window. She could sense Alison wanted to say something more.

'You know, you probably should take it easy with the talking. I have a notepad downstairs. I could get it for you?'

Beth was reminded of what the nurse had said before she was discharged. Baby steps. Her voice had barely come back, and she didn't want to lose it again. She nodded and watched as Alison left the room.

She sat on the edge of the unfamiliar bed, the scent of fresh paint and the distant hum of traffic outside were a world away from the bloodstained walls of her own home. She ran her fingers over the soft duvet, trying to find some sense of peace amidst the chaos in her mind.

She could hear Alison moving downstairs as she looked for a notepad. There was a part of Beth that wanted to stay hidden in the room, but if there was any chance in finding the truth, she would need to suppress her anxiety and be clear-headed.

Weren't people always telling her that?

She went downstairs and found Alison.

'I was just coming up. Here.' Alison held out a thick notepad and some pens. Beth took them. 'The living room is through there. Why don't you go in, and I'll get us a drink?'

Beth took in the pictures on the wall as she headed into the living room. A small boy with a big smile was in most of them, Alison's son. He looked happy. No pictures of his father, though Alison had said they were separated. The living room was welcoming. Neutral colours and a large, plush three-seater, which Beth sat on.

Alison came in and sat next to Beth, handing her a cup of tea. Beth accepted it gratefully, the warm liquid soothing her frayed nerves as she took a sip.

'Thank you for letting me stay here.' Beth managed a whisper.

Alison placed a reassuring hand on Beth's shoulder. 'Don't mention it. You're safe here.'

Safe. The word hung in the air like a lifeline.

Beth opened the notepad and began writing.

If I ask you a question, will you be honest with me?

'Of course. I know trusting me is going to take time, but I only want to help you...'

What do you think happened? That night. You know Joe. What did he tell you was going on?

Alison shifted in the seat. 'Well, he said you were struggling. That you'd been drinking a lot and mixing it with your meds. He thought you were— Are you sure you want to hear this?'

Beth nodded. She couldn't believe that Joe had been so open with this woman.

'He thought you were hallucinating at times, as well as being paranoid. He mentioned that you had said you were getting hang-up calls and notes or letters... But when he wanted to see the letters, you couldn't find them. He never heard the calls. He checked your mobile once and there was nothing in the call log.'

Beth looked away before picking up the notepad and sharing with Alison her truth.

You know me from our sessions. I wasn't drunk then. Did I come across as paranoid?

'I don't want to confuse the two scenarios. I didn't get the impression you were under the influence when we spoke, but...'

But what?

'Well, that was an hour a week. I'm not saying I believe Joe over you but somewhere in the middle of both of your versions is the truth, and I guess that's what we need to figure out. You and I were little more than strangers and you remember the old joke? "I didn't know he drank until I saw him sober".'

Beth could appreciate what Alison was saying, even though it angered her – she was angry at how she had messed things up, at how Joe had perceived the situation. She was fuming at everything that had led up to this. It was incredible just how differently she and Joe saw the same situation.

As the afternoon wore on, the sky outside darkened, and Beth's anxiety mounted. The police had said that once she was discharged, they wanted to question her further, and she feared the repercussions of her foggy memories.

I need to speak to my employers

She wrote, her eyes fixed on the mug of tea which was now cold.

They might be able to help me. Maybe a phone call would be better.

Alison nodded. 'That's a good idea. They know you, and they might be able to recommend a good solicitor, if that's what is eventually needed. I imagine it could be perceived as a conflict of interests for them to represent you.'

Beth bit her lip, as Alison came in with the landline phone. 'I'll just be in the kitchen if you need me' She handed it to Beth. 'Don't strain your voice – keep things brief.'

Beth mustered up the courage to dial her work number, her breath hitching as she waited for someone to pick up.

'Good afternoon, Lynch, Walker, Travis and Co.'

Beth recognised Glyn's voice and took a deep breath, hoping her whisper would be enough to convey her turmoil. 'Hi. It's Lisbeth Stanford. I ... I need to speak with someone about a legal matter.'

'Oh, Beth, sweetheart. How are you? Never mind, we can catch up another time, I'll just connect you. Two secs.'

Moments later, a soothing voice came on the line. 'Lisbeth, thank God you're okay,' Cassandra sounded relieved. 'We've all been worried sick about you. We tried to reach out sooner but were told you didn't want any contact. How are you holding up?'

Beth's lip trembled. She suddenly felt wary. Her boss had her 'fake voice' on. Was she just going to placate her, or would she help? But Beth knew she had to start trusting people if she was going to get herself out of this mess.

'I'm out of the hospital. My voice... I have to be careful ... it's only just returned, but I can't remember a lot of what happened.' Beth's heart pounded as she explained the situation, her words a hushed confession of her fears and uncertainties. 'The police want to question me further about Joe. They think I hurt him, but I don't remember everything clearly. I ... I need help. Joe attacked me. I'm ... sure of it... Well ... pretty sure. I was only defending myself.'

'Mmm... Okay. I definitely can help, and your call indicates you want to retain the firm's services so tell me what you can recall.' Cassandra's tone turned serious. 'You didn't hurt Joe, did you?'

Beth shook her head vehemently even though her boss couldn't see her. Tears streamed down her cheeks. 'No! I would never hurt him.'

'Okay. I'd offer to represent you myself, but so that there's no potential conflict of interests, I'll give you the details for one of the best criminal barristers I know. They'll help you navigate this situation, all right? Don't speak to the police any more without having someone there, okay?'

Relief washed over Beth as Cassandra gave her the details. 'Thank you. I'm scared, the police have been twisting things and I don't know what to do.'

'Stay strong,' Cassandra encouraged. 'While we've been talking, I've sent an email giving them the heads up about your situation. They're offering you an appointment tomorrow to discuss your case in detail. They will guide you through this process. If the police contact you again, direct them to the firm. They'll handle everything.'

Tears welled up in Beth's eyes, she thanked her boss before ending the call and placing the handset on the side table.

Now she just had to figure out what she would tell them, so that they believed her.

Chapter Seventy-Nine

BETH

The night passed slowly. Beth tossed and turned, haunted by that day. As the first rays of dawn filtered through the curtains, she knew she couldn't stay in this limbo forever. She got dressed and headed downstairs.

Alison was in the kitchen and Beth could smell the coffee brewing.

'How are you feeling this morning?'

Beth managed a small smile. 'I'm scared, but I can't hide forever, can I?' She looked around. 'Is your son not here?'

'He's with his grandparents. I thought it might be a good idea if he stayed with them for a little while. It will give you some privacy and, to be honest, I think the press have caught wind of where you are staying because someone knocked on the door this morning. I just don't want to give my ex any excuse to try and take Nicky away from me. I don't have work today, so if you like, I can take you to the appointment with your solicitor – go in with you, too, but only if that's what you want.'

'I'm so sorry about what I've gotten you into. I can go and stay with my aunt in Leek, if that makes things easier for you.'

Alison shook her head. 'It's fine. Nicky loves staying with his grandparents.' She smiled. 'So, what about that appointment?'

'I guess that would be okay. Thank you.' Beth smiled back. 'I'll just finish this coffee and get my things together.'

As they pulled into a parking space, Beth clutched her handbag so tightly, her knuckles were white. A moment of dizziness washed over her, and she wanted to turn around and bury her head in the sand.

'It will be fine.' Alison parked and they got out.

Beth's pulse quickened with each step towards the building. The sleek, glass structure loomed before them, and as they entered it, she couldn't help feeling she was betraying Joe as he lay helpless in the hospital, but she also wasn't prepared to take the fall for something she didn't do.

The solicitor's office was elegant and professional, creating a sense of stability amidst the turmoil. They were greeted warmly by the receptionist, who informed them that Mr Carter would see them shortly.

As they sat in the waiting area, Beth clung to the hope that Mr Carter could shed light on her situation, give her the guidance she needed. Finally, he emerged from his office, extending a hand to Beth. 'Ms Stanford, it's a pleasure to meet you. Please, come in.'

Inside his office, Beth felt a sense of reassurance. She shared her story, her whispers filled with raw emotion as she recounted the night that turned her life upside down. She held back nothing, unsure of what details could or would be crucial to her case. 'I want to tell the police about the hang-up calls, but I'm afraid they'll think I'm just trying to deflect blame since I didn't mention them earlier.'

Mr Carter listened attentively, his eyes never leaving her face as she spoke. When she finished, he leaned back in his chair, his expression thoughtful. 'I understand that this is a difficult time for you.'

Beth nodded, wiping away a tear. 'I just want to know what happened that night. I need to know the truth.'

'We'll do everything in our power to help you find that truth,' he assured her. 'It's important to share all the information you have. We can request the phone records to try and trace the origin of those calls. It might provide valuable insight. And the letters, do you still have them? Did any of your neighbours see them being dropped off? We could also check CCTV in your neighbourhood. The police should have all this in evidence and if that's the case...'

Beth could tell Mr Carter was talking more to himself than to her as he jotted things down on the yellow legal pad in front of him.

He looked up at her. 'It'll be helpful to know what the police have on you. The fact you haven't been arrested or charged, makes me believe they have very little, if anything. Remember, if the police contact you again, direct them to us. They shouldn't be pressuring you without proper legal representation.'

Gratitude surged within Beth, she finally felt she had someone on her side who believed in her innocence. She didn't even care that she was paying him for that reassurance. Her heart felt a little lighter as she left the solicitor's office with Alison.

As they walked back to Alison's car, a loud, shrill ring cut through the air, and Beth jumped at the sudden sound. Alison held out her mobile, showing Beth as it flashed with an incoming call. Beth noticed the number coming up as UNKNOWN and this triggered something in her memory.

She grabbed Alison's arm, stopping her from answering the call. 'Remember the calls I was getting before the attack? I think they're connected to everything. They must be. What if Joe was making the calls to scare me. Make me feel like I was losing the plot?'

Alison's expression darkened. 'I suppose that's possible, but Joe wasn't controlling, Beth, was he? I just can't picture him resorting to such tactics. Not the Joe I know.'

'That's just it. Can't you see. He's good at hiding what he's really like. I mean, even I wouldn't have thought that he would do something like this, and yet here we are. He could have been setting this up for some time. Did he ever really love me?' Beth's throat started to ache.

Alison hesitated. 'Are you okay? Here, have some water.' She pulled out a bottle from her bag and handed it to Beth. 'Maybe Joe wasn't the one who attacked you. Maybe he was trying to protect you from someone else. I think we must be really careful and not dismiss the possibility that both you and Joe are the victims and there is someone else out there who the police need to find.'

Beth's heart clenched with conflicting emotions. Her throat felt raw, so she pulled out her notepad and started writing.

I don't know what to believe anymore.

Alison's phone rang again, and this time she answered it, her voice tense as she spoke to the caller. 'Hello? Who is this?'

Beth heard a sinister laugh echo through the call before whoever it was hung up. Alison's face turned pale, and she stared at the screen. 'It's him. My ex, Pete. He's been tormenting me like this for months. He must have got hold of someone else's phone or used a landline.'

Beth's mind was racing, connecting the dots. What if she and Joe weren't the main victims. What if Alison was tied into this and they were just pawns.

Should she say something? Was this just her paranoia creeping back? She'd been hiding too much for too long and the worse that could happen was Alison would point out the inconsistencies in her thinking.

If he's capable of doing this to you, then what else is he capable of? Did he know Joe?

Beth held up her notepad and Alison shook her head, her voice trembling. 'I don't think so. I don't know. But I'm scared. He just won't stop.'

Chapter Eighty

BETH

Back at Alison's place, they were both emotionally exhausted. Beth sat in the living room while Alison made them coffee. The room felt suffocating, and Beth needed answers, closure. But with Joe in a coma, she feared she might never get either. Her attempts at getting information from the hospital had been fruitless. Beth was told they could only share information about him with Joe's parents. It looks like they didn't believe her either.

'Here.' Alison held out a mug and Beth took it, needing caffeine to keep her eyes open and her mind focused.

'The police investigation is dragging on. Why won't they tell us anything?' she whispered hoarsely.

'I think you just have to be patient. I know it's frustrating but let them do their job. Detective Johnson seems like he knows what he's doing, unlike his partner.' Alison rolled her eyes. 'If it was up to that other one, you'd probably have been arrested by now, even without evidence.'

Beth's eyes widened. 'Why would you say that?' She

shifted in her chair. Maybe she was right to not trust this woman. Was Alison only helping her so that she could throw her under the bus? Protecting Joe...

'Sorry. I didn't mean it the way it sounded. DC Thompson is just a real prick. He seemed to want to make an arrest without the facts. At one point, the way he was speaking, I thought he was going to put me on his list of suspects.'

Beth took a sip of the coffee and didn't answer Alison.

'Look, I need to go out and run some errands. You can stay here or come with me if you'd like.'

Beth tapped the couch. She'd stay and look at trying to figure out her next move.

'Okay. I won't be long.'

Beth took her coffee up to the spare room and sat in the chair, looking out the window, Alison waved as she reversed out of the drive.

Beth had this strange feeling she was being watched, that someone wanted to keep her silent, to bury the truth, but had no idea who would want that or why. It wasn't like before, with her substance-induced hallucinations and paranoia. Every now and again she would catch sight of journalists snapping pictures of her, and those that did try and speak to her were met with silence. But this wasn't them. This was different.

She turned on the small telly and the news. She was caught off-guard when she saw Mr Brewer smiling as he left the courthouse, apparently found not guilty on all counts. Charges were now pending against his wife.

He had been telling the truth.

The news went on to say that Mrs Brewer had been co-conspiring with a 'friend' for financial gain. Beth felt a brief tinge of sorrow for her – she had still been assaulted, just not at the hands of her husband. She was surprised that Cassandra hadn't mentioned the case when they spoke. But then Beth was suspended from work, no longer privy to such information.

She yawned and turned off the TV. She took the blanket off the bed, wrapping the fleece around her. As sleep finally claimed her, she hoped the nightmares would stay away. As much as she wanted closure, she also wanted to be able to sleep without Joe's angry face haunting her.

Chapter Eighty-One

BETH

Beth woke with a start at the sound of her mobile ringing. The police had returned it, but not before, Beth suspected, making a copy of its data. She'd seen that happen in cases she'd worked on. Forensic cloning they called it, or something like that.

Her breath came in short bursts. She got up and grabbed the phone from the nightstand, clutching it tightly, her finger hovering over the answer button.

'He-hello?' Her voice was scratchy, a burning sensation tearing at the back of her throat.

'Ms. Stanford? It's Detective Johnson here. Glad to hear you've got your voice back.'

'Uh ... yes. Well, it comes and goes.'

'Okay. I won't keep you long. We'd like you to come into the station for further questioning. We have some new information, and we'd like to clear some things up.'

She could feel the dread in her stomach. 'Could you tell me

a bit more about what you need me for? Maybe I can answer your questions now.' Beth's throat ached and she coughed.

'I'd rather not do this over the phone. When can you come in?'

'I'm going to have to call you back. There's someone at the door.' Beth hung up before the detective could say anything else. She'd just lied to him, but with her heart pounding in her chest, she couldn't concentrate.

She called her solicitor. 'Mr Carter, It's Beth Stanford. The police want me to come in. What should I do?'

'I'll meet you at the station,' he said. 'Tell them you're on your way in. And remember, don't discuss anything until I'm there.'

'Okay.'

Beth gathered her things and was about to call a taxi when Alison returned home.

Alison offered to accompany her, but Beth declined. She needed to face this on her own. She also wanted to stop by her house and pick up Joe's car. Although the thought of driving triggered her anxiety, she needed some independence. She had to start somewhere.

The taxi dropped her off and she went inside. Maybe being there would prompt a memory, anything that could help her piece together the missing parts, and she could share that with the police.

As she stepped into her house, the memories hit her again. Despite the house having been cleaned, in her mind she still saw the blood on the walls, the broken furniture, and felt the pain and fear of that day – it was all too overwhelming. She closed her eyes, trying to push back the flood of emotions threatening to consume her. This was a bad idea.

She grabbed the spare car keys and drove to the station. It had been a while since she'd driven, so she took her time and ignored the glares from annoyed drivers.

When she arrived, Mr Carter was waiting for her with a supportive smile. Beth took a deep breath, thankful for the solicitor's presence. Together, they entered the station and were led to an interview suite.

The room was stark and cold, the atmosphere tense as Beth took a seat at the table. The two detectives entered the room, and Beth's heart sank. Detective Thompson, the sarcastic one, gave her a smug grin, while DC Johnson maintained a formal but respectful expression.

'Hello again, Beth.' Johnson sat down opposite her. 'Thanks for coming in.' He went through the purpose of the interview and disclosed she was free to leave at any time. 'We have some questions for you.'

Mr Carter spoke before Beth could respond. 'I hope you have new evidence, or an update on the case for my client. She's still recovering, and you wouldn't want to set her back, would you?'

Detective Johnson nodded. 'We do. We found some interesting things in Joe's phone records. I'm just going to come straight to the point. It seems you called Joe just before he arrived back at the house on the afternoon of the attack.'

Beth's mind raced as she tried to recall that moment. 'I ... I don't remember making that call. I was not myself. Everything's still hazy.'

Sitting beside Johnson, Detective Thompson scoffed. 'That's convenient, isn't it? But that's not all. There are numerous texts from you to Joe that suggest you were trying to convince him to come home. Get him there so you could get rid of him for good, perhaps?'

'That's not true! While you are pointing the finger at me... You're ignoring the truth.' Beth's leg shook under the table. She needed to deflect the attention away from her while she figured things out.

Her solicitor intervened, his voice firm. 'This all seems a bit far-fetched, officers. Beth was unwell, grieving the loss of her father and struggling mentally at the time. She has never hidden the fact that she was under the influence a lot of the time leading up to the attack. Wanting her partner home because she was struggling, does not equal wanting to harm him. Even if she had messaged him, without other evidence, these are just wild accusations and you're wasting our time.'

The detectives exchanged glances, and then Johnson leaned forward looking directly at Beth. 'We just want the truth. Maybe something happened that morning that you can't quite remember and led to the events of the afternoon? Maybe you're afraid to tell us something ... worried about how it might look? If you cooperate, it will be easier for you.'

Doubt crept in Beth's mind. Was she hiding something? The constant questioning, the accusations, it was all too much to bear. She began to wonder if she was indeed hiding a darker truth.

Did I do this?

Carter interjected again, his voice unwavering. 'I think we're done here. You're just going over the same old ground, and my client has answered these questions repeatedly. If you have any new evidence or charges to bring against her, do it. Otherwise, she has nothing more to say. And next time, please don't waste our time with a new point as trivial as this one.'

Detective Johnson sighed. 'All right, we'll be in touch.'

As the detectives left the room, Beth's shoulders relaxed. She was emotionally drained. She turned to Mr Carter. 'I don't know what to believe anymore.'

He placed a comforting hand on her shoulder. 'I know it's tough. Don't let them get to you.'

Beth nodded, thankful for the reassurance. 'Do you think they really have evidence that shows I'm responsible? I know how the police work, and they often—'

'Look. From what we've seen today, it doesn't appear they have anything but speculation. Don't let them play mind games with you. They might try to trick you, so let me do the talking in future. I know you want to help, but they will twist things.'

With the meeting at the station concluded, Beth stepped outside and took a deep breath.

One way or another, she knew she'd have to work out what happened that fateful night. She'd somehow need to jolt her memory so that everything came back to her. There was no other way.

Chapter Eighty-Two

BETH

As she drove away from the police station, Beth worried she'd never work out what had happened. She approached her home slowly, and a shiver ran down her spine. Beth hesitated for a moment before taking a deep breath and pushing the door open. Once inside, the air felt heavy and her stomach tightened, as flashes of a knife seared her vision.

Her mobile rang and she saw it flash: UNKNOWN NUMBER. She answered the ringing phone, her voice steady. 'Hello.'

The voice on the other end was distorted, cold and mocking, though she detected a familiar twang in the accent. 'Did you think you could escape from me, Beth?'

Beth's heart raced, she looked around and out of the front window to see if anyone was outside, but there was no one there, not even the press. She almost wished a journalist was there in the bushes taunting her, but this time she refused to allow her fear to paralyse her. She backed away from view and bumped into the chair.

His Truth Her Truth

'Who is this? Why are you doing this to me, you fucking coward!'

There was no answer and she hung up, her breathing becoming quicker, her head throbbing. She took a screen shot of the listed call to show her solicitor – prove that the harassing calls were still happening and this time she was stone cold sober.

She went outside for some fresh air, and then she saw the flat tyres on the driver's side of the car. Three paces later, she saw the passenger-side tyres were the same. A look up and down the street revealed nobody. No neighbour standing at their window, or in their doorway, watching her. There was just the violated car and a house filled with bad memories.

A spike of fear went through her, and she reached out, pressing her palm against the rough wall of her house to steady herself. With her other hand, she fumbled with her phone, finding the contact number she needed and hitting call – the glaring screen burned her dilated pupils in the darkness.

'Alison?'

The chilling silence that followed was punctuated by the howling wind whipping around her. Beth's heart began to slow down with each deep breath she took. A snippet of memory snapped into her mind's eye like a cruel puzzle piece.

The hang-up calls. They had to be significant. If connected, that would mean Joe was also a victim. Someone else had been in their home that day. But who?

Her attention was pulled back to the call as she heard Alison's voice.

'Hey, are you all right? Where are you?'

'I can't do it.' Beth confessed. 'I'm at my house, and it's too

331

much. I was only inside for a minute when someone slashed my tyres.' She took a deep breath. 'And I got another call.'

'I knew it would be traumatic for you, you weren't prepared. It's still too soon.'

'But ignoring it, hiding from it, only makes me look guilty. Makes me feel guilty... I need to be here to remember what happened.' Beth heard a sound, like someone was there with her, and wished she'd kept her mouth shut.

The rough voice on the other end of that call, it had been eerily familiar.

Perhaps it was important. 'I should tell the police,' she said.

Alison had other ideas.

'I don't know. We need to keep this to ourselves, at least for now. They don't even believe you had any calls, what if they think you are making it up to get their eyes off you?'

Beth was worn out, but Alison did have a point.

'What happened at the police station?'

Beth looked around and saw her neighbour peering out of the window next door. She couldn't speak here. 'I'm sorry to ask you this, but can you pick me up? I'll be waiting outside. I can't go back in there. I'll tell you everything then. Too many eyes on me at the moment.' She glared at her neighbour as the words came out through gritted teeth.

Beth could hear keys jangling.

'I'm on my way,' said Alison.

She was sitting at the end of the driveway, clutching her bag close when Alison pulled up twenty minutes later. Beth hopped into the passenger side and buckled her seatbelt. Closing her eyes she took a deep breath as Alison pulled away.

'So, what did the police say when they questioned you?'

'Just give me a minute.' Beth couldn't think clearly.

'Uh, sorry. Of course, whenever you're ready.' Alison stared straight ahead as she drove. 'We'll talk back at my house.'

Beth was grateful for the reprieve. She had been bombarded with so many questions today, she just needed it to stop.

When Alison had parked the car, she turned to Beth. 'Get settled and I'll make us a cuppa. I won't pressure you to tell me anything you don't want to. Sometimes I find it hard to switch from therapist to friend. I want to be here for you as a friend.'

Beth smiled and squeezed her hand. As wary as she was of everyone around her, Alison seemed like the only friend she had at the moment. 'Thanks.'

Once inside, Beth took off her jacket and went into the living room, putting her mobile on charge before sitting down. She was tempted to turn on the TV, but was afraid to see herself plastered all over the news.

Alison joined her with tea, and Beth took it gratefully.

'The police obviously think that I'm responsible. They say they have evidence, and with Joe in a coma and unable to tell the truth, I don't know what's going to happen to me.' Her voice trembled.

Alison's brow furrowed. 'I know it's easy for me to say, but you can't let their tactics get to you. Have you heard any more from the hospital? I could try and find out – maybe go and see Joe?'

'Once his parents find out I am staying with you, you'll be on the block list, too – I don't want to give them any more ammunition to hold against me. There must be another way.'

'What about your aunt? Would she be able to speak to Joe's parents?'

'I doubt it. I'm not sure she believes I didn't do it either.' Beth's shoulders shook as the tears came. 'What if I'm wrong? What if I am the monster they think I am?'

'From our conversations as your therapist and from what I know of you now, I don't think that's the case.' Alison placed a gentle hand on Beth's shoulder. 'The truth will come out, and let's hope Joe comes out of the coma and clears this up once and for all.'

Chapter Eighty-Three

BETH

Beth's thoughts were spiralling again, back to the call with Alison just before she'd picked her up. Dread welled up within her. Why would Alison tell her not to let the police know about the threatening call and flat tyres? She looked over at her and wondered whether her paranoia was returning. Her hands began to tremble. She thought her medication was keeping her level, but the intrusive thoughts were poking again.

Alison's landline rang.

'You don't mind if I take this do you?'

Beth shook her head. 'It's your house, why would I mind?'

Alison put the call on speaker while she did something in the other room.

Beth heard a little boy's voice, but then worry morphed into suspicion when she heard an adult male voice. It must be Alison's ex but there was also something else. The tone, laced with bitterness and deceit, chilled her blood more than the wind outside. A realisation flashed in her mind, and goosebumps formed on her arms.

It's him.

Alison returned to the room.

'Sorry about that. Nicky just wanted to say goodnight. Pete didn't have to jump on the call, see what I mean about him?' Alison rolled her eyes.

'Your ex... His voice sounded familiar,' Beth said, staring at her.

Alison's gaze was steady, but she swallowed before she answered. 'What do you mean?'

'I'm sure he was ... he was the one at my house that afternoon. The one watching me.'

The one who slashed my tyres.

Alison's eyes widened, but then she quickly regained her composure, shaking her head dismissively. 'Beth, I think you're just stressed out. You're making connections where there are none. Why would Pete be doing this to you?'

Rage, quick and fierce, flared within Beth. Her words sharp by design. 'I'm not some sponge, absorbing other people's problems and claiming them as my own. I know what I heard.' The tension in the room was heavy. 'This was a mistake. I can't be here. I'll just go upstairs and collect my things. It must be the connection between you and Joe, maybe I was just in the wrong place at the wrong time.' As she heard the words out loud, she wondered if there was any truth in what she said.

Alison sighed, a note of resignation in her voice. 'Fine. I'll drop you back. It doesn't make any sense for you to call a taxi when I can easily do it.'

When Alison pulled into her drive, Beth turned to her, feeling guilty now. She shouldn't be taking her anger out on Alison, as she was only trying to help.

'Do you want to come in for a coffee?' she asked.

'Yes, please. It's freezing. Look, Beth. Are you sure you want to be here? I'm sorry about earlier. I didn't mean to sound dismissive.' Alison rubbed her hands together.

'I know, but I need to stop running from my memories. If this house can unlock them, this is where I need to be.' Beth ushered Alison into the living room and took her few belongings upstairs in silence. When she returned downstairs, she boiled the kettle and made them both a steaming hot coffee.

'This should help warm you up.' Beth passed Alison a mug and sat across from her so she could look at her, really look at her. Beth's mind was awash with conflicting thoughts. Just how well did she know Alison, and could she really trust her?

Sometimes you have to keep your enemies close.

Chapter Eighty-Four

BETH

Half and hour later, as Beth watched Alison drive off, her phone jolted to life. The screen illuminated the dim hallway, the sudden brightness making her squint. Part of her wanted to let it go to voicemail, but her curiosity won out.

'Lisbeth, I want to help,' her mother's voice crackled. 'Let me come over and help you tidy the house. I want to be a part of your life. Please, love.'

Beth's fingers tightened around the phone, her knuckles whitening. She'd told her mother not to contact her, but she should have known Janis would ignore that. Beth had survived this long without a mother in her life, there was no way that she was letting Janis waltz back in as if nothing had happened. But maybe … she could use her to get information about Joe.

Beth sighed deliberately heavily. 'I've had a company around to do it, but okay,' she conceded, her voice catching on the word. 'Come round in an hour. We can talk. Do you need my address?' As much as Beth didn't trust this woman right now, it would be good to find out what her real motive was for making contact. For a fleeting moment, she wondered if her mother could have had anything to do with the attack on her and Joe. From what she remembered of her temper; she wouldn't put it past her. Did she know Alison's ex too?

'I've ... uh got it ... from Kay. See you shortly.'

Beth walked around the house aimlessly. It no longer felt like a home. Every room echoed with silent accusations and unspoken words. Her phone buzzed, the vibration sending a jolt through her already shaky nerves. The number was withheld.

'Hello?' Her throat ached from talking way too much already but she didn't want to put off the call.

'Ms Stanford.'

It was Detective Johnson. Beth got a bad feeling, an icy hand gripping her heart.

'Yes. What's the matter?' Her voice was a shaky whisper.

'I'm afraid I have some bad news,' he began, and Beth felt faint. She knew what he was going to say before he said it.

'It's Joe, isn't it. He's ... gone?'

'I can't really say anything over the phone. Can you come to the station?'

'No. No more questions. Just tell me ... has Joe died?'

'This is highly irregular but... I'm so sorry, yes, he has. I know this isn't the best time, but I thought you'd appreciate knowing this is now a murder investigation. We're going to need to speak to you again. It might be of some comfort to know that Joe died peacefully about a half hour ago.'

Her hand released the phone, leaving it to land on the carpet with a dull thud.

Joe is dead.

The words echoed in her mind, a chilling reality that she

was now alone. She staggered, gripping the back of a chair for support. She felt the ground give way beneath her and could hear a voice emitting from the phone on the floor. Her hands trembled as she picked it up.

'Ms. Stanford? Beth? Are you still there?'

'Sorry...' She took a deep breath. 'I'm ... here. I just ... I don't...' She couldn't find the words.

'Listen, one of my officers is on his way to collect you. I shouldn't have said anything to you.'

'Now? I want to go to the hospital. Say my goodbyes. Please ... you have to let me do this. I will come in and talk to you for as long as you want after that—'

'I'm afraid that's not possible.'

Someone knocked on the door. 'Excuse me, I have to go.' Beth hung up on Detective Johnson and ran to the door.

It was her mother.

'What are you doing here?'

'Uh... Hello to you, too. You invited me.' Janis crossed her arms.

'I don't have time for this.' Beth couldn't think straight. She looked around and spotted the taxi her mother had come in still parked outside. She grabbed her bag and ran down the drive to catch the cab before it pulled away.

'Can you take me to St Peter's Hospital?' She took a moment to catch her breath.

The driver turned to look at her. 'Still waiting for her to pay.' He pointed at her mother standing in the doorway.

'I'll pay for her trip. I need to get to the hospital as soon as possible.' She jumped in the back seat, ignoring the shouts from her mother.

The taxi screeched away, and Beth searched in her bag for

her wallet. She hadn't bothered to check if she had any cash, but when she opened it, she was relieved to find some. There were no signs in the car to say it took cards and stopping at an ATM machine would cause further delay.

Detective Johnson wouldn't be happy once he realised Beth had left her home, but at the moment, she needed to see Joe, and nothing was going to stop her.

Chapter Eighty-Five

BETH

Beth sat in the back of the taxi, her heart pounding like a drum. Despair gnawed at the edges of her mind, but she pushed it away, focusing on one goal: getting to Joe.

'Miss, we're here.'

She spotted the press, milling around the front like vultures. 'Could you just pull around to the other entrance at the side. Thanks.' She pulled her hood up and tucked in her hair before paying, her eyes riveted to the hospital's grim entrance. A cold gust of wind whipped around her as she stepped out, and she pulled her jacket tighter around her.

Inside the hospital, the smell of antiseptic was overpowering, a sterile mask that failed to ·hide the undercurrent of human suffering. All she could think of was Joe's face, the soft curve of his smile. All she could hear was his laughter, now forever silenced. The knowledge was like a weight, dragging her down with every step.

Navigating through the maze of corridors, avoiding anyone she thought could be from a newspaper or telly, she finally arrived at Joe's room. However, it was the stern faces of the police officers blocking the doorway that caught her attention.

'No! Joe! I need to see him. Please!' Beth's voice echoed off the walls of the hospital corridor. She lunged towards the room, desperation lending her strength. But the firm hands of the officers held her back, their expressions devoid of any emotion as she screamed Joe's name, her pleas falling on deaf ears.

'Please let me in. You've no right to keep me away. I didn't do anything!' She whimpered, sinking to the sterile tiles, the cold seeping through her jeans. 'I ... didn't do ... anything.' Her words trailed off into sobs, her body shaking with the force of her grief.

More police were advancing towards her now, their footsteps echoing in the silent corridor. Not now, she willed herself. Beth tried to pull herself together, tried to suppress the flashes of the attack that flooded her mind. But the flashes were already there, a brutal attack playing out in her mind. She saw a knife. She remembered her own screams, the pain.

But Joe was dead. The puzzle pieces didn't fit, and she didn't have the time to make sense of it. It couldn't have been Joe, which meant the killer was still out there and with Joe gone, was she next?

'I had another threatening call,' Beth's voice shook. She needed them to listen, to understand the meaning behind her words. They'd then see she was also a victim and needed protection from whomever attacked her and Joe. Her words were cut off, as cold, unyielding metal encased her wrists. Joe's parents in the distance, shaking their heads and blame in their eyes.

The handcuffs were a chilling confirmation of her worst

fears. The hospital lighting seemed to dim, the edges of her vision darkening as she felt consciousness slipping away. The last words she heard would haunt her.

'Lisbeth Stanford, you are under arrest for...'

Her world crumbled around her. The last vestiges of her strength ebbed away, and the ground rushed up to meet her as she fainted.

Chapter Eighty-Six

BETH

Beth didn't know how long she'd been out when she woke up. A sickly-sweet smell filled her nose and the room around her was draped in shadows, the only light coming from the buzzing strip overhead. She looked around, her vision blurred... The police officers, the hospital, all seemed like a far-off nightmare.

She sat on a bare mattress, the cold seeping into her bones. Her gaze fell on the peeling paint from the walls and the metal door with a small slit that reminded her she was in a holding cell at the police station. The silence in the room felt thick, pressing down on her like a physical weight.

How had she ended up here? She ran her fingers through her hair.

Her throat burned with a yearning for a stiff drink, the irony not lost on her. After all, it was her slip back into alcohol after her father had died that had started this whole mess in the first place. She needed to find Joe's killer, and she wouldn't find them at the bottom of a bottle. This time, her grief would have to wait.

The jangle of keys startled her from her thoughts. The cell door screeched open, and a female officer gestured for her to get up. Numbly, Beth followed her down the narrow hallway to an interview room.

The room was small, with a single metal table and four chairs. Beth's solicitor, Mr Carter, sat on one side, his face serious. He nodded at her, and Beth sat beside him, steeling herself for the discussion to come.

Once they were alone, Mr Carter leaned over, his eyes probing. 'They're going to drop the breach of the peace charges, but say they now have evidence regarding Joe's murder. Something substantial enough to point to you as his killer. Is there anything I need to know?'

'They can't have anything. How many times do I have to say I didn't do it.' Beth's voice, still healing, was raspy. 'And I had another call ... a threatening one... just before I found out that Joe was dead.' Despite her mind being foggy, the realisation her fiancé was gone, made her chest tighten. Her shoulders shook and she wiped her eyes with her sleeve.

Before her solicitor could reply, the door swung open. The two detectives walked in, their presence filling the small room. Detective Johnson tried to offer a comforting smile. The other, Detective *Arsehole* Thompson, pierced her with his sharp, bird-like gaze. Beth stiffened, her hands clutching the edge of the table.

Johnson took the lead and Beth was grateful.

'Before we ask you anything,' he said. 'Joe's parents have requested we let you know they don't want you at the funeral. They'll be taking care of everything, but they did say that you may visit the graveside only once everyone else has left. We'll be asking you some questions now and we need you to be forthcoming.'

Beth got the impression he was unsure of where he stood in terms of her guilt or innocence. But that soon changed once he started firing off his questions.

'Phone records show that you called Joe just before he arrived at your house and the attack occurred. What can you tell us about that?'

'Really? We've already been through all this. I'd like to advise my cli—' began Carter.

'It's okay. I have nothing to hide. I'll answer.' Beth interrupted, and Carter let her proceed. 'I couldn't have called him. I was being attacked myself. Don't you see? I'm being set up. Someone else did this; *they* probably called Joe using my phone, to lure him to the house. You're wasting your time with me, when whoever did do this is out there, literally getting away with murder.' Beth looked directly into Johnson's eyes, hoping he would see the truth in her words.

'Okay, let's take on board your theory. Who have you had problems with? Why would they attack you and then lure Joe to the house? If they were setting you up, surely the idea would be to have you out of the way and to come home and find Joe?'

The officer had a point. Beth felt her solicitor's hand on her arm. He leaned into her. 'I strongly recommend you go *no comment* going forward,' he murmured, then leaned back in his chair.

'Well, I was receiving letters that said Joe was having an affair. Maybe whoever sent me those letters did this. Anger, jealousy ... those are motives, aren't they? With Joe out of the way, they could punish their partner and leave me to get the blame.'

Johnson looked at Thompson and Beth saw them note something down. 'But we never found any of these so-called letters and you haven't been able to produce them. Do they really exist?'

The question felt like an assault, the words chipping away at her resilience.

'I know. I couldn't find them, but I'm not lying.' She looked down at the table when something else dawned on her. 'It could have been my mother... She suddenly wanted to be back in my life, and I was having none of it. Maybe she snapped. She's always been jealous of other people's happiness.'

'And why haven't you mentioned your mother before?' Thompson said smugly, tapping the table with a pen.

This guy annoyed Beth, and he knew it. Revelled in it.

'It never dawned on me. I've had a lot to deal with, officer. Forgive me for not trying to solve this case for you.' Beth immediately regretted her outburst when the kindness previously there in Johnson's expression vanished.

Detective Thompson slid her mobile records across the table, the paper cold under her fingertips. The time-stamped messages showed her pleading for Joe to come home, all sent in the relevant timeframe. One call in particular stood out, apparently answered by Joe.

'What did you say to him?' Thompson sat back and crossed his arms.

'I told you. I didn't call him,' Beth insisted, her heart pounding in her chest.

'Let's get back to your mother for a minute,' put in Johnson.

'You said you were attacked by Joe initially. So, are we right to assume your attacker was male?'

'Well ... yes. I never said my mother attacked me, but maybe she hired someone. She knows quite a few people who would probably do it for the promise of a good drink or drug binge.'

Thompson's gaze bored into her. 'You've been watching too many true-crime shows by the sounds of it, Ms Stanford. What about the previous domestic-violence call out? Or Joe losing all your savings in bad investments. Finally, you'd had enough?'

'What? That's… What are you talking about?' Beth looked at Detective Johnson, urging him for an answer and though her solicitor shot her a warning look, Beth's anger surged. 'Why aren't you listening to what I'm saying. I didn't do anything. Tell me what you know.'

Carter sighed next to her. 'Let's be real here, detectives. Everything you have is circumstantial.' He looked at Thompson, 'Or made up and irrelevant. There are explanations for it all. Either charge my client or let her go.'

Detective Johnson looked at her with sympathy, but Thompson seemed pleased. He rose, smoothing out the creases in his suit. 'You're free to go for now,' he said. 'But I wouldn't plan any trips abroad if I were you. You'll be back soon enough.'

His words echoed in the room as the two cops exited, leaving Beth and her solicitor alone. Beth sat there, the reality of her situation sinking in, a hollow feeling in her gut.

To them, she was a killer.

Chapter Eighty-Seven

BETH

Beth could taste fear on her tongue as she stepped out of the police station. The world outside was just as unwelcoming, and the allure of a nearby pub tugged at her, just one drink to calm her nerves.

She veered towards it, craving for an escape with each throbbing heartbeat. But a hand on her elbow stalled her. 'Is that really wise?' Her solicitor's voice was low and stern.

He had a point, Beth begrudgingly admitted to herself. As much as she yearned for the numbing embrace of alcohol, the last thing she needed was to give the police another reason to doubt her innocence.

Mr Carter offered to drive her home and Beth took up the offer, sliding into the passenger seat of his sleek black car. The ride was silent, the humming engine a stark contrast to the storm of thoughts in Beth's head.

'Did Joe spend all your savings?' Carter asked, staring at the road ahead.

She frowned. 'No. I mean, I noticed he'd been moving

money back and forth over the last few months, but nothing is missing. The cops are just trying to give me a motive.'

Carter nodded. 'Okay.' And he left the topic alone.

Arriving home felt surreal, Beth pushed her way through the cluster of journalists standing outside and locked the door behind her. In the living room, the photo of her and Joe at their engagement party stared back at her from the mantelpiece and Beth felt herself crumble. She fell to her knees, sobs tearing through her as the cruel reminder of the future she'd lost overwhelmed her.

Janis stepped into the room, startling Beth. Her mother's face was drawn, worry etching lines on her forehead. 'You need to rest,' Janis said. 'Have those arseholes outside left yet. I threatened them with the police if they didn't leave.' She guided Beth to the couch.

Beth, dazed, allowed herself to be ushered. 'Why are you still here?' Was her mother determined to finish the job someone else had screwed up?

'You left your front door open, and I thought I'd just wait for you to get back – I wasn't sure if you had your keys, and after everything you've been through...' Janis put a tentative hand on Beth's leg. 'I'm so sorry about Joe. Plus, and I'm embarrassed to say this, but I have no money. I'd never be able to walk back into town.' Janis coughed as if she needed to prove a point.

Beth squirmed at her mother's touch. A gnawing suspicion told her that Janis's sudden attentiveness wasn't just about maternal concern. She remembered Janis's cold silences, the years of indifference too vividly to be convinced otherwise.

'Has Kay called?' Beth looked around for the hands-free landline. Although they had their ups and downs, she couldn't deny that Kay was like the mother she'd never had and she would want to know about Joe.

Janis hesitated for a moment, then shook her head. 'No calls.'

Beth eyed her mother. The hesitation, the averted gaze – something wasn't right. But she was too exhausted to confront her mother right then. 'I need to be alone. I want you out of my house.' She pulled out her mobile. 'What are your bank details, I'll transfer some money to you, but after this no more.'

Janis gave her a curt nod before giving Beth her account number and heading out. Beth made a mental note to have the locks changed in the morning.

The second the door closed behind Janis, she reached for her mobile and called her aunt. Kay picked up on the third ring. Her voice was full of sorrow at the news of Joe's death.

'I've been trying to get a hold of you all night,' Kay said then. 'That woman – your bloody mother – wouldn't tell me anything and I was sick with worry. When I said I wanted to come down, she raised an almighty stink so I just gave up. There was no way I was going to put up with her... She's only contacting you because your father said he'd leave her some money if you reconciled. How did she know your address?'

'She said you gave it to her.'

'Absolutely not!'

Janis had been lying. Not only had Kay been calling repeatedly, but she'd also been kept away.

Money. It was always about money with that woman. And it wasn't just Beth her mother had been manipulating. According to Kay, Janis had been harassing Joe before his death. Beth recalled a conversation when she was in the hospital, when Janis made it seem like Joe had been conspiring with her behind Beth's back.

'Did she tell you how she was threatening him?' said Kay. 'Harassing Joe for months about getting you to reconcile with her or she would expose him. The nerve. What could she possibly expose poor Joe for?'

Beth couldn't hear any more and ended the call, her mind whirling. Anger surged, red-hot and blinding. For too long, she'd let her mother's behaviour slide. But not anymore. Janis was in for a confrontation she wouldn't forget.

Beth was going to demand answers, and this time, her mother had nowhere to run.

Chapter Eighty-Eight

BETH

The pub's neon sign flickered enticingly through Beth's living room window. The comforting numbness of alcohol promising to blur the sharp edges of reality.

I can't.

She resisted and tightly clenched her phone instead. Beth had never considered herself naive, but Kay's revelation about her mother felt like a sucker punch. The sudden concern for her wellbeing, it was all about Pops's will, that was all Janis was after. Always the money. And Beth had nearly fallen for her false promises.

Beth rang Janis.

'I'm so glad you called.' Her mother's voice was sickly-sweet. Fake.

'Stay out of my life. Don't ever contact me again or I'm going to call the police.' Beth's voice was flat as she spoke through clenched teeth.

Janis's caring facade dropped as quickly as it had come.

'You ungrateful bitch!' she hissed. 'After everything I've done for you!'

'What you've done for me? You mean lie to me? Manipulate me?' Beth shot back. 'I know about the will. I know what you're really after. You're always hiding behind your lies – you wouldn't know the truth if it hit you in the face.'

Her mother's mask crumbled, revealing the woman Beth remembered from her childhood. The woman who was never there, unless it served her interests. 'You don't know anything!' Janis spat out. Then, as if the revelation of her greed wasn't enough, she twisted the knife deeper. Her laughter was bitter, venomous. 'You want honesty? How about this? Your precious Joe was a cheater – and he was stealing money from your joint account. How's that for honesty?'

Beth recoiled as if she'd been slapped. Janis was just trying to get under her skin. She had to be the one behind the hang-up calls and the letters. It was too much of a coincidence, she knew too much. But then, a chilling realisation dawned upon Beth. This could be why the police suspected her. Why had they asked her about Joe's finances when she was last at the station. Janis has been setting her up all along.

Beth was pulled out of her thoughts when the shouting began.

'I need help! My daughter's lost her mind!' Janis screamed down the line.

'Who are you talking to? What the hell are you playing at?' But instead of answering her, the line went dead.

Beth dialled her solicitor's number with shaking fingers. As she waited for Mr Carter to pick up, her mind whirled. She felt like she was moving backwards, back into that dark place she had fought so hard to get out of. When he finally answered, Beth filled him in, her words tumbling out in a rush.

'I need to know what to do.' Her voice caught on a sob. 'I think my mother is behind all of this and now she is setting me up again.' Beth walked towards the front window, but her foot caught on the rug, sending her tumbling to the floor. Pain exploded in her skull as she hit the hard wooden floor.

Everything went black.

When Beth came to, she found herself staring into the concerned eyes of a man.

'Looks like you had a bit of a fall.' He held out his hand and helped her up.

Beth glanced around, expecting to see her mother there but she was nowhere in sight.

'How did you get into my house?' She rubbed her aching head.

'My name is PC Bradshaw.' He pulled out his ID. 'I was one of the officers who responded when you were attacked. We received a call from someone saying you're in a bad way and might harm yourself? Your fiancé's recently died, is that right? We're just doing a safe-and-well check. Your door was open. Is everything all right?'

The officer's face looked familiar. If his beard had been trimmed and his hair a little shorter, he could be Joe's brother. Beth stopped herself from reaching out and touching his face.

Her heart dropped. This had her mother written all over it.

A woman popped her head round the living room door. 'Nothing looks out of place,' she said.

'Do you remember my colleague? PC Harper.' He nodded towards to the doorway.

Beth had a vague recollection of the woman but wanted them gone. She was sure PC Harper had attended when the neighbours had called the police, but she didn't have the brain space to deal with all those fuzzy memories again.

'Everything's fine.' She tried to keep her voice steady.

PC Bradshaw didn't look convinced. 'Well, in case you change your mind.' He handed her his card. 'We're here to help, Ms Stanford, and we're sorry for your loss.' He looked over at the engagement picture.

He gave her a final, appraising look, before turning to leave. Beth watched them go, a sick feeling in her stomach. Just when she thought things couldn't get worse, her so-called-mother had found a way to drag her deeper into the mess.

As the door closed behind the detective, Beth glanced down at the card PC Bradshaw had given her. There, scribbled on the back, were five words that made her blood run cold:

Be careful who you trust.

Chapter Eighty-Nine

BETH

Beth watched through the window as the two officers climbed into their car and PC Bradshaw pulled away, his colleague staring back at her. The five words scribbled on the back of his card echoing in her head.

As she turned, her eyes swept over her living room, the quiet a chilling reminder of the night's events. An image of her mother's snarling face made her flinch, but she welcomed the sting. It was a tie severed; a toxic presence forever removed from her life.

Her mobile phone buzzed on the coffee table, breaking the silence. Alison's name flashed up on the small screen. Beth hesitated, her thumb hovering over the decline button. They hadn't spoken for a while, but something inside her shifted when she answered. And she could really do with a friend.'

'How are you?' said Alison.

'I'm exhausted.' Beth shut her eyes. 'Joe's dead, Alison.'

'What?' Alison's shock seemed palpable. 'Oh, my God,

Beth. I can't… Poor Joe. Poor you.' Beth heard the sob in Alison's voice.

'I'm sorry,' said Beth, though her voice came out as a monotone. 'I know you two were close colleagues.'

'Yes, it's heartbreaking,' said Alison quietly. 'But you were his fiancée. I'm so sorry, Beth.'

'Thank you.' Beth swallowed. Look, I'm going to get to bed now, but there are things I should catch you up on in person.' She paused. 'I have an appointment at the hospital tomorrow afternoon.'

Alison interrupted. 'I have to work first thing, but why don't I pick you up at the hospital when you're done. We can talk then.'

'Okay, I'll see you tomorrow.'

After ending the call with Alison, Beth couldn't face sleeping in the bed she and Joe had shared, so she grabbed a blanket from the cupboard and curled up on the couch. She thought she would struggle to sleep but her lids were heavy and before she knew it, she was out for the count.

A loud bang woke her, and Beth sat up, her heart fluttered with multiple palpitations. She looked around the room, her eyes slowly adjusting to the darkness when a second bang made her jump. A flash of lightening lit up the sky outside. A storm was gathering.

Her mobile was on the floor and the time said 4am. She got up and stretched her legs. Coffee was what she needed, and she suddenly had an urge for a cigarette. She hadn't smoked since she was a teenager and wondered if all the stress was dragging her back in time. A former addiction was now rearing its head.

After a quick shower, she dressed and made herself a coffee before returning to the living room, placing her coffee on the side table. She bent over and picked her phone up off the floor. It needed a charge before she went out later today.

She turned on the television and when a picture of Joe, lying in his hospital bed, flashed up on the screen she gasped. The news was suggesting that Beth knew more than she was sharing with the police, and she quickly changed channels to *The Big Bang Theory*. She'd seen it so many times she could have it on in the background as white noise.

She must have dozed off at some point because when she next looked at her phone, it was 11.30am – she needed to be at the hospital for 1pm.

Shit.

Beth looked around for her power pack and popped it into her handbag before rushing out to catch the bus.

Forty minutes later, she found herself at the hospital with a bit of time to spare before her check-up. Her throat, though not entirely healed, was definitely feeling better. But every now and again, there was a raw ache, a grim reminder of her ordeal. Speaking was bearable, unless she strained her voice or screamed.

The consultant inspected her wounds and assured her that she was healing well.

'Just remember not to strain your voice. If it becomes too sore or you find it difficult to speak, listen to your body and rest it, okay?' The consultant's head tilted to the left.

Beth nodded. 'Will it ever go back to the way it was?'

'I can't say for definite, but you've recovered remarkably well so there's no reason that shouldn't continue, and you'll find it easier over time. If there are any changes, and you're concerned, book an appointment.' He got up, said something to the nurse and left.

Beth picked up her bag and sent Alison a text telling her she'd wait out front. Her hands were clammy, and she wiped them on her jacket. When Alison pulled up outside the hospital entrance, Beth got in and thanked her for the lift.

'I wondered – and feel free to say no – but my son is with his grandparents, do you want to come around? We can just have a chilled evening; I can drop you back when you want, or you can stay over. My ex has been at it again and I really don't want to be alone.'

'Sure.' Beth wasn't too keen on being alone at the minute, herself. 'Might be wiser to go to mine, though, in case he comes round to your door.'

'That works.'

The ride back home was filled with comfortable silence, punctuated by Alison's attempts at small talk. Beth could see the strain in her friend's eyes, the tension in her jaw. Joe's death and whatever was happening between her, and her husband was clearly taking a toll. They ordered takeaway curry, and when it arrived, the aroma of garlic and spices filled the kitchen.

As they were about to settle down for a movie, Alison's phone rang. Beth watched as Alison's facial expressions changed – her brows furrowed, her mouth opened wide.

'Yes ... I'll be there.' She ended the call. 'That was the police.'

'The police?' Beth sat up straight. 'What do the police want with you?'

Alison shook her head. 'They want me to come in and explain why I was here, at your home, at the time of the attack.' She let out a nervous laugh. 'Someone's got it very wrong.'

Beth stared at her. 'That's ridiculous,' she said. 'I'd never met you in person before I saw you at the hospital... And it was a man, not a woman, who was here. I'm sure of it.' Beth felt panicked, though, unsure of her memories.

The scratch of a beard, the gruff voice... It couldn't have been Alison.

Beth was more sure than ever that both she and Alison were being set-up. Alison had nothing to do with the attack.

Her mother. It had to be. The sudden reappearance, her interest in the inheritance from Pops's will... Janis must have hired someone to carry out the attack, and she was feeding the police lies to keep them off her back.

Beth shared these suspicions with Alison, her voice a thin whisper.

Alison was silent for a moment before letting out a shaky breath. 'A few weeks ago, I might have worried that you were putting two and two together and getting five, but now I think you might be onto something. We're definitely being set up. Christ, what are we going to do? I need a drink; do you want one?'

Beth was dying for a drink but declined. 'Probably not a good idea.'

'Shit. That was really dumb of me. Do you mind if I make some coffee, then? Best if I go to the station now and clear this all up.'

As Alison went to the kitchen, Beth's phone pinged. UNKNOWN NUMBER. Opening it, her blood ran cold. The message contained only four chilling words.

Watch your back, Beth.

Chapter Ninety

BETH

Alison wasn't long at the police station long before she popped back to Beth's.

'You didn't tell them about our theory, did you? They probably think we're crazy.' Beth closed the door behind Alison.

'Do you mind if I just wash up?' Alison held up her hands.

'Sure, you know where to go.'

Beth turned to head to the living room when there was a knock on the door. Her eyes widened when she saw who was in front of her. 'PC Bradshaw. What are you doing here?'

'I'm sorry to disturb you, Ms Stanford, but we need you to come down to the station. We've made an arrest in the case involving your fiancé.'

Beth felt her heart skip a beat. 'Wait, what? Why are you telling me this? Where's Detective Johnson? I'd better call him.' Beth didn't trust the officer, he was looking around and his partner wasn't with him. Something felt off.

'He sent me here. Said you needed to come right away.'

'Who has been arrested?'

PC Bradshaw looked at her, his expression unreadable. 'Janis Stanford. We've arrested your mother for Joe's murder.'

Beth was in a state of disbelief, the reality of officer Bradshaw's words refusing to settle in her mind. 'You've arrested my mother?'

PC Bradshaw's gaze was steely. 'I shouldn't be saying this...' He leaned in closer. 'But we found evidence at her residence that ties her to the attack on you and Joe. It's best you come to the station.'

'Hang on a moment, I just—' Beth turned to let Alison know where she was going only to see Alison, her face pale and her arms crossed defensively across her chest, step into the hallway.

'What the hell are you doing here?'

Beth turned back and noticed PC Bradshaw's composure slip for a moment, his gaze flicking to Alison with a spark of anger. 'This is official business, nothing to do with you,' he snarled. There was a grit to his voice, a raw edge of emotion that gave Beth an uncomfortable feeling.

'How do you two know each other?' Beth looked between the pair, her confusion deepening.

Alison's gaze met hers, a flicker of trepidation in her eyes. 'He's my ex. Pete. The one I've been telling you about.'

Beth's stomach turned. This was a nightmare. She could see the tension in Bradshaw's face, the tight lines of his mouth.

'Where's our son?' Alison demanded, her voice rising in

pitch. 'And since when do you deal with murder cases? You're a field officer.'

Bradshaw's face hardened. 'I was called in to help,' he shot back, the words laced with venom. 'And Nicky is with my parents.'

'You have no right to just leave him when you are supposed to be spending time with him.'

'I have every right. I'm his father!'

The argument escalated, their voices bouncing off the walls. Beth could hardly process what was happening. Finally, she'd had enough. 'You'd better leave, PC Bradshaw,' she said firmly, 'or I'll call Detective Johnson and find out what is really going on here.'

Bradshaw shot her one last furious glare before he stormed off. Beth closed the door behind him, her hands trembling. If there had been an arrest, DC Johnson would have come around himself to tell her, she was sure of it.

Alison was still standing there, her arms wrapped protectively around herself.

Beth turned to her. 'Tell me what's going on. Tell me about him.'

Alison drew in a shaky breath, her gaze distant. She spoke of her husband's controlling nature, his obsession with knowing her every move. She told Beth about the harassing hang-up calls she'd been getting, how he had been watching her for months.

The story mirrored Beth's own. 'Why haven't you reported him?'

Alison's tone was a scoff when she answered. 'He's one of them. A cop. Who would believe me?'

Beth felt a chill run down her spine. A memory clicked into

place. Bradshaw was one of the officers involved in the Brewer case she had worked on at the law firm – she recognised the name now. And he'd said he was one of the first responders when she and Joe had been attacked. The pieces fell into place with a sickening clarity.

Beth and Alison locked eyes, a mutual understanding passing between them.

'I feel sick.' Alison raced to the downstairs loo.

As Beth reached for the landline, intending to call the police, the power suddenly cut out, plunging the house into darkness.

The real monster might not be Beth's mother, but Alison's ex, and he was the police.

Who could they trust?

Chapter Ninety-One

BETH

Beth's heart hammered in her chest like a wild thing, adrenaline flooding her veins.

'Alison? Where are you?'

A shadow came from the direction of the kitchen. 'Here.'

Beth gestured to Alison, her voice a low hiss. 'Check if the back door is locked. I'll get the front.'

Together, they moved through the house, once the doors were secured, they hurried upstairs and barricaded themselves in the master bedroom. The air felt heavy.

Beth's ears strained for any sounds from downstairs. Suddenly, a crash echoed through the house, a cascade of shattered glass. Beth felt a cold rush of terror. Alison's hand bumped her arm. 'Call the police.'

Beth's hand went instinctively to her back pocket only to find it empty. Her mobile was still downstairs. But Alison was already fishing hers out, the screen's faint glow illuminating her wide, fearful eyes. The battery was dangerously low, the battery icon showing only a single bar. With shaky hands, Alison punched in 999.

The operator picked up. 'Emergency services, what is your emergency?'

Alison quickly handed the phone to Beth.

Beth's words tumbled out in a rushed croak. 'My house ... broken into... PC Pete Bradshaw ... after Alison...' Each word was a struggle, her throat dry and constricted. She took a deep breath to steady herself and continued, but her words were cut off as the sound of creaking stairs echoed from the hallway. Beth pointed to the built-in wardrobe, urging Alison to hide.

'Hello?' The operator's voice buzzed in her ear, grounding her.

She raised her voice, hoping it carried through the house. 'PC Bradshaw! You should know I'm on the phone with the police right now.'

The call operator was saying something else, her words lost in the thundering beat of Beth's heart. The bedroom door handle twisted violently.

'He's coming in here! Please, you need to tell them to hurry!' Beth yelled into the phone.

Suddenly, the room was bathed in the bright white light of a flashlight. Beth squinted against it, her heart in her throat.

It wasn't Bradshaw. It was her neighbour, concern etched on his face.

'Beth? Is that you? I saw all the lights go off in your house, then heard glass breaking ... so I thought I'd better check on you. I used the spare key Joe gave us a few months ago.'

Relief washed over Beth like a cold shower and Alison emerged, shakily, from the closet, her face was ashen.

'Thanks, Bob. Sorry... This has all been a big

misunderstanding.' Beth ushered the neighbour out, assuring him they were fine.

Moments later, the wailing sirens filled the air. The police officers listened to Beth's hurried explanation of what had happened with PC Bradshaw, the power cut and her mother's arrest. Their expressions unreadable. Beth watched as one of them stepped away to speak into his radio. He came back with a strange look on his face.

'Ms Stanford, your mother hasn't been arrested,' His tone was careful. 'And PC Bradshaw is off duty this weekend.'

Beth looked at Alison, her mind racing. Alison gave a slight shake of her head, her eyes wide with a silent plea. Beth kept what she knew to herself. This was bigger than both of them and Beth wondered which, if any, of the police attending were in on it. Protecting one of their own. She clamped her mouth shut.

The officer did a quick sweep of the house and helped to secure the broken window. 'Get it fixed as soon as you can,' he advised. 'Likely a burglar taking advantage. Been a recent spate of incidents in the area.'

When the police had left, Beth and Alison exchanged a look. They were both certain of one thing: Pete was somehow involved.

'How did Joe and I get wrapped up in your domestic situation, Alison?' The question hanging heavy in the air. She didn't have the answer, and neither did Alison. But one thing was clear – they were far from safe.

Chapter Ninety-Two

BETH

The morning light spilled through the cracks of the covered broken window, casting jagged shadows on the kitchen floor. Lines of exhaustion were etched deep on Beth's and Alison's faces, making them look like weary soldiers on a battlefield. The scent of coffee hung heavy in the room, a feeble comfort amidst the turmoil.

'Look at us,' Beth croaked, her voice still raw. 'We look like the walking dead.'

As she poured them both a mug of coffee, Alison's gaze was intent on her, unwavering and steadfast.

'We need a plan.' Alison's voice was low. 'We need to convince the police that Pete's behind this.'

They huddled over the kitchen table, their faces drawn in contemplation. Over the rim of her mug, Alison's eyes glistened.

Beth stared at the dark liquid, swirling, just like her thoughts. 'But how?'

'In my line of work, I often use hypnosis to uncover

repressed memories,' Alison suggested, her gaze unwavering. 'Maybe we can unlock something you've forgotten. I didn't think you were ready to go down this avenue before, but maybe you are now.'

Beth hesitated, her heart thudding hard against her ribs. But her desperation for answers was stronger than her fear. 'Do it.'

They moved into the living room, usually a haven of tranquillity, it seemed to bear silent witness to their desperation. As Beth settled onto the couch, the leather soft beneath her, she began to have second thoughts.

Alison squeezed her hand. 'If I think it's becoming too much for you, we'll stop. I promise.'

Alison's voice, soothing and steady, guided Beth deeper into her subconscious, each question peeling away layers of her memory like the petals of a bloom. The images began to surface, fragmented, and disjointed.

Beth saw herself on the phone, her eyes wide with shock.

'It was Joe,' she whispered, her voice shaky. 'He called me right before ... right before...' There was a scent, a cologne. She thought it was *Joop* like Pops wore. She recalled thinking it was strange of Joe to be wearing it.

A wave of horror washed over Beth as the memory of the attack flooded back. She writhed on the couch, her breath coming out in ragged gasps. Alison quickly brought her out of the hypnotic state, her voice cutting through the fog of Beth's memories. Beth awoke, shaking and sweating, the bitter taste of fear still lingering on her tongue.

'I'm sorry.' She shook her head. 'I didn't see who did it, only that Joe was on the phone as I was attacked. It couldn't have been him. Plus, that smell.' She rubbed her nose.

Beth's breath hitched, her body trembled, and silent tears streamed down her face.

'What smell?'

'*Joop*. Joe hated it. I bought it for him for our first Christmas together because I thought he'd like it, but it smelled awful on him.' Beth almost smiled at the memory of Joe's scrunched-up nose.

'Jesus.' Alison stood up and started pacing the room. 'I can't believe he went this far.'

'What are you talking about?'

'Pete. He wears that. It has to be him – what with that and everything that happened last night. Joe and Pete look similar, it's now easy for me to see why you've been confused. We need to tell Detective Johnson.'

Beth looked around. 'Have you seen my phone? I'll ring him.'

'They'll just fob us off. We need to go in person, make them listen.'

'I'll get my coat.'

Chapter Ninety-Three

BETH

They drove to the police station, the familiar scenery passing by in a blur of anxiety. 'What if they don't believe us?' Beth turned to look at Alison.

'Detective Johnson, he seems quite understanding... Maybe if we can speak to him alone we'll be able to convince him. After what happened last night, he has to believe us.'

'Why would your ex do this to me and Joe, though?' It didn't make any sense to Beth. 'If it's you he's mad at, what would he gain by hurting us?'

'Haven't you figured it out?'

Beth didn't like the way Alison had said that. Like Beth was stupid or blind. It was the way her mother spoke to her. 'Obviously not. It's why I asked.' Beth crossed her arms, tense.

Alison shot her a quick glance. 'Sorry. I didn't mean for that to come out the way it did. Of course you wouldn't know. Pete was always accusing me of having an affair. I'm sure he was following me, and I mentioned this to Joe once when we were out at lunch. He must have thought I was *with* Joe.'

'Were you?' Beth had to ask because she'd wondered after the letters whether Joe was cheating on her.

'Absolutely not. I've told you. Joe was my boss, a friend and colleague, nothing more. He loved you, Beth. I thought we were past this.'

'Sorry, it's just... Never mind. Why would he attack me, though?'

'I think he was trying to set Joe up, maybe even me... The police took my DNA – they must have found something to make them believe I was there.'

'I don't know. The more we talk about it, the more none of it makes sense and sounds too far-fetched. Maybe we should just tell Detective Johnson about what happened last night and leave them to it.' Beth was beginning to doubt their theory and the last thing she wanted was the police to go on a wild goose chase and waste their time.

Alison pulled into a parking space just outside the station. 'I need to know you will back me if I tell them. If we're wrong, I will take the brunt of any flack that comes our way.'

Beth realised she had asked so much of Alison that to turn her back on her now wouldn't be fair. 'Okay,' she said. 'I'll have your back.'

They waited in reception while the woman at the enquiries desk called Detective Johnson. 'He'll be down in five. Take a seat,' she told them.

They both stood instead. Beth staring out of the window at the town centre, watching people go about their daily business, while Alison paced the small area.

'Ladies. Would you like to come through?'

Beth groaned when she realised it was Detective Thompson who had called their names.

'Detective Johnson will be with us in a moment. Follow me.' He led them into a casual interview room. 'Coffee? Water?'

'No, thanks,' they both whispered. Beth looked at Alison and she shrugged in response. Detective Johnson walked into the room.

'Sorry about that. We understand you have some more information?'

As Beth and Alison shared their theory and evidence about Pete Bradshaw, the revelation was unsurprisingly met with scepticism by Thompson.

DC Johnson, who had always shown Beth a modicum of empathy, attempted to appease them. 'We'll look into it, ladies,' he assured them, his tone softer than his stern exterior suggested.

On the other hand, Thompson, his smirk more biting than his sarcastic words, scoffed at their claim. 'How convenient, blame the ex, who also happens to be a police officer. Any reason why you hate us so much?' His scorn was palpable.

Beth ignored him. She refused to lower herself to his level and knew he'd only turn anything she said around and use it against her.

As they were led down the corridor to the exit, a figure in uniform caught Beth's eye. Pete Bradshaw. Consumed by anger, she screamed at him, her accusation echoing through the station. 'You're a murderer! And you won't get away with it!'

Bradshaw turned, his eyes meeting Beth's. A sly grin played on his lips, his audacity chilling her to the bone. And then, the world spun around her. The floor rushed up to meet her, and then darkness.

When Beth awoke, she was in the hospital and her head pounded.

As she lay there, her mind raced with possible plans. She and Alison had to find a way to catch Bradshaw, to end this nightmare once and for all.

We'll stop him, no matter what it takes. I promise, Joe...

Chapter Ninety-Four

BETH

Beth was held overnight for observation and was surprised to see Detective Johnson in the chair next to her bed when she woke up.

'What are you doing here?' Her throat was dry, and she looked around for something to soothe it.

Johnson stood and poured her some water. 'Here.' He handed her the cup. 'Your reaction to seeing PC Bradshaw at the station yesterday made me think about what you told us.' He scratched his head. 'Who actually came up with the idea that Bradshaw attacked you and Joe?'

'It was me ... I think... I don't know.' Beth wasn't sure who had put the pieces together. 'What does it matter? Are you here because you believe me?' Under the harsh white glare of the hospital lighting, she felt exposed.

'I need to be honest with you before we proceed.'

Beth sat up in the bed.

'I'm here in my own time. Unofficially.' He pulled the chair closer. The metal legs screeched against the linoleum flooring, echoing in the otherwise quiet room. 'I want to believe you, but can you see why we are finding it difficult?'

Beth could understand Johnson's scepticism. The similarities between Bradshaw's behaviour towards Alison and what Beth was experiencing: the hang-up calls, the feeling of being watched, odd things that seemed to align between both of their lives but that could also be coincidental?

Beth told Johnson that everything pointed to a deep-seated malice PC Bradshaw harboured and he was using his experience as a police officer to avoid detection. He must have seen Joe as a threat and she'd just got in the way.

Detective Johnson listened, nodding periodically, his expression revealing nothing.

'Look, I'll take on board what you've said, but no guarantees. It will all have to be matched against what we have and referred to the CPS, they decide whether there is enough evidence to charge and convict. Not us.'

'What evidence do you even have?' Beth challenged, her voice wavering slightly. 'If it were substantial, wouldn't someone have been arrested and charged by now?'

Johnson sighed, rubbing his temples. 'I can't disclose any specifics,' he confessed. 'But I believe an arrest *is* imminent. Just. Be careful. You can't trust everyone.' Detective Johnson stood. 'I hope you're feeling better soon, and promise me you're not going to do anything foolish, okay? Let us do our job.'

Beth smiled but committed to nothing as the detective left. His words of warning stuck in her head. There was nobody to trust, but she needed someone.

Later that day, Beth was discharged and Alison was waiting to take her home.

'I hope you don't mind, but I got your window fixed and installed one of those doorbell camera thingies. You can see who's there, without having to open the door.'

Beth felt a swell of gratitude. Alison was being a good friend and Beth could now see what Joe had seen. 'I really appreciate that.'

She told Alison about Detective Johnson's visit.

'Do you think you can believe him? Maybe he was just fishing to see what we actually do know. I think we're onto something and the police are not going to want any bad press. They'll do whatever they can to suppress information and protect their own.'

'I didn't get that feeling from him,' said Beth. 'Besides, my outburst at the station means everyone there knows what I'm thinking.'

'I guess so.' Alison pulled into Beth's drive.

'Do you want to come in?'

'I can't. I have to pick up Nicky. You don't have to stay here you know. There's always a room for you at my house.'

Beth shook her head, declining the offer. 'My aunt texted to say she'll be coming round, so I'd best be here. She'll be mad if I cancel.' Beth got out of the car and waved as Alison reversed out of the drive.

Beth and Kay's relationship had been strained since Pops's death, and everything that had followed since. She wondered if it would just be better to smooth things out – Kay was the only family she had left that mattered to her.

Right on time, there was a knock on the door and Beth used the new security cam that Alison had installed to confirm who it was. She could see Kay looking around, fixing her coat, and peering through the window.

She opened the door and stepped aside. 'Come in. I've put the kettle on.' She returned to the kitchen and poured the hot drinks. 'Let's go through to the living room.' Kay followed and they sat opposite each other. Kay in the chair, Beth on the couch, gripping their drinks as if their life depended on it.

The reunion was a mix of awkward silences and apologies. Beth apologised for her recent behaviour and Kay admitted she could have been around more when her niece needed her.

'You kept pushing everyone away, and well... I was just reminded of—'

'I know. Let's not keep dwelling on things, okay. We'll only go round in circles. I just want you to know and believe that Joe's death had nothing to do with me. Despite our troubles, I would never hurt him. I love ... loved … him.'

'I never doubted you. Just promise me you'll keep your mother at a distance,'

Beth told Kay about the recent events concerning her mother and her own suspicions that Janis could've had something to do with the attack, though now she wasn't sure at all. 'I made it crystal clear that I want nothing to do with her. I even gave her some money and told her that if I ever see her again, I'll take her to court for harassment and extortion. The only thing that woman responds to is threats.'

Kay's brow furrowed at the suggestion. 'That's opening a Pandora's Box.' Kay sipped her coffee. 'She'll just want more.'

The sound of a knock on the door cut through their conversation. Beth checked the doorbell app, but the screen was black. Whoever was at the door was covering the camera.

'Stay here.' Beth stood and handed Kay the landline

handset. 'Be ready to call the police.' Beth put the chain on the door before she pulled it open.

Standing on the threshold, her icy gaze piercing through the dim light, was Janis. And it was evident she wasn't there for a family reunion.

Chapter Ninety-Five

BETH

The stench of alcohol clung to Janis Stanford. Her eyes, bloodshot and dark-rimmed, glared at Beth with an unsettling intensity.

'Should've known you'd show up drunk.' Beth didn't move. There was no way she was letting her mother walk all over her again.

Her mother's slurred words came out like poison, each one dripping with resentment and bitterness. 'It's your fault,' she spat. 'You think you're better than everyone else. Living in your nice house. Money coming out of your wazoo while the rest of us struggle. Your father did a shit job at raising you. Such an entitled brat. If it wasn't for you, we'd have stayed together, been happy, he would never have died.' Her words, though slurred and venomous, bit into Beth, causing her hands to tremble.

'If I'd known you'd blow the money on booze, I wouldn't have given it to you,' Beth said. 'Pops left you exactly because of this. Have you looked at yourself in the mirror lately? You're a drunk, abusive narcissist. You don't know the meaning of love, and only care about yourself, Mother dearest.'

'Oh, yeah? And what about you? All those fights when you were younger? Kevin told me about everything. He was ashamed of you, all the drink and drugs. I know all about you, missus. Bet the police would like to know, too. You probably offed Joe for the insurance, to add to your inheritance from your dad. You don't deserve any of it.'

This was a threat to expose Beth's past, to convince the police she'd set up everything to inherit Joe's money on top of her father's. Fury surged within Beth, and she lashed out, the slap landing hard on her mother's cheek.

'Lisbeth!' Kay's voice cut through the tension. 'Enough. I'm calling the police.'

But as she moved to do so, Janis waved her off with a dismissive hand, her words slurred and threatening. 'Don't bother. I'll just share this latest assault with the police myself. Let them decide what to do. You may be called as a witness, Kay.'

She turned and walked unsteadily down the path, and Beth watched her stumble into the road.

'Stop being a bitch and be a mother for once in your life!' she shouted after Janis.

Her mother paused, swaying slightly as she turned back towards her. As she opened her mouth to retort, a dark-coloured car roared into view, its headlights momentarily illuminating her mother's shocked face before it careered into her and struck her down.

Time seemed to slow as Beth stood, frozen in horror, the sound of the car hitting her mother echoing inside her head. Inside, Kay's frantic voice on the phone to emergency services snapped her back into reality and she raced down the path. The car was long gone, leaving nothing but a chilling silence in its wake, and her mother was lying on the pavement, her body twisted at an odd angle. Blood was pooling around Janis's head; her eyes were cloudy and distant.

Beth fell to her knees beside her mother, her hands hovering over her body, her mind screaming not to move her. Her mother's breathing was laboured, shallow, and Beth watched as Janis tried to speak, the words garbled and swallowed up by a gurgling choke. Then, as if a light had been switched off, her mother's eyes rolled back, and her body went limp.

Time seemed to slow down; every detail amplified. Beth could hear Kay still on the phone, her voice faltering as she relayed their location to the call handler.

Minutes later, the piercing sound of sirens filled the night. As the paramedics scrambled out of the ambulance, Beth could only watch them work in a state of numb shock, her ears ringing. But her mother was dead. The paramedics ceased their attempts, and a heavy silence fell over the scene. Beth felt her heart drop, the reality of the situation crashing down on her. Her mother, despite everything, was gone.

And the secrets she held had died with her.

Chapter Ninety-Six

BETH

The flashing blue lights painted an eerie glow against the facade of Beth's home. An unwanted spotlight illuminating the tragic scene. She could hear the police officers questioning the gathered onlookers, their voices floating towards her on the chilled night air.

Beth was aware of the officer approaching her and what his questions would be.

'We need you to recount what happened, Ms Stanford,' the officer began. 'Anything you can remember about the car, or the driver.'

Beth shook her head, frustration bubbling within her. 'It was too dark, the car was small, I think. And it might have been black or navy. It all happened so quickly. I didn't see the driver.' She stumbled through her answers, carefully leaving out the heated exchange that had taken place in the moments before her mother's death.

How many more people are going to die?

'My mother said she knew something about my attack, and about Joe.' Beth's voice was barely a whisper, the words tangled in her throat. 'She knew something. You have to find out what it was. Someone wanted to kill her.'

Beth was certain that her mother's death was no accident. Had someone followed her mother. Killed her to silence her? What did she know?

The officer gave Beth a sympathetic glance. 'What makes you think that?'

Kay interjected, her voice firm. 'That's enough. Can't you see she's in shock?'

Seeing the officer off with a glare, Kay ushered Beth inside the house. The door closed behind them, effectively sealing off the outside chaos. Beth looked down at her hands, stained with her mother's blood. The sight sent a jolt of nausea through her stomach.

Kay fetched a bowl of warm water and a cloth from the downstairs bathroom, gently wiping away the blood. 'Do you have any sleeping pills?' she asked, her concern evident.

Beth shook her head, the memory of her past struggles with addiction still fresh. 'I don't want any.' Her last binge is what had got her into this mess in the first place.

'I'll make you a cup of tea, and then you need to get some sleep. We can talk about this in the morning.' Kay led Beth into the living room and sat her down.

Beth's mind was unwilling to shut down, but Kay was persistent, making her cups of tea, coaxing her to at least try to rest. As Beth lay on the couch, Kay's soothing voice offered a momentary distraction.

Beth allowed sleep to claim her. But her dreams were

troubled, haunted by the faces of those she had lost. Her father's gentle smile, Joe's loving eyes, and now her mother's hard, accusing stare.

Who would be next?

Chapter Ninety-Seven

BETH

Two weeks had passed since the death of Beth's mother, and she still felt nothing. The funeral arrangements were a blur of signatures and papers, each one a stark reminder of a relationship that could never be repaired. She had no desire to attend the ceremony itself. That chapter of her life was closed, sealed away and soon to be forgotten.

The police did little to alleviate Beth's concerns. Even as they updated her on the hunt for the hit-and-run driver, she felt a strange disconnection from it all.

The police assured her they'd keep looking for the driver and keep her posted, but something told her this was just going to end up another cold case on their pile.

She gathered her coat to meet Alison in town.

They sat in a cosy café, the comforting aroma of fresh coffee intermingling with the delicate scent of freshly baked scones.

Over steaming mugs of coffee, they chatted in hushed voices, needing to get back on track. Joe's killer was still out there.

'Pete's been keeping a low profile.' Alison's voice was tinged with worry. 'He hasn't even kept up with his supervised visits with Nicky, and...' a tremor shook her hands, 'I found a dead bird on my doorstep. The door camera wasn't working, my internet was off.'

Beth's heart skipped a beat. The mention of Pete Bradshaw, the man who lately seemed to weave a web of terror around her life, sent a jolt of fear through her.

'A dead bird at your front door, Alison? Sounds like a warning. It could be him.'

'I don't know. It's definitely something he'd do, but without evidence...' Alison trailed off.

The two women spent the next hour formulating a plan, a desperate gambit to lure Bradshaw into a confession. Neither questioning the other's belief. Everything that had happened couldn't be a coincidence.

'I could get him to come around. Maybe tell him I want to work on things, give us another go. That's what he wants, to get back into my life so he can control me.'

Beth wasn't too keen on Alison being used as bait, but they didn't seem to have any other options.

'What if he was the one who killed your mother?' Alison threw the new accusation on the table. 'He could have rented a car or stolen one.'

Beth sighed. 'I think we need to be careful we're not seeing murder in everything that happens to us. The police are sure it was a hit and run and if it wasn't, that would mean someone has been following my mother. Let's not go all *X Files* with the conspiracy theories. The police think we're crazy enough without adding fuel to that flame.'

'You're right,' said Alison. 'Let's get back to what we can control...'

———

The plan was risky, but the need for answers drove them forward. They agreed on a pact, an unspoken vow, and Beth's adrenaline drowning out the voice of reason which was begging her to let the police do their job.

That evening, back at Beth's with the bushes rustling in the wind as if whispering secrets, Alison made the call. She left it on speaker and as the phone rang, Beth thought she heard Joe's voice whispering for her to just 'leave things be.'

'Hello?' Pete Bradshaw's voice was as cold as ice, causing a chill to spread through the room.

'It's me.' Alison held the phone out. 'We need to talk.'

A pause, then a soft, menacing chuckle. 'About what? All these stupid accusations you and your sidekick are making? Is she there? Beth ... who else are you planning to kill?'

'Don't be ridiculous. I thought you wanted to work things out. Be a family again, but if you just want to keep playing these stupid games,' Alison snapped, her anger breaking through.

The line went dead, the silence a heavy weight that settled over them. Beth and Alison exchanged a look, they had set the wheels in motion, and there was no turning back.

The game was about to begin.

Chapter Ninety-Eight

BETH

After Alison had left, a nagging thought tugged at Beth's mind: should they speak to Detective Johnson first? He'd hinted he already had concerns about PC Bradshaw and might be willing to help them. The question spun in her head, but she quickly dismissed it. The police would only twist things and she was tired of people thinking she had lost the plot. Who knows what Pete would do between now and when the police took her seriously. No, they were doing the right thing.

With a heavy sigh, Beth sank into her favourite armchair, a worn piece of furniture that had cradled her through many storms. Her eyelids felt heavy. She was on the edge of sleep when the shrill ring of the phone jolted her awake. She picked it up to see an unknown number flashing on the screen.

'Hello?' Beth's voice wavered.

'Beth, you've got it all wrong.' The cold, emotionless voice of PC Pete Bradshaw cut through the line like a knife, sending a shiver down her spine.

'What are you talking about?' Beth's voice trembled as confusion and fear danced within her.

'AJ … Alison. She's not who you think she is.' Bradshaw's voice oozed with conviction. 'There are things you don't know, related to Joe's case and connected to you. She's been speaking to Mr Brewer. Why would she be speaking to a man who was accused of nearly killing his wife when Travers House was working with Mrs Brewer? Did you know she was counselling Mrs Brewer, the same way she was counselling you?'

Beth's mind reeled, the room spinning around her as she tried to comprehend what she was hearing. 'No, that can't be.' She shook her head. 'She was right about you. Always needing to be in control, twisting things. You're lying and I'm not falling for it.'

'I wish I were. But think back to your therapy sessions. She didn't disclose that she worked with Joe, did she? She should never have been counselling you.'

'She didn't know who I was. I mean, I used my professional name, I never mentioned Joe by his name... She couldn't ... didn't know.' Beth's voice rose, desperation and disbelief warring within her.

'Oh, she knew. She knew all along.'

The certainty in Bradshaw's words were chilling.

'What? Alison didn't have a motive to kill Joe or try to kill me. Stop deflecting your guilt onto her.' Beth's voice was breaking, she felt dizzy.

'Her motivation is to frame me. She wants me out of her life, and my son's, for good. She's been making up lies and that's why she's manipulating you into getting me arrested. She has something bigger planned, and I need to know what it is. If not for me, for Nicky. He needs stability in his life, to be safe from her twisted mind. You need to tell me everything.'

'Wait. How do you know Alison isn't here? How did you know when to call?' Beth's voice was a whisper.

'That's not important. Please, you need to tell me what you two are planning. Don't let her involve you in this. You're not...'

She didn't hear what he said next. Her head was spinning, her thoughts a tangled mess of confusion and doubt. She glanced at the mug of tea Alison had made for her before she had gone home. A strange taste lingered in her mouth, and a sudden wave of dizziness washed over her.

'I...' Her voice trailed off, the world tilting as darkness closed in.

The phone fell from her trembling hands, the sound of Bradshaw's voice a distant echo as the room spun and everything went dark. The last conscious thought that flitted through Beth's mind were questions. Had she been drugged?

Is Bradshaw right?

Chapter Ninety-Nine

BETH

Beth woke up on the couch with a banging headache, she sat up and glanced at the mug of tea on the table next to her. Getting blearily to her feet, she took it in the kitchen and poured what was left of it down the sink.

She was exhausted. Pete Bradshaw's call had tipped her over the edge. She couldn't be sure who was lying to her. Him or Alison.

When Alison called later, wanting to meet up, Beth bit the bullet and challenged her.

'Did you put something in my tea?' she asked. 'It knocked me out.'

To her surprise, Alison was upfront.

'I crumbled a sleeping pill into it,' she said calmly. 'Your aunt suggested it. She's been worried and called me to check how you are. You've been so wired. I thought having some sleep might help, but I didn't really think it through. I should have told you. I guess I didn't want us to fall out when we're so close to getting justice for Joe.'

It sounded plausible. Caring.

'Yes. You should have told me...' She decided she wasn't going to tell Alison that Pete had called but instead she'd stick to their plan. She needed to find out the truth and this could be her only opportunity. She agreed to meet with Alison.

Pete's previous behaviour showed how manipulative and controlling he was, and Beth wasn't prepared to fall into his trap. They had him now, and soon this nightmare would be over. As a safeguard, Beth sent an email to herself, detailing everything Pete had said and outlining what they were planning to do to get his confession. If anything happened to her, the police would look at her laptop and everything would be uncovered.

When they had first started dating, Joe had once shared some information about one of his clients and explained it had been what kept the man from being sent to prison for fraud. Perhaps Joe was being the voice of reason, still protecting her even though he was no longer at her side. She gave a wry smile at the comforting thought.

The muffled rumble of taxi tyres on wet pavement accompanied Beth's heavy breathing as she headed to Alison's home. She glanced out of the rain-streaked window.

As the taxi pulled up to Alison's house, the yellow glow from her windows promised warmth but not comfort. With a whispered thanks to the driver, Beth paid the fare and stepped out into the chilling rain.

Alison opened the door, her eyes wide. 'He's coming.' Alison's voice was edged with tension. 'I can't believe it, he actually agreed to meet up after his shift. Nicky's with Pete's parents for the night.'

Beth felt the goosebumps form on her arm before she saw them. They quickly discussed where she would hide and how they would record the encounter. The plan was simple, yet fraught with danger.

'If he tries anything, I'll call the police, right away. I'm not having someone else die in front of me.' Beth's voice wavered, the enormity of what they were doing settling in.

'I won't let that happen. Alison assured her, her hand trembling as she closed the door behind them.

The wait was painstaking, time stretching out like a slow-motion nightmare. And then, the sound of a car pulling into the driveway. Pete was here.

Beth ran to hide behind the heavy, full-length curtain at Alison's front-room window. She could hear her heart, hammering in her chest, as she watched from her hiding place. Bradshaw's face was drawn, his eyes scanning the room as if sensing her presence, only he didn't see her.

'I want your phone,' he demanded, his voice cold and hard. He held out his hand to Alison, waiting.

'What? Why?' Alison's voice quivered and Beth had to stop herself from intervening. She was beginning to question whether they were doing the right thing.

'Don't play games with me,' Bradshaw snarled, lunging forward and grabbing the phone from Alison's hand. 'I'm not risking you recording me and then editing it to distort the situation. Like you've done before.'

Beth's breath caught in her throat. What did he mean by that?

'You're afraid of *me*?' Alison's voice rose, fury and accusation lacing her words. 'I know what you've done. Joe,

Beth, her mother – all those murders and violence... I knew you were controlling but never thought you could go so far. You're trying to frame me so you can have Nicky!'

'Wait, what? *I'm* trying to frame you? You're delusional.' Bradshaw's voice was a thunderous roar, and peeping out, Beth saw his face was contorted with rage. 'It's you who's trying to frame me! I know about everything. The calls to my colleagues. Telling them all the bullshit about Beth, Joe, stalking. You need help. Let me help you...'

'I'm not delusional. You're a master at gaslighting, aren't you. Your abuse against me would have the courts give me full custody. Why would I need to frame you?' Alison spat back, her voice dripping with scorn.

Beth saw their faces twisting with anger. What had Bradshaw said? Alison had told the police about her? Could she trust either of these people?

The yelling escalated, and suddenly they moved out of view, their shadows dancing on the wall as the argument intensified.

'Leave me alone.' Alison screamed, her voice breaking with terror.

'You've lost your mind! Enough now.' Bradshaw's voice was a full-blooded yell.

'Get your hands off me!' Alison cried out as Pete moved closer to her and tried to grab her arms.

Beth's instincts took over. Keeping herself hidden, she carefully took her phone out and dialled the police, whispering urgently into the phone, the sounds of Alison's scuffle with Pete drowning her out.

'Please hurry! There's a serious assault going on,' she told the call handler, her voice was frantic, terror gripping her.

Ending the call, Beth rushed out from behind the curtain, and as she grabbed a lamp from a table her eyes took in the sight before her.

Pete Bradshaw lay on the floor, his eyes wide in shock, a knife protruding from his chest.

'Alison. Oh my God. What have you done?'

Chapter One Hundred

BETH

The wailing of sirens grew closer, louder, Alison's eyes were cloudy, unseeing, her face pale, the blood on her hands a stark contrast to her skin.

When the police arrived, they moved swiftly, their eyes taking in the scene, their hushed voices a mere murmur against the backdrop of chaos. Beth and Alison were ushered into different rooms, and Beth found herself sitting across from Detective Thompson, his eyes searching her face as he began to question her.

'What happened here tonight, Ms Stanford?'

Beth struggled to find the words. 'I... I was hiding. We ... Alison and I, we were trying to get Pete... PC Bradshaw to confess.' She hated the stammer that had crept into her speech.

'Confess to what?' Thompson's eyes narrowed.

'To ... to the murders. Joe, my mother. Alison thought he was trying to frame her ... us ... no, *her*.' Beth's voice was shaky, she no longer believed what she was saying herself as the words left her mouth.

'And did he confess?' Thompson's gaze unwavering.

'Uh... Well, no. Not exactly. They started arguing, and then ... then there was a scuffle, and I heard Alison scream. As soon as I heard that, I rang the police ... then ... then I found him on the floor.' Beth's voice broke, the horror of the scene replaying in her mind.

The officer continued to probe, and Beth answered as best as she could, unsure of what Alison would say, she didn't want to lie.

Beth was taken to the police station, her eyes catching Alison's as they were driven in separate cars. Alison's face was drawn, Beth saw her mouth the words: *Don't say anything.*

At the station, the interrogation continued, the officers' questions probing deeper, their faces revealing nothing of their thoughts.

'Can you tell us exactly what you saw?' DC Thompson asked.

'I already told you. I ... I saw PC Bradshaw on the floor, the knife, all the blood... Alison was standing there, but I didn't see how it happened.' Beth's mind replayed the scene over and over, but she had nothing more to add.

The questioning seemed to go on forever, each answer leading to more questions, Thompson's face impassive as he pushed her for more. After what seemed an age, both women were released, the police advising them that they may have more questions later.

'What did they ask you?' Alison's voice was hushed, her eyes filled with relief as they waited for a taxi.

'They wanted to know what we were doing, what I saw, what I heard.' Beth's voice was weary, the events of the night taking their toll. 'I told them the truth, Alison. I told them everything.'

Alison nodded, her face pale as she recounted her own interview.

Beth listened, her mind turning over the details, a nagging doubt creeping in. Alison was so calm despite having just killed someone.

Was Bradshaw telling the truth? Had Alison been manipulating her all along?

As they waited for the taxi, Detective Johnson came out, his face filled with concern.

'Can I have a word, Ms Stanford?' He pulled her aside, his gaze flickering to Alison as he spoke quietly into Beth's ear.

Beth's eyes widened as she digested what the detective had to say. A cold chill running down her spine.

After Johnson had walked away, a taxi arrived and Beth walked over to Alison, her mind filled with a thousand questions.

'What was that all about?' Alison squeezed her arm a little too tight, her eyes searching Beth's face.

Beth looked at her, her eyes searching for a reaction. 'They know who killed Joe and my mother.'

Chapter One Hundred One

BETH

Alison's mouth hung agape as they sat in the taxi, its engine idling. 'Well?' she asked.

Beth was uneasy, telling Alison what she wanted to know. 'They confirmed it was Pete. Detective Johnson is going to meet with me tomorrow and go through the details, there's going to be a press conference and he wanted me to know before the details were released. As for my mother, they've arrested two boy-racers. It was a hit-and-run, after all.'

'We were right. I knew he was twisted but a part of me still didn't want to believe he would go to these lengths.' Alison shook her head.

The silence that fell between them was palpable.

'Did Johnson say anything about me?' Alison's voice was a mere whisper, her face pale under the harsh light.

Beth shook her head. 'No. He just told me that they have enough evidence to show Pete was behind it.'

Alison looked at her, her eyes filled with a mix of relief and disbelief. 'Are you sure?'

'Yes. I don't think they would have released us otherwise. Anyway ... it was self-defence. Wasn't it? What you did earlier?' Beth's voice wavered.

'Of course. You were there. You heard him attack me. Let's just go. I've had enough of this place.'

Beth hoped this nightmare was over. She looked back at the police station and caught Detective Johnson watching them. She turned to Alison and studied her, noticing a strange calmness that seemed to have descended over her friend. Something about it unnerved her, but she was too emotionally exhausted to explore it further.

'Do you want to come over?' Alison's voice pulled Beth out of her thoughts.

'No. I ... I think it's best I just go home. I need to process all of this ... alone.' Beth's voice was quiet, almost lost in the hum of the taxi's engine.

The taxi pulled up to Alison's house first and Beth watched as her friend got out, her silhouette a dark shadow against the glow of the light above the door. As the taxi pulled away, Beth noticed Alison watching her leave. Something in the way Alison stood, sent an unwanted shiver down Beth's spine.

Once back home, Beth tried to make sense of everything. Why would Pete kill Joe and try to kill her, too? Was he really trying to frame Alison? It still didn't make sense. How had Alison convinced her it did?

She closed her eyes, the memories of the night of the attack on Joe returning in terrifying flashes. The dark figure, the chilling fear, the cold steel against her skin.

It had been a man. She was sure of it. But was it Bradshaw? Beth couldn't be certain.

Her mobile pinged, pulling her from her thoughts. It was

Kay, checking in. Beth reassured her aunt that she was okay, the lie sticking in her throat.

She lay on the couch, closing her eyes, the exhaustion taking over, but she was interrupted by another text. Annoyed, she picked up her phone and saw the message wasn't from Kay but was from Alison.

It's finally over. Sleep well. x Alison

Beth stared at the message.

Was it really over?

Chapter One Hundred Two

BETH

The police station loomed ahead, its grey facade a stark contrast to the otherwise quaint North Warwickshire landscape. Beth's grip tightened on her phone as the taxi pulled over to let her out. With each step toward the building, her heart pounded harder in her chest, fear threading its way into her veins. She hoped this would be the final time she had to be here.

Detective Johnson greeted her, his face a neutral mask, and led her to an interview room. As she sat down opposite Johnson, her anxiety spiked as Detective Thompson sauntered in. She held her breath, bracing herself for the inevitable onslaught of probing questions and thinly veiled accusations. She thought this was over. Were they tricking her, too?

To her surprise, it was Thompson who started speaking. 'We have evidence, both forensic and circumstantial evidence'—he shifted in his chair—'that points to PC Bradshaw. I owe you an apology and once again offer my condolences.'

Beth blinked, her mind whirling at the words – unsure whether she was more shocked at the information about Bradshaw or the fact that Thompson had apologised.

'Bradshaw's alibi didn't hold, and his colleague confessed they'd lied about their whereabouts when we questioned them.' Thompson's gaze never wavered from Beth's.

'But Bradshaw's partner had been in our house before, when … when our … my … neighbours had called in the argument Joe and I had. I don't understand?' Beth said, her words spilling out in a rush. Both detectives glanced at each other, and Thompson's next words only served to heighten her unease.

'All part of his plan. He sent his colleague there. He didn't want any connection made between you, Joe and him but he had asked about the details of your home. That officer wasn't supposed to answer that call, but Bradshaw threatened a junior officer to keep her mouth shut and she subsequently came to tell us.'

'Oh my God.'

'The evidence was mounting against him,' Johnson chimed in. 'We searched his home and laptop. He was convinced that Alison and Joe were having an affair. He manipulated their joint bank accounts to look like Alison paid someone to attack you both. The guy came forward and confessed it all. Bradshaw was obsessed with Alison and wanted her to suffer for leaving him and keeping his son.'

The details of their findings rolled on, their words painting a horrific portrait of a man driven by hatred and vengeance. Beth felt her stomach churn. They even had Bradshaw's phone records, positioning him near the scene of each crime.

When Thompson finished, a chilling silence descended on the room.

Beth felt the room spinning. 'What happens now?' She still found it hard to process the details of Bradshaw's plan. If he hadn't been a police officer, Beth wondered if he would have been found out earlier. He must have initially contaminated any evidence against him.

'With Bradshaw dead, the case will be closed.' Johnson leaned back in his chair. 'We'll be holding a press conference this afternoon.'

Thompson smirked at her. 'Guess you got your justice after all, didn't you?' Despite his earlier apology, he couldn't resist one last dig.

Beth thanked them tersely and made her way outside as she called for a taxi.

Out of the corner of her eye, she thought she saw a familiar car and the figure inside – Alison, a self-satisfied smirk on her face.

Her taxi arrived and when Beth looked back, Alison was gone.

'Can you take me to Mount Pleasant Cemetery?'

The driver nodded and Beth got in.

The drive was a blur, the events at the station echoing in her mind.

With a sigh, she paid the driver and walked through the large cemetery gates, her hand automatically reaching for the necklace that held her father's ashes.

She spoke to Joe at his grave, the details of her meeting with the detectives spilling out in a rush. She could grieve properly now, for Joe, for her father, for the mother she lost twice. Once as a child and once as an adult. Her shoulders shook as she let out the pent-up emotions that had been pushed so deep, she forgot they were there.

When Beth returned home, she took a long, hard look at the house she had shared with Joe. With a deep breath, she made the call to an estate agent, setting the wheels in motion to sell the house. It was time to leave the past behind, to let go of the ghosts that haunted her and begin again.

Epilogue

Two Years Later

Beth Stanford's life had settled into a rhythm as steady as the tick of the old clock in her father's hallway. After she'd sold the home that she had shared with Joe in Gladstone, the house where she'd grown up – now half sanctuary, half construction site – was hers. Beth was determined to weave her own legacy into the fabric of her new home. She was building bridges with Aunt Kay, who was now on her own after weathering her husband Frank's death with a quiet grace.

The renovation was an exercise in transformation, a stripping away of the old to make room for the new. And then came the letter, an unwelcome echo from a past Beth had hoped was sealed away.

Beth,

If you are reading this, I am dead. This letter is what I guess could be considered a confession, to help you understand why I had to do what I did. You see, and you may have already figured this out, our friendship was a facade I maintained to make sure you never uncovered the truth while I was still alive. I'm not even sure why I felt the need to write these words. Maybe I'm seeking forgiveness or maybe I think you deserve to know. Maybe it is neither of those things.

It was you, Beth, not Joe, who was always my target. His presence that afternoon was a tragic error, an unplanned variable and I do deeply regret that. I tried to stop him, when he was on the phone hearing your scream as you were being attacked... Rushing home to you ... to prevent the inevitable, but it was too late. The wheels were already in motion, and he didn't listen. Stupid Joe.

What I told you about Pete was only half true. I needed him out of my life, Nicky's life and when Joe had mentioned your issues, I had found the perfect victim. I could put you out of your misery and reunite you with your father, while making sure Pete got the blame. It was really something charitable, if you think about it. I could have made Joe happy.

Unfortunately, Pete saw through me early on in our marriage and tried to change me, control me, ruin me. He said I was a narcissistic sociopath. Takes one to know one.

He had to be stopped. It wasn't Pete who had hired a killer, it was me. Helping the police and pointing them in Pete's direction when I realised what he knew was tricky, but it worked. If you do some research, you'll find out the man I hired is dying from cancer, may already be dead — the money he was paid, given to his own young family. He was a client of Travers House, and I used his drug habit to get him to do what I needed. He had nothing to lose.

I guess Pete wasn't so bad at being a cop, after all. You should have believed him. But that doesn't matter now. His flaws, his weaknesses, were things I couldn't tolerate. Just like yours. You were all just obstacles, weaknesses that needed to be removed.

As you read this, you may find it in your heart to pity me, or perhaps you'll be glad I'm gone. I would understand either. But know this, Beth — I regret nothing. The truth was always about who told the most convincing story, so whatever you decide to do with this information is up to you. The truth is now yours to bear.

Alison

Alison's words were laced with such a cold venom that made Beth's blood chill. The letter revealed a heart that held love only for power.

Aunt Kay's voice from the doorway pulled Beth back from the vile words that invaded her thoughts. She folded the letter with shaking hands, the weight of Alison's confession pressing down on her.

'What's that?' Kay pointed at the letter.

'It's ... nothing.'

Beth was glad Alison was dead because if she were here now, she would have to resist the urge to end her with her own bare hands.

She walked into the living room and eyed the burning fire. Her arm outstretched, she nearly threw the letter into the flames. Instead, she decided she'd send it to Detective Johnson who would do the right thing. Nicky deserved to have his dad's name cleared.

Beth had always wondered what had happened to Alison and now that she knew she was gone, she didn't have to worry anymore. The truth was finally out.

Acknowledgments

I'd like to thank everyone who has cheered me on and supported me so far on my writing journey, especially my family and friends. I'm so grateful to be able to share my stories, and I can't do that without any of you spreading the word.

A massive thanks to my editor and the One More Chapter team for all that you do.

Special thanks to my beta readers: Graham Smith, Claire Knight, Sarah Hardy and Sharon Bairden. Your brutal honesty and constructive feedback helps me see those gaping plot-holes and turns my chaos into calm. I may curse you under my breath, but I know you're right.

A heart-felt thank you to all the authors, crime writing/reading community and festival peeps who have been so incredibly supportive, inspirational and kind – you have no idea how much it means to me.

To the blogging, bookstagram and booktok community – your friendship and support has been incredible!

Finally, a massive thanks to all the readers. There are just no words to convey how much your support and reviews have meant to me. You make me believe I can keep on doing this and give me a reason to write.

ONE HOUSE
EIGHT KILLERS
NO WITNESSES

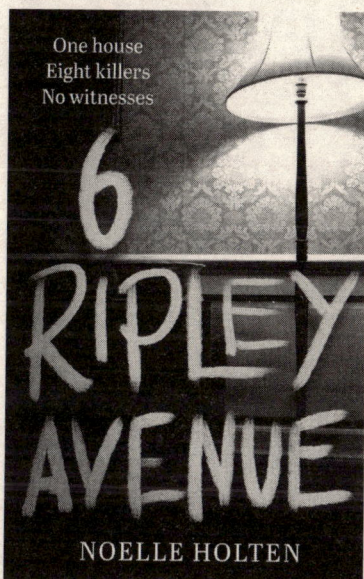
Jeanette is the manager of a probation hostel that houses high risk offenders released on license.

At 3am one morning, she receives a call telling her a resident has been murdered.

Her whole team, along with the eight convicted murderers, are now all suspects in a crime no one saw committed…

Available now in paperback, eBook and audio!

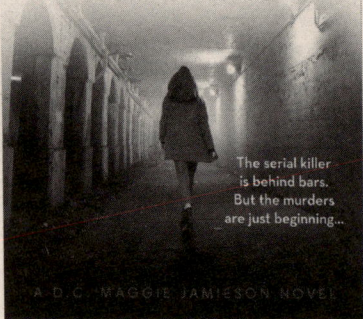

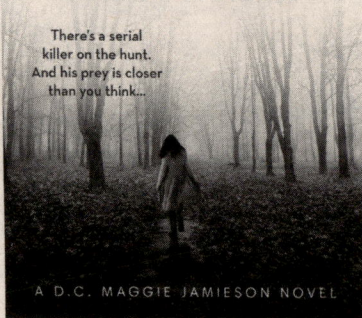

ONE MORE CHAPTER

YOUR NUMBER ONE STOP

FOR PAGETURNING BOOKS

The author and One More Chapter would like to thank everyone who contributed to the publication of this story...

Analytics
James Brackin
Abigail Fryer

Audio
Fionnuala Barrett
Ciara Briggs

Contracts
Laura Amos
Laura Evans

Design
Lucy Bennett
Fiona Greenway
Liane Payne
Dean Russell

Digital Sales
Laura Daley
Lydia Grainge
Hannah Lismore

eCommerce
Laura Carpenter
Madeline ODonovan
Charlotte Stevens
Christina Storey
Jo Surman
Rachel Ward

Editorial
Kara Daniel
Charlotte Ledger
Ajebowale Roberts
Jennie Rothwell
Caroline Scott-Bowden
Emily Thomas
Helen Williams

Harper360
Jennifer Dee
Emily Gerbner
Ariana Juarez
Jean Marie Kelly
emma sullivan
Sophia Wilhelm

International Sales
Peter Borcsok
Ruth Burrow
Colleen Simpson
Ben Wright

Inventory
Sarah Callaghan
Kirsty Norman

Marketing & Publicity
Chloe Cummings
Grace Edwards
Emma Petfield

Operations
Melissa Okusanya
Hannah Stamp

Production
Denis Manson
Simon Moore
Francesca Tuzzeo

Rights
Helena Font Brillas
Ashton Mucha
Zoe Shine
Aisling Smyth
Lucy Vanderbilt

Trade Marketing
Ben Hurd
Eleanor Slater

The HarperCollins Distribution Team

The HarperCollins Finance & Royalties Team

The HarperCollins Legal Team

The HarperCollins Technology Team

UK Sales
Isabel Coburn
Jay Cochrane
Sabina Lewis
Holly Martin
Harriet Williams
Leah Woods

And every other essential link in the chain from delivery drivers to booksellers to librarians and beyond!